Fallout in Georgia

S.E. GLEN

ISBN: 9798992196207

DEDICATION

For Tina—who braved the storm of my rambling, rode shotgun through every plot twist, and never once told me to shut up.

1 Into the Swamp

Had I stayed home that weekend, a 5,000-degree fireball would have incinerated me, vaporizing me before I could even scream. Instead, oblivious to the coming apocalypse, I shoved my *HappyKamp* two-person tent—thank you, Temu lightning deal—into my Ford Explorer, slamming the hatch shut with a thud.

The car groaned under the weight of cans, pots, dishware, and propane tanks. My Scottish grandmother used to say, *"Always be ready for company, lass. You never know who might pop by."* It sounded like advice for another life, and my SUV agreed, sagging under the strain of carrying too much for far too long.

I trudged to the mailbox, gravel crunching under my boots. As I reached for the handle, a blur of black and white swooped in, landing on the box's rim. The magpie cocked its head, its obsidian eyes fixed on me like it knew more than it should.

"Okay, okay, I get it." I didn't need a lousy omen bird to tell me what trouble lurked inside the mailbox. I waved the magpie off, and it flapped into the sky with a squawk.

I yanked out the mail and glared at the red stamp on the top letter from my auto loan company:

FINAL NOTICE.

Happy Friday, y'all.

"Thanks for nothing, Mr. Magpie." I crushed the letter in my fist. Some old rhyme floated through my head—something about greeting magpies to keep the bad luck away. *How are you today, Mr. Magpie? Yeah. Too late now.*

I tossed the crumpled letter into the trash can and sifted through the rest of the mail. My fingers froze on an envelope with a return address stamped in bold, black letters:

DEPARTMENT OF CORRECTIONS, PALMETTO SPRINGS.

My stomach tightened into an icy knot. I had to resist the urge to tear the envelope open right then and there. But I wasn't in the mood to see whatever crap my ex-husband had managed to spew out from his prison cell. *Not today.* Eric always knew how to stir the ashes, even from behind bars.

Across the street, Mr. Hughes rolled his mower out of the garage, gave me a wave, and pulled the cord. The engine choked, sputtered, then burst into a steady roar. Its growl filled the quiet street and drowned out the giddy whoops of kids playing next door. Some people had it easy: I'd kill to trade my problems for a lawn that needed to meet the homeowner's association's three-inch rule. But life didn't work that way. My problems spread like weeds in a derelict lot—tough, thorny, and rooted deep. It would take a tractor-mower just to cut through them.

I stuffed Eric's letter beneath the pile, then added the next one from the Florida Bureau of Emergency Medical Services. I didn't need to tear it open to know what it said: *License revoked.*

My hands trembled as I gripped the letters, crushing them into a crumpled wad. The letters were anchors to everything I wanted to leave behind—Eric's betrayal, the wreckage of our marriage, and the unforgivable mistake that had cost me the one thing I thought I was still good at. Tossing the letters in the trash wouldn't change a thing, but at least I wouldn't have to see the proof of my failures staring back at me.

Wasn't that the way life always worked? When life sucks, the universe keeps piling it on. Ruined marriage? Here—have a repoed car and house. And just in case you're still hoping—let's trash the job too.

I hurled the stack into the trash, but my hand hovered over the edge of the can. With a curse under my breath, I reached in and fished out two letters. Maybe I did need to read them. Maybe seeing the words would make it real. Or perhaps it wouldn't change a damn thing.

"Crap," I said. Indecision—that's what always got me into trouble.

I shook the envelopes, dislodging slimy chunks of fruit that might have been an apple a week ago. A sour-sweet rot clung to the paper, staining my fingertips with a sticky residue. The letters were heavier in my hands than they had any right to be, as if they carried the weight of all my failures, taunting me to open them. Like another test I wasn't sure I could pass.

My phone buzzed in my pocket, breaking me from my thoughts.

I stared at the notification, my thumb hovering over the screen. I wasn't in the mood for a forced break when I could be job hunting.

Should I feign illness and cancel? Or stick to my promise? Even the smallest choices sparked a debate in my head, looping endlessly until I wanted to scream.

I opened my message app. My stepsister had fired off a text with her usual flair for emojis: "ETA?" followed by a smiley face, bunny, and kissy face.

I released a quiet huff and glared at the screen. Button was in her thirties but acted sixteen. When would she grow up? I typed back:

"Be there in 20 mins."

I glanced at the crumpled letters one last time before shoving them into the Explorer's glove box and slamming it shut. Sliding into the driver's seat, my hand hovered over the keys. *Don't start. Please don't start.* I could already hear myself calling Button with the excuse: *Sorry, Button! What a shame, huh? Guess I'll have to miss all the fun.* My fingers trembled as I turned the ignition, half hoping for silence, half dreading what would come next.

The Explorer rumbled to life, the engine catching with a rough cough, like it didn't want to wake up. The magpie shrieked again, circling overhead in the late afternoon warmth. If it was a sign, it sure as hell wasn't a good one.

* * *

Button flounced down her front steps ten minutes late, all energy and glitter. She looked like a kid dressed up for her first dance, unaware of the clouds gathering both in the sky and in my mood. I'd bet anything that Button hadn't packed a rain jacket, so I always packed for two.

Button hopped into the passenger side. "Hey, before we go, I wanted to, uh, talk to you about something."

I drummed my fingers against the steering wheel, my annoyance increasing with each tap. "Okay, what's on your mind?"

"Give me a sec," Button said, adjusting the seat backward.

I took in Button's flawless facade—foundation caked on thick, lipstick a crimson smear, hair flat-ironed to a smooth gloss. My hair was a tangled mess, a wild mane that defied gravity. I'd spent a grand total of five seconds yanking it into a sloppy ponytail, a desperate attempt to tame the beast. A trip to the salon was out of the question—a luxury I couldn't afford. My beauty routine was more modest: bargain-bin shampoo and a quick trim in my bathroom mirror.

I waited, my patience thinning as Button stared at the gravel driveway as if the answers might rise from the ground. "Well?"

Button pressed her lips together, eyes darting back and forth on the dashboard. "I just... it's nothing. Well, sort of."

I twisted the key and started the engine. "Just say it, Button."

Button fumbled with the seatbelt. "I was, uh, wondering if you..."

The seat belt jammed as usual. Button yanked at it once. Twice. The third time, it came loose with a clunk. She let it hang for a second, then glanced over. "Um... heard anything about the house yet?"

My foot hovered over the gas pedal. "Not since the last time you asked me." *Yesterday.*

"Oh," Button said, jabbing the seat belt latch into its socket. She adjusted the rearview mirror, tilting it back and forth until it was just right. She inspected her lipstick, then rubbed at the corner of her mouth like something was there. "Did you bring anything to do?"

Do? Wasn't the point of camping to do nothing? "A book. You?"

Button grinned, though it didn't reach her eyes, as she held up her phone like a prize. "My phone. Does that count? Don't worry, I downloaded plenty of playlists." Then she added, as if it were the most essential part of the trip, "I'll keep us entertained."

I put the Explorer into gear, wondering for the hundredth time why I'd agreed to this trip. Maybe I could've handled a beach vacation—Mai Tais, a killer novel, and sunshine—but an entire weekend with no one around for 50 miles except Button?

Had I taken a page out of Gatsby's guide to poor life choices? It had seemed like such a good idea months ago, back when the sun was higher and life was less suffocating.

Five minutes later, we barreled west down I-10, the highway crowded with traffic under the waning afternoon light.

Button leaned forward, fiddling with the radio until static crackled through the speakers, followed by snippets of an insipid pop song. She turned it up, nodding to the beat.

I reached to switch the station back, only to have Button swipe my hand away with a laugh. "Come on, Ellena, this is a road trip. Let's keep it fun."

I rolled my eyes but let the pop music flood the car. It reminded me too much of growing up, of Button always taking the lead, always getting her way. Or was it I had never learned how to push back? No, that wasn't true, and I knew it. The lie was pretending I couldn't remember—pretending I didn't see myself fold, again and again.

4

I remembered it perfectly. Christmas morning, fourteen years old, Button squealing so hard over Spice Girls tickets she nearly passed out. Dad's big gift to the family: the entire clan on a road trip to Atlanta for the show at Lakewood Amphitheatre, Button's dream come true.

I had unwrapped my mother's gift minutes later—two tickets to The Nutcracker. The glossy program cover with Clara in mid-leap had sent my heart soaring. The note inside said, "Just us, sweetheart. It's our night." But the second Button saw the tickets were for the same night, the pleading began. "Please, Ellena, please! You're my best friend in the world!" And before I could even say I didn't care for the Spice Girls, Dad had decided it. One show for the family, no splitting up.

My mom hadn't fought. She never fought, even in the divorce. The tickets to *The Nutcracker* disappeared back into the box, tucked away with everything else Mom had lost in the proceedings. I nodded and said okay, like it didn't matter. What's one more disappointment? I clutched the glossy program to my chest as if it might shield me from Button's whirlwind of excitement.

And now here I was, speeding west down I-10 on a camping trip I didn't want to be on, with a stepsister who was, for better or worse, my only remaining family. *"Please, Ellena, please! I need a break!"* The words had worked again, Button tugging at my heartstrings and dragging me into another compromise. Except this time, the big event wasn't the Spice Girls; it was a trip to the wilderness accompanied by Beyoncé, Taylor Swift, and whatever pop dreck Super Hits FM was pumping out.

The thought crawled up the back of my mind and wouldn't let go: Why can't you ever say no?

Button leaned back in her seat. "Turn that frown around, Ellena. You're making it feel like a funeral in here. The world's not going to end if we miss a turn or two."

Her words were light, but something in her tone needled at me, like a pin slipping under my skin. Was that a jab? Or was I imagining it?

We passed brightly lit gas stations and rivers of cars, the sprawl of Jacksonville clinging to the highway like it didn't want to let go. About 30 miles from the city, it was as if time had slowed down. Newer developments gave way to weathered buildings and homes that whispered of another era. A giant Walmart loomed beyond the 'Welcome to Macclenny' sign, the last glimpse of civilization before rural North Florida swallowed the road.

We turned off the exit and veered north. Within minutes, the open spaces began. Fields stretched out on either side, dotted with scrub and pine. The route grew quieter, the air thick with an earthy scent. Miles passed without another car on the road, and with each stretch, the swamp loomed ahead, beckoning us deeper.

Button's phone, previously alive with notifications, had fallen silent. Her thumb drifted over the screen, hunting for a signal that wasn't there.

A wisp of static broke through the radio, followed by a robotic voice: "—monitoring global tensions—" before it crackled out again. Another burst of static, then a clipped voice: "—unexplained animal deaths reported near Yellowstone National Park—officials cite possible geothermal activity—" The signal warped and died.

Button frowned and let her hand fall from the dial. "You hear that India and Pakistan are trading fire in Kashmir again? Because that's just what the world needs—more powder kegs."

The usual doom and gloom, I told myself. Nothing worth worrying about. On my therapist Sal's advice, I'd stopped keeping up with the headlines months ago. "Instead of scrolling the BBC app," Sal had suggested, "Try drinking tea in your garden. There's research showing that people who binge on the news feel more anxious and depressed."

And then Sal had added, "Staying off social media wouldn't hurt either."

Button, of course, was the exception to all of that. She didn't just thrive on bad news—she was a walking, breathing Page One. A moment's peace was impossible when Button was around. "Did you hear Japan is threatening to bomb China? Oh my God, Thailand just joined the Korean Alliance. They just found a Russian missile silo in the Falklands!" But Button wasn't just my stepsister; she was my friend, too, in that messy, intertwined way only family could be. After my firehouse buddies had drifted away like debris in an ebb tide, Button was the only friend I had left.

"Feels like there's rain coming," Button said, squinting at the horizon. "Hope it doesn't soak us when we get there."

My grip on the wheel tightened as I glanced up. The clouds stretched thin and frail, like a curtain ready to tear. Rain wasn't the problem, per se, but setting up camp in the rain would be a pain in the ass.

The quiet turned restless as the dark pressed closer. Shadows pooled at the roots of the trees, their crooked limbs clawing at the last scraps of daylight. In the ditch, a vulture lay crumpled and still, its wings bent at unnatural angles, its lifeless eyes catching the fading light. I looked away, but the thought was cold and unshakable: nature was pulling the strings out here, and it didn't care if they snapped.

* * *

The sun sank low as we entered the heart of the Okefenokee Swamp, a bird and nature sanctuary stretching over seven hundred square miles from northern Florida into southeastern Georgia. It was a labyrinth of blackwater and towering cypress trees, their limbs draped in Spanish moss.

Button wrinkled her nose, pressing closer to the window as we rumbled over a bridge. "It just goes on forever."

I nodded, taking in the sprawling scenery. "This place has its own rhythm, doesn't it? I wonder if we'll see bears?"

Button gave me a sidelong glance, half-smiling. "I hope its 'rhythm' doesn't include eating us alive."

I opened my mouth to reply but stopped, distracted by the rippling shadows in a flooded gully by the roadside. The water's surface was dark glass, smooth and impenetrable until a ripple broke across it—a sign of something moving just below. Shadows shifted, and then an alligator's eyes broke the surface, unblinking, before sliding back into the murk.

As I drove the last mile, my mind drifted. Out here was its own world, where survival had different rules. The idea was both daunting and comforting—maybe here, I could escape the mistakes that followed me like shadows everywhere else. I could hear Gran speak as if she were there: *Aye, right, lass. And haggis are wee creatures ye can catch with a butterfly net.*

I turned off the main road onto a narrow gravel path. Another alligator rested in the roadside reeds, still as a log, waiting for its sunset snack. The sight reminded me I was starving. *Did I eat breakfast? I did, right? Or maybe not. Lunch? Definitely not.*

Button, glued to her phone, missed the creature completely. Seconds later, she dropped the phone into her lap. "Signal's gone. Are we seriously almost there?"

I pointed to a small clearing at the end of the winding road. "We're close."

But Button didn't seem to hear; she reached for her phone again and tapped the screen.

The silence between us felt alive, like static prickling against my skin. Three years ago, Button's energy was a bright and boundless lifeline when my marriage circled the drain. Now, it was discordant—like the radio hovering between stations. Something was wrong, but its shape stayed just out of reach.

Outside, the landscape swallowed the fading light, shadows stretching like tendrils. We passed the park entrance and checked in at a wooden hut that doubled as a rustic shop stocked with Band-Aids, firewood, and camper van Christmas tree ornaments. The air inside carried that unmistakable tang of old pine and damp earth—like every rustic cabin ever built. A sign by the register read: *No grocery store for 20 miles—plan ahead!* If I had relied on Button to pack supplies, we'd already be heading back to Argon, Georgia—a blip on the map with one gas station and a cell tower trying its best to look like the Eiffel Tower.

With the parking pass in hand, we hopped into the Explorer and turned right into the campground. It stretched out before us, as still as a backyard after the party's over. Gray ash and half-burned wood lay inside fire pits, cold and lifeless. A flier reading "Stargazing Tonight!" fluttered limply from the damp air on a bulletin board. Somewhere in the distance, a bullfrog gave a low, foghorn croak that echoed through the stillness of the evening.

I spotted a lone Airstream tucked beneath the towering cypress trees. One neighbor. Hopefully, not football fans. My last camping trip—Hanna Park, two years ago, back when my mom was still alive, and diabetes chewed through her like termites in an old beam—had been the kind of misery I couldn't forget. A group of tailgaters had turned the beachside campground into their own private stadium, blasting college football so loud it rattled my tent poles. I'd been too timid to tell them off after quiet hours kicked in. Instead, I'd spent the night cringing every time someone screamed, *"Touchdoooown!"* It'd still be too soon if I never heard that word again.

As we pulled into site 26, Button's earlier complaints gave way to a spark of excitement. She hopped out of the Explorer and stretched her arms wide, a grin spreading across her face. "Back to nature! This is gonna be fun," she said, spinning in a slow circle as she took in the landscape.

I raised an eyebrow. "Fun?" I asked, my voice flat. Not the word I'd use. Solace, perhaps. A chance to let my thoughts roam unchecked, to devour me like an alligator dragging its prey under.

Or maybe loneliness, stretched thin over the vast, empty wild.

* * *

Two hours later, the firepit roared as the logs burned and sizzled, sending bright embers dancing into the dark sky. I sat on the worn picnic table, cradling a hot toddy—Gran's chilly night special. The whiskey's smoky bite blended with the soothing sweetness of honey and lemon, coating my throat with warmth that radiated into my bones. Gran always called it "*a wee hug in a cup*," and as the warmth spread through my hands, I could almost hear her voice.

The evening came alive with a hidden orchestra tuning up: crickets chirped in a high-pitched hum that filled the still air, cicadas droned with a mechanical buzz—blending into the background until I forgot they were there. Occasionally, a splash echoed—a fish leaping or something larger slipping into the dark water. Overhead, a barred owl let out a questioning hoot, answered by silence that pressed against my ears like a living thing.

The meditative symphony let my thoughts close in, bringing the empty pain of everything that had fallen apart in the past year. My marriage, my job, and my hopes for motherhood. My failings played on repeat like an earworm, every soundbite as clear as the day it happened. Even now, surrounded by trilling insects and starry skies, I was moving through motions: Eat. Breathe. Sleep. Repeat.

"Borrr-ing," Button said, her voice slicing through the heavy silence like a nail dragged across a porcelain cup. Her messy bun bounced as her foot tapped the ground to music only she could hear through her earbuds. She took a bite of her sandwich and grimaced. "Ugh. This tastes like wet sock."

I took a sip of my hot toddy, the warmth and weight of the mug grounding me amid Button's theatrics. Just hours ago, my stepsister had been hyped about being outside. Now, she was air-slapping mosquitoes—muttering curses when they darted out of reach—and flinging bits of sandwich into the bushes with a flair that bordered on the absurd.

Button swatted at her hair. "Why did I think this was a good ah-deah?" Her drawl stretched the word like taffy—sticky, and cloying. "I mean, a weekend in Savannah would've been more my speed. Air conditioning, Wi-Fi..."

The sugary edge in her words set my teeth on edge, but I bit back a response. Instead, I tilted my head toward the stars, where Sirius smoldered through the gauzy clouds—an unblinking eye in the dark.

Button flung the last bite of her sandwich into the bushes, the crinkled wrapper following close behind. "Ellena, seriously. How much longer we gonna sit out here, lettin' these bugs eat us alive? They're feasting on me."

"You wanted to get in touch with nature. Looks like nature's getting in touch with you."

Button sighed and dropped her hands into her lap. "Whatever."

I pointed toward the tossed sandwich. "You should probably get that. Unless you want bears sniffing around in the middle of the night."

Button froze, staring at the bushes, her eyes wide. "Oh, my God. There's ticks in there. I'm not gonna add them to the list. Why didn't you tell me not to do that?"

What was she, twelve? The thought flared, but I pushed it down. Picking a fight would only stretch our tension into something taut and ugly. "You know now."

I stood, switched on my headlamp, and bent to gather the sandwich scraps. The bushes rustled, and I froze, sweeping the beam into the undergrowth. Two amber circles glinted back at me from the dark. A raccoon. Harmless. *If it's yellow, friendly fellow; If it's red, you're good as dead.*

I dumped the scraps into the critter-proof can and pushed the lid down hard. Or tried to, anyway. The stupid thing popped back up, flipping open like it was having a laugh at my expense. I swore under my breath, jammed the lid down again, and twisted it until it latched.

"Good luck now," I muttered, glancing toward the bushes where the raccoon's eyes glinted. *You're not getting an easy meal tonight.*

I turned back toward the fire, brushing my hands against my jeans. Button's smile tilted enough to suggest she'd been watching the whole ordeal. That smile had changed since before Eric went to prison. I couldn't say precisely when—not with those first months lost in a grief-drenched fog. Now, it looked like flimsy armor that didn't fit.

The sound of distant thunder made me shift uneasily as the night closed in. I looked up at the last stars twinkling out behind the thickening clouds. *Great, here comes the rain.*

Button said, "I heard something weird on Blaze Radio this morning. Something about Defcon 2. Then Uncle Hank called and told me to get to Colorado. He said, 'You wanna be in the mountains when this shit goes down, Button.' He sounded dead serious."

I gripped my mug, the warmth failing to touch the icy knot coiling in my chest. The world churned with chaos—it always did, much like my own life. But if Button's colonel uncle was worried, there might be a reason.

I stared at the fire. "I don't want to think about it right now. We came here to escape."

But the feeling wouldn't leave me, the sense that another blow awaited. *Bad luck comes in strings, doesn't it?* Maybe a frantic dash to Colorado would be strike twenty.

Button looked at me for a long time as if she were searching for something unsaid. Then her grin reappeared. "You're always so calm and collected. I mean, I'd be a mess if I had so much on my plate."

Calm? Was this the same Button who had seen me crumpled on the kitchen floor, sobbing until my voice broke? The same Button who'd watched me shatter my phone against the wall after one of Eric's collect calls from prison?

Sure, I kept it together at work—at least, I had until I hadn't. I'd tried pushing past my limits, signing up for the paramedic exam, hoping it would mend the fractures in my life. While I aced the written portion, practical skill stations exposed my most profound flaw: hesitation cost me more than a passing score—it cost me confidence and, eventually, my license.

My mind lurched back to that terrible night—the pouring rain, the twenty-car pileup, my failure to act—before I willed myself to breathe and listen to the chirp of crickets instead.

"I should have downloaded a movie," Button said, dropping her phone into her Hermès bag with a thud.

And maybe I should have come alone. The words simmered beneath the stifling heat pressing down on us.

Button pointed across the road, a sudden excitement lighting her face. "At least we're not completely alone. Do you see that guy? He's a cutie."

I squinted into the shadows toward the glow of the man's lantern. The light wavered, casting flickers over the border collie curled at his feet. The man stood still, staring into the dark like he was waiting for it to move first.

"Don't forget the Airstream," I said, feigning indifference. "There's them too."

"Uh huh. But do you think he's out here on his lonesome? He looks like one of those survivalist types—did you see his gear? Military I bet. And did I mention he's cuu-ute?" Button dragged out the word like an announcer shouting over a Hail Mary pass, her voice bright with enthusiasm.

Of course. She's my personal play-by-play commentator now.

Button gave me a playful, insistent nudge that begged for agreement, for a shared moment of gossip to shatter the tension between us.

I gripped my mug tighter, my knuckles turning white. "I'm not... ready. To notice anyone, I mean."

"It's been over a year. You gotta let it go, Ellena."

Not that simple. It never was. Button hadn't been there when I'd confronted Eric about forging my signature on the second mortgage—hadn't stood in the kitchen as he cried and apologized. Hadn't been there when the first delinquency notice arrived for the house my grandmother had bought in 1941, the one now slipping through my fingers thanks to Eric. If Button had been there for any of it, she wouldn't have tossed out "let it go" like a handful of glitter meant to magically wipe the pain away. Lost in my thoughts, I barely noticed Button waving a hand in front of my face.

"Hello? NASA to Major Tom," Button said, snapping her fingers.

I blinked, pushing aside the thick clouds of guilt. "I heard you," I said, my voice a steel door slamming shut. I wouldn't unload my thoughts onto Button—not now. "It's 'Ground Control,'" I corrected with a sigh.

Button squinted, not comprehending the David Bowie reference. We hadn't even made it through the first night, and Button was already testing my patience thin.

Button said, "Stop overthinking. We came out here to escape, remember?"

I forced a smile. "I'm fine."

"Sure you are." She yawned and stretched. "I'm turning in. You comin'?"

"In a bit." A shooting star traced the sky in a gap between the clouds. For a breath, I thought of making a wish but held back, thinking that dumb superstition wouldn't wave its magic wand and make everything okay.

Button disappeared into the tent. The fire snapped and crackled, sending embers spiraling upward like tiny signals to the stars.

I thought of the letters burning a hole in the glove box. I pushed myself to my feet, the need to know chafing my nerves. At the Explorer, I yanked open the glove box. My mouth was dry and gummy, like I'd chewed on a cotton ball, as I pulled out Eric's letter. A brown apple guts stain smeared the crumpled envelope. I flattened it out and tore it open.

The notepaper crackled like dry autumn leaves as I unfolded it beneath the dome light's yellow stain. It was the usual crap. *Sorry. Didn't mean for it to happen, never meant to hurt you, blah blah damn blah.* I scanned over the letter, but my focus locked on the last paragraph.

"Lizzy said she was going to tell you, so I'm writing to say don't blame her. It wasn't her fault. I know you can't forgive me, but I hope you can forgive her? She's good people, Ellena. Take care."

I read it twice. The jagged words bled into one another as my tinnitus swelled to a cacophony. Lizzy? Button's real name was Elizabeth. But Lizzy?

Not a pet name. Please, God, not a pet name.

The fire hissed and popped, sparks curling upward before fading into the dark. Somewhere in the distance, a mournful sound, low and hollow, threaded through the cypress trees, an echo of something lost.

2 Protocols Pending

The morning sun filtered through the trees as I crawled out of the tent, my body dragging with exhaustion. Sleep hadn't come—not with Eric's letter looping through my mind, the words as persistent as the rain that had pounded the canvas all night. Although the rain had stopped, the swollen clouds brooded overhead, restless and bruised, as if ready to strike again.

A leak had formed along the cheap stitching in one corner of the tent, matching the nagging thoughts in my head—drip, drip, drip. The tent bulged at the top, where water pooled from the rain. Like everything else in my life, it felt ready to give out at any moment.

The morning chorus swelled to life: the throaty bellows of bullfrogs, a red-winged blackbird's piercing trill, and the slow rustle of something unseen moving through the reeds. A black rat snake slid across the damp trail, its dark body glistening like oil on water.

I brewed my coffee, the aroma battling the swamp's peaty scent. I forced myself to eat a granola bar. It was dense and gummy, like chewing on raw oats.

As soon as Button woke up, I'd ask about the letter. Or should I wait until we got home? *No, now is better.* "*Takin' yer time's just another way tae say no,*" Gran would've said. The letter could be innocent. Right? *Forgive Lizzy for never returning that book you lent her. Forgive Lizzy for forgetting your birthday last year. It could be anything. Or it could be...*

I stood up, brushed off my pants, and decided making vegetable soup from scratch might settle my nerves. The prep would keep my hands busy, I thought, but it didn't work. I chopped onions and wondered about the letter. Peeled and diced potatoes, imagining the worst. Chopped herbs, thinking of what I'd say if Button admitted to being close enough, too close, to my ex-husband to have a pet name. Lizzy.

I smashed the garlic, the pungent scent cutting through the damp morning air. The thud of the blade against the cutting board was my only defense against my spiraling thoughts. I glanced at the tent, the flap still

zipped tight. Button wasn't an early riser, but the waiting nagged at me—
like the other letter calling to me from the glove box.

The one from the Bureau of Emergency Medical Services.

Maybe it's good news, I told myself for the hundredth time. Maybe it
isn't what I think. Maybe they had reinstated my license, and the letter
explained the error. The investigation found you weren't at fault, it would
say.

"And there's a tree near Loch Lomond that grows blood pudding sausages,"
Gran would've said.

I gritted my teeth, my chest tightening as if my T-shirt had turned into
a corset. I couldn't face another scrap of bad news. Leaving the letter
unopened meant it could still hold hope—and hope, however threadbare,
was the only thing keeping me together that weekend.

The rustle of fabric broke my focus. I set down the knife and wiped
my hands on my pants as Button emerged from the tent, stretching with
an exaggerated yawn before collapsing into a camp chair with a dramatic
sigh.

I straightened the already neat pile of vegetables. Words were too
elusive; anything I might say risked spilling the turmoil simmering beneath
my skin. Instead, I grabbed a water bottle and took a swig, the plastic
crinkling in my hand. The lukewarm water, tinged with plastic, did little to
wash down the dryness in my throat. I would talk to Button later, when I'd
figured out how to say what I wanted to say.

The hours dragged by, each one slower than the last. I busied myself
with a familiar camping routine—reorganizing gear, cooking soup, flipping
through my worn copy of *The Andromeda Strain*. But the words swam on
the page, the plot lost to the tug of my thoughts. Eric's letter in my pocket
grew hotter with every passing second, as if it might burn a hole clean
through my jeans.

By late afternoon, the air had cooled, golden light spilling through the
dense canopy.

Button grabbed a water bottle and stretched. "Let's go for a walk. I
need to move. This place is stiflin'."

I hesitated, then nodded. I had no desire to walk with Button, much
less listen to her drone on about the weather, the bugs, or her
uncomfortable sleeping bag. Still, a walk might help me focus on what
needed to be said.

Button led the way to a narrow path that wove through the southern edge of the wetland. The squelch of our boots in the mud and the hum of cicadas filled the silence between us.

Button swatted at a mosquito and groaned. "Remind me why I thought this was a good idea."

"You said you wanted to escape the city. I only came because you begged me after that awful blind date."

"Fine. But Connor wasn't that bad—if you ignore his lizard obsession and green hair."

I forced a thin laugh. Button's dating catastrophe jokes usually lifted my spirits, but not today. I glanced at my stepsister, searching for a hint of guilt or unease, but Button's face gave nothing away. It was infuriating how calm she seemed. I wanted to ask her about the letter, but every time I opened my mouth, the words stuck. Tonight, I told myself. A tot or two of whiskey, and then I'd confront her.

The trail curved, the dense canopy above deepening into shadow. Button froze mid-step, her voice dropping to a whisper. "Uh, Ellena..."

I followed Button's gaze to an alligator, its black eyes fixed on us with the surety of a sniper zeroing in on a target. "They won't bother us," I said, though my voice wavered. "Just don't get too close."

"Are you sure?" Button's voice was thin, her usual bravado stripped away. She took a cautious step back.

"Pretty sure," I said, but I kept my distance as we moved on. The world buzzed with life, every sound amplified, every snapped twig and wingbeat screaming in my ears like nails on a chalkboard.

A barred owl flapped its wings in the branches above us, startled into motion. Its call echoed through the trees, low and mournful. *Who cooks for you? Who cooks for you-all?* The sound had always been comforting, but today it felt ominous, a warning I couldn't place.

Button flinched at the noise. "What was that?"

"A barred owl. Harmless. Usually."

"Usually?" Button frowned, taking a slow step back. "What do you mean, usually?"

"They've been known to get territorial. Nesting season and all that. If you get too close, they'll let you know."

"Great. Killer birds. What's next?"

I said nothing, unwilling to get dragged into a conversation about killer birds, killer alligators, or—God forbid—zombies on the loose in

Uzbekistan just because Button had gotten a cell phone signal that morning.

The path meandered toward the campground, and that's when I noticed him, six feet away—a figure perched near the water's edge, sharpening a hunting knife on a rock. The unhurried rasp of steel against stone carried in the humid air. His border collie lay sprawled at his feet, its white coat broken by black patches that gave it a lopsided, mischievous look. Its tail thumped the ground in lazy intervals.

The man I had glimpsed the night before wasn't a typical camper. His short hair and precise movements, paired with scuffed military boots, suggested someone who belonged to a different world. He glanced my way, his expression unreadable. I resisted the urge to look away first.

"Hi," I said, feeling backed into a corner.

He nodded with a hint of a smile. "Out for a walk?"

I shifted my weight, debating whether to humor a stranger with a knack for the obvious. "Something like that."

Button dove right in. She crouched beside the dog, reaching out before the man had time to say no. "What's his name?" she asked, her voice honeyed and too bright.

"Winter. Full name's Winter is Coming."

Button laughed, bright and carefree. "Game of Thrones fan?"

He chuckled, the sound warm and familiar, an old friend passing through. "Until the last season."

Button let out a bright, too-loud laugh, the kind that bounced off trees and felt just a little forced. She and the man started chattering about dragons, episodes, and favorite characters. Winter nudged my hand, and I scratched behind his ears, trying to tune them out and hoping Button would wrap up the flirting before I lost my patience and stomped back to camp on my own.

I pictured it: the two of them laughing over drinks at his campfire while I sat alone at base camp, sipping a hot toddy and kicking myself for not saying something first thing that morning. Hell, I should've shaken Button awake as soon as I read the letter.

My hand worked over Winter's head with such force that the dog backed away, giving me an accusatory glare. Hey, lady, not so hard, eh?

When I finally looked up, the man was there, standing so close it made my breath hitch.

He extended a hand. "I'm Jax."

For a second, I thought about leaving him hanging. Instead, I gave his hand a quick shake. "Ellena."

Button grinned, the kind of smile that made men lose track of their better judgment. "We're stepsisters."

And which one's wicked? I kept my expression neutral.

Button tilted her head, leaning in just enough to signal her interest. "So, Jax, you from around here?"

"Got a cabin further up the swamp. But the stars are better out here—when the clouds don't get in the way."

Button said, "I love stargazing. Orion's my favorite. What's yours?"

I resisted the urge to roll my eyes. *Oh, please. The only stargazing you enjoy is inside the pages of People magazine.*

"Well, Orion's not technically a star," Jax said, a grin tugging at the corner of his mouth. "But I'll let that slide. Mine's Algol."

Button blinked, her smile fading like she'd just lost five grand on red. "Oh. I don't know that one."

"It's the second-brightest star in the constellation Perseus."

"The Demon Star," I said, the words automatic—a game show contestant hitting the buzzer too soon. "Pretty bad omen, if you believe the lore." I winced, cursing myself for starting a conversation with someone I had no interest in talking to.

"I like it because it winks—every three days or so," Jax said.

Did he just wink at me? No, probably not. Or maybe? My mind spiraled for a second before I shook it off. I was already calculating the fastest way to extricate myself from the conversation when Button piped up, "You should join us for dinner, Jax. We've got plenty."

I shot Button a glare that lingered long enough to make my point. Unwanted company was not part of the evening plan. Then again, Button wasn't a mind reader—unless she was. Had Eric tipped her off he was going to tell me their secret? Was that her way of avoiding the fallout? Either way, even if I couldn't summon the courage that night, one thing was certain: I wasn't spending the evening talking about stars with a stranger.

I said, "I don't think you'll like what we have. Veggie burgers. And I'm not sure we've got enough."

"Rubbish," Button shot back, not missing a beat. "You always pack for a week even if we're gone two days. You up for veggie burgers, Jax?"

Jax glanced between us, his expression caught somewhere between suspicion and unease, like he had just cracked open a vampire's casket and couldn't decide whether to check if it was empty or run for his life.

He held up a hand. "I don't want to impose."

Button dismissed his hesitation with a casual wave. "I insist. Come on, Jax, we're starvin' for company. Join us for a beer, at least."

My mouth opened, but no words came. I should have said no, should have shaken my head, or shot it down with something firm and final. But out of some misplaced sense of politeness, I found myself nodding and smiling. I was furious—at Button, at Jax, and at myself most of all.

"If you're sure..." Jax said.

Button said, "We will not take no for an answer. Come on over when you're done sharpenin' that knife."

* * *

By the time we returned to the campsite, the sun had dipped behind the trees, and a cool breeze threaded through the air. I fired up the camping stove while Button set the table, humming under her breath.

"Unusual name," Button said, glancing at him as she popped open a beer.

"Oh, it's short for Jackson. My dad wanted something southern. Let's just say he had... opinions about the Old South."

"Like a Civil War buff?" Button asked.

"Something like that," Jax said, his tone clipped.

I stirred the pot of pasta, filing the information away. I couldn't say why, but the name didn't fit the man. Dexter, perhaps. Or Hannibal?

Bet he's sizing me up for dinner.

Over burgers and pasta salad, Jax appeared to let his guard down, though his answers to Button's questions stayed just vague enough to keep my curiosity simmering. I liked unanswered questions about as much as I liked an impossible Wordle. Jax mentioned being stationed in Jamaica, but when Button pressed him, his responses tightened like a knot pulled taut.

"What were you doing there?" Button leaned forward, her voice bright with curiosity.

"Navy SEAL stuff." Jax's tone was too casual, like he was testing the waters.

Button's eyes lit up, her enthusiasm undimmed. "Ooh, where did you train?"

He paused for a moment too long. "Parris Island."

19

I frowned, swirling my pasta salad around my plate with my fork. The name struck a chord, but something about it was... off. "Parris Island?"

Jax's expression didn't falter. "That's right."

I set my plate down. I knew little about military bases, but I was pretty sure Parris Island was for Marines, not SEALs. Wasn't *Full Metal Jacket* set there? Maybe I was wrong—but the gnawing sense that I was right wouldn't let go.

His calm, measured demeanor reminded me too much of Eric when he lied—smooth on the surface, roiling underneath.

Who is this man? Isn't this how slasher movies start? The audience would've been screaming, "Run," the moment they stumbled upon him sharpening that knife.

Thankfully, the conversation shifted to lighter topics—camping mishaps, favorite hikes, the brightest stars in the sky—and the tension eased just enough for me to tuck my distrust into a far corner of my mind.

After dinner, Jax excused himself, disappearing into the trees. The fire crackled, its light flickering over Button's face as she turned to me.

Her smile slipped away, like she'd just stepped offstage and out of character. "What's with the weird attitude, huh?"

"I could ask you the same."

Button frowned, her mouth pulling into a tight line. "What's that supposed to mean?"

The words tumbled out before I could stop them. "Eric wrote to me. He mentioned you."

Button froze, her usual composure cracking like a windshield hit by hail. She turned abruptly, rummaging through her bag with frantic motions, as if searching for something that might buy her time to think.

I stared, my pulse quickening. Was this it? The confession? The moment of truth—the *Culminare*? I braced myself for whatever Button would pull out.

But it wasn't a letter or some piece of damning evidence. It was a lipstick. Button stared at it, her fingers tightening around the tube, and then she shoved it back into the bag. She took a slow, deep breath—as if she was trying to stay calm.

"I wanted to tell you myself," she said finally, her voice a whisper.

My throat tightened, the firelight casting deep shadows across Button's face. Before I could complete the thought, the sound of boots on gravel broke the moment.

Jax's footsteps crunched closer, and Winter padded into the firelight ahead of him, tail wagging. The dog's presence dulled the tension—not enough to smother it, but enough to push it into the background.

Button gave a bright, practiced laugh—the kind that sounded too big, too cheery to be real. "Jax! There you are. I was just sayin' it's time for dessert."

I didn't move. Dessert? A pie in the face would be perfect. I could already picture Button's ridiculous makeup smeared with cream topping and pumpkin slop.

Jax declined Button's dried fruit offering and sat down. He steered the conversation toward the Leonid meteor shower, which was supposed to peak that night. But I barely listened. The truth lingered like heat from dying embers, left by Button to smolder.

And then, as if Jax had predicted it, the sky opened up. A break in the clouds revealed a patch of inky black, where a streak of light blazed across the darkness—a meteor, brilliant and fleeting. Then another, and another. The meteors carved mesmerizing, bright paths through the exposed sliver of night.

Button gasped, pointing skyward. "A meteor shower!" She turned to Jax, her voice dripping with playful charm. "What are you, some kinda genius? I should make a wish!"

I snorted. *Sure, because nothing screams "good luck" like fireballs streaking through the sky.*

Then came the buzz. It cut through the silence like a dentist's drill hammering a molar—a shrill, needling whine that made the hairs on my neck prickle—a sound too insistent to ignore, too high and thin to mistake for anything but a chime engineered for panic.

My phone lit up on the table, followed by Button's and Jax's.

Button picked up her phone and stared at it like it was a Mensa test. The soft glow from the phone cast a spectral sheen on her face, accentuating the furrows of confusion etched between her brows. She tilted the device at different angles, as if clarity might emerge from a shift in perspective.

"What does it say?" I asked. I could've checked my own phone, but I'd long since trained myself to ignore every buzz, ring, or ping—it was always spam or bill collectors, anyway. Jax hadn't so much as glanced at his phone, and I wondered if he was dodging the same relentless calls.

"I have no idea, but it don't sound good." Button's voice trembled with an unease she couldn't hide. "Usually, it's a missing kid or something, right? But this one... it just says, 'Wait for further instructions—protocol engagement pending.'"

"Protocol what?" I asked, glancing at Jax, searching his face for answers he might not have.

Jax looked at me, his face expressionless. "We do exactly what it says. We wait."

Wait? For what? Who is this man?

I forced my attention away from Jax's knowing stare and onto a crackling piece of wood in the fire. My mind scrambled for procedure, for answers—anything grounded in logic, anything but this vague, formless threat. I wished for my old EMT badge, the solid heft of it, a reminder of times when action was the only option. That badge had meant purpose, something tangible to do. Now, trapped in a vacuum, my instincts flickered between fear and control.

But here, in that moment, there were no wounds to dress, no bones to set. Just the stifling uncertainty of *what*? A mishap at FEMA? Someone pressing the wrong button, like that time in Hawaii when an employee sent an inbound missile alert instead of a test message during a shift change. Hawaii residents had hidden in sewers for 38 minutes. But surely this was no missile alert. But if that was true, what was it, exactly?

The stupid message had shattered a fleeting illusion of calm, leaving my mind spinning in a storm of confusion and dread. I kept my words locked behind clenched teeth, holding back the rising flood of panic.

Button stared hard at her phone, like sheer willpower might drag answers out of the screen. My hands twitched with the urge to grab her, to shake her free of that trance and demand an explanation. Inside my head, fears spun and collided, each louder than the last. We were sitting there, waiting for—what? A tornado warning? A chemical spill? Some other disaster?

A second alert shattered the quiet, pulling me back to the present. Each phone buzzed out of sync in a jarring, overlapping cacophony. Button's hand flew to her chest, clutching her phone like it might shield her from whatever was coming.

"Seek shelter immediately. M-m-more information to follow."

The words hung in the air, thick and foreboding. My pulse quickened, the instructions simple but overwhelming. Seek shelter immediately. But why? From what? I needed answers. I needed Google.

I glanced up at the storm clouds creeping in. Stars blinked through breaks in the dark canopy, and a meteor blazed across one gap, brighter and larger than any I'd seen. Its fiery tail carved a glowing scar through the night sky.

"Jax. What... what's going on?" Button whispered.

He jumped to his feet. "We need to find cover."

Button nodded quickly, like a bobblehead doll snapped into motion, her focus still glued to the phone.

Jax said, "Can we take your truck? There's a motel in Argon. Might be able to get a couple of rooms."

I stood and grabbed my phone and mug off the picnic bench. The thought of taking action felt good. I didn't trust him—not by a long shot—but action was something solid, something to hold on to. It was better than sitting here with swirling thoughts and no plan. "You don't have wheels?"

"I took my canoe down," he said.

Before I could say no, Jax bolted over to his campsite. He ducked into his tent and reemerged seconds later with a bulging seabag, jogging back with Winter in tow. Button and I gathered our bags with tense, wordless efficiency.

I just couldn't say no, could I?

I barely had time to toss the bags into the Explorer when thunder rolled through the thick, claustrophobic air. A blinding light exploded out of the darkness, sudden and searing like a camera flash on full blast. It washed over everything, bleaching the world in an instant, leaving me disoriented and stunned, as if the night had been stripped away in one violent stroke.

3 Name That Nuclear Tune

I locked eyes with Jax, the air between us taut and unspoken, thick with the tension neither of us dared to name. Button stood to the side, her usual chatter absent, as if she felt it too—nature coiled tight, like a diamondback before the strike.

The sounds of the swamp didn't fade into silence but into something heavier, a stillness that thrummed at the edge of awareness. It reminded me of the way the air held its breath before a tornado, a moment stretched thin with anticipation.

Jax looked away first. He tilted his head and scanned the sky, his brow furrowing. He was searching for something. A pressure in the air I couldn't name.

What's he looking for? My mind couldn't settle. The way he searched the sky reminded me of scanning my surroundings under duress during training.

The memory slipped in without warning: riot training, the gas chamber, the sting of CS gas in my lungs and eyes. Two of my colleagues had panicked, clawing at their masks and bolting for the door. But not me. I'd stayed rooted, clinging to the science. Tear gas couldn't kill me. The pain was a lie, designed to break resolve. I hadn't let it.

But this wasn't tear gas.

Another flash lit the horizon, cold and electric, slicing through the darkness. Not as bright as the first, but enough to make my heart slam against my ribs like a trapped bird. My mind scrambled to place the source: Tallahassee? Lake City? The light vanished as quickly as it came, leaving an afterglow that pulsed in my vision. Moments later, the rumble came—low, distant, and wrong. *Another flash? What the heck?*

I froze. A bat jerked through the clearing—a black needle stitching crooked through the night air. When it swept past my face, so close I felt the wind from its wings against my cheek, I screamed.

Jax turned, his eyebrows raised. "You okay?"

I pressed a hand to my chest, feeling the hammering of my heart. "Bat. Just a bat." I forced out the words, my voice cracking.

My mind raced. I had trained for emergencies, but not this. Not for flashes on the horizon. Not for rumbling that sounded like the sky splitting open.

"We've got minutes before the shockwave hits," Jax said.

Shockwave? The word sucked the breath from my lungs.

Button's eyes widened in panic. "Minutes? Why...?"

Jax said, "That second flash might've been Tallahassee. But the first one is what we need to worry about right now. Mayport? King's Bay? Either way, we're close enough to feel it." He crouched down and grabbed Winter by the collar, pulling him close. "Get down. Stay low."

"Why...?" Button repeated, her voice high-pitched, on the edge of a shriek. "Shockwave from...?"

Jax shot her a steely, unhinged look. "A blast."

Button's breaths came shallow and quick, her eyes flitting around like moths slamming against a lampshade, a beat away from full-blown hysteria.

An overwhelming feeling of dread consumed me as every second passed. My mind urged me to do something—anything—but my legs refused to move, cemented in place.

Come on, move! My hands shook as I fought to break free from the paralysis creeping over me. I crouched down seconds before a powerful wall of air swept through the campsite, nearly knocking me to the ground.

The air trembled before a second gust swept through, carrying with it the scent of dust and something metallic, like hot iron. Loose leaves and dirt swirled in the wind. Even the trees, their branches groaning in protest, were uneasy, their leaves trembling as if they, too, were desperate to escape. The smell shifted again, acrid and biting, clinging to the back of my throat.

The campfire's flames guttered and spit, sending a handful of embers spiraling upward before the air went still again. The air carried a sound of its own—an almost imperceptible hum that burrowed into my ears, stretching the moments thin and leaving me braced for something to shatter it, even as I prayed it wouldn't.

Winter sprang to his feet, his fur bristling. A low growl rumbled from his throat.

I turned toward the eastern horizon, where the glow of the blast still hung in the sky. A pressure settled in my chest, heavy and unrelenting, like fear made solid. *What if this is it? What if this is how it all ends?*

In the back of my mind, my EMT voice urged me to take control of the situation, but I couldn't move from my crouched position as I processed the horror of it all.

"Felt like an earthquake," Jax said.

Button's lips parted like she was about to speak but couldn't find the words. She glanced at Jax, as if waiting for him to explain, to fill the silence.

I glared at Jax. *An earthquake? Seriously?* The ground had shaken with something far more sinister, and we all knew it. I bit back a retort, my mind racing. Was Jax downplaying it, or was he trying to keep us from falling apart?

I said, "No. That... that felt like something big. Maybe... a bomb, even nuclear." I trailed off, the words sinking in like lead into water as my mind spun with uncertainty. I chastised myself for stating the obvious—the same thing I'd accused Jax of back at his campsite.

The King and Queen of Obvious. Let's play Name That Nuclear Tune, the stupid game we are apparently playing now.

Jax glanced at me. There was something in his eyes that might have been pity—or resignation. "Yeah. A nuke. But panicking won't help. Not now."

No point in panicking? Jax had no idea how close I was to losing it right now—and Button was even closer.

Her hand flew to her mouth, tears carving pink trails through her foundation. "A nuke? Lord, are we fixin' to die?"

I took a shaky breath, battling the panic rising within me. This wasn't the time to lose it—I had to at least try to look composed. "No," I said, hoping my voice sounded steady. "We... we'll figure this out. We just need to stay calm."

Stay calm? Wasn't that what Captain What's-His-Name said on the Titanic, right before the ship split in two?

Winter pressed against Jax's leg. The firelight cast dancing shadows across Jax's face, which was lined with tension.

I scanned the campsite, my mind buzzing as I honed in on movement at the Airstream, about a hundred feet away. A bearded man in the baseball cap—mid-twenties, I guessed—bent over a picnic table, turning something over and over with hurried motions. I squinted, making out the shape of what looked like an emergency radio. Something about the way he rocked there, shoulders hunched like a carrion bird, punched through years of buried memories.

A scene flashed before me: the fiery wreck of a bus crash, a chaotic tangle of twisted metal and flames where twelve lives had been lost in an instant. One man had survived, sitting untouched by the highway, his body trembling as he rocked back and forth, tugging at his sleeves. I'd tried speaking to him, but his wide, empty eyes had looked straight through me.

The jittery man at the picnic table wore that same look—haunted, teetering on the edge.

Just like me. I am going to lose it any second.

"Stop," I muttered under my breath. "Focus. This is not the time."

Button shot me a confused glance. "Stop what?"

I shook my head. "Nothing."

Across the way, a woman stepped out of the camper and placed a hand on the man's shoulder. Her long black hair, streaked with gray, was wild and untamed. His mother, I guessed. Or perhaps just *"auld enough tae be his mum,"* as Gran would have said—a cougar in hiking boots. *Good God, why am I thinking like this when we are in—what* is *this? The middle of an apocalypse?*

The radio crackled to life. "This is not a test," the voice announced, its words traveling across the campground's dead quiet air. "This is an emergency alert. A nuclear explosion has been detected in your area. Seek immediate shelter and avoid windows. Stay indoors and await further instructions."

The announcement hit like a dull blow, driving the air from my lungs and smothering any words. Button's grip tightened on my arm, and Winter let out a soft whimper at Jax's feet. Heat rushed to my face as fear scraped at the edges of my mind.

This. Is. Not. Real. Now. Is. Not. The. Time. Don't fall apart.

I said, "We should... try to get organized. Maybe check our supplies, see what we've got."

Jax said, "Agreed. We'll need better cover. If the fallout reaches us— and it could, in a couple of hours—we'll need insulation from the radiation. Fast."

"What about the motel?" I asked.

Jax pushed himself up from his crouch. "Not enough time. And we can't risk them being full."

Button raised her hand as if she was asking for permission to speak. "We could drive home? Couldn't we?"

Jax said, "Sure. If you want to drive straight into the path of the fallout."

Button's hopeful expression crumbled. "Oh."

Out of the shadows, the black-haired woman appeared as if summoned. Beaded necklaces and trinkets hung around her neck and wrists, softly clinking as she came to a stop a few paces away. She looked over my tent with a skeptical lift of her brow. "Looks like you could use a better shelter, eh?"

She pointed to the Airstream. "I'm Maggie and that's our home. Me and my son, Greg. We've been living off the grid for a while now, so I s'pose we've got a few things that could help us all."

In the flickering firelight, her black hair melted into the shadows, with just a few silver strands catching the glow. Her face was lined, not just with age, but with the kind of stories you don't tell unless someone's earned the right to hear them.

Jax eyed the trailer. "Think it'll fit all of us?"

"It won't be luxury, but it's solid. One bedroom and one bath, but we'll make it work, you betcha."

Jax said, "I appreciate the offer. But aluminum walls aren't much better than tent fabric."

"Ah, but we winterized it. It's no lead vault, but there's enough insulation to keep Greg and me toasty in Alaska. Might just be your best option—unless you're thinking about breaking into the camp shop and using a bucket for a bathroom."

Jax frowned. "Insulation won't stop gamma radiation."

"I hear you young man. But it's better than being out in the open, eh?"

Button's nose wrinkled as she glanced up the road that led to the camp shop. "A bucket? No thank you, ma'am. The trailer has a bathroom, doesn't it?"

Maggie nodded. "One bath. Small, but it does the job."

Jax raised a hand, cutting off any further debate. "It's not ideal, but I agree, it's our best option. A log cabin or a tent would be suicide in this."

I said, "Suicide? I thought you said the fallout might not even hit us. So, which is it, Jax?"

For a moment, he didn't meet my eyes. "I said it *could*. It depends on the wind. Fallout spreads fastest with the jet stream, but ground-level winds can carry it in unpredictable directions. If it's a surface detonation, the radiation plume could travel hundreds of miles, depending on how the wind shifts. We need to plan for the worst, and hope for the best."

I crossed my arms and stared at him, his torrent of information washing over me without fully sinking in. "In other words, you have no idea if it will come our way."

Button glanced between us, her brows furrowing. "Can we not do this right now?"

My hands hovered in the air, fingers stiff and claw-like, gripping at nothing—like I was throttling a phantom neck. I tipped my chin toward the sky in a silent *God give me strength* plea. Before I could snap at Button, Maggie stepped in.

"Well, come on over with whatever you've got, eh? Greg and I'll be inside."

As we gathered our gear and prepared to follow Maggie, the air thickened with tension. My thoughts focused on one thing: time. We were running out of it. Every second we spent exposed in the open meant more danger, more risk, one step closer to fallout.

Jax rifled through his seabag, pulling out supplies with a mechanical precision that set me on edge. His hands moved too fast, each motion clipped and exact, like he was on autopilot. Something about the way he worked unsettled me. I didn't think he had all the answers—but then again, none of us did. At least he knew *something*, though how deep his knowledge went or where it came from didn't matter. Not right now.

I broke the silence. "Assuming the fallout reaches us, how long will we have to stay inside?"

Jax didn't look up, his hands still moving with that unsettling precision. "Depends. Could be a few days. Could be weeks. Hard to say without knowing the yield or where it hit." His tone was even, detached, like he was reading instructions off a manual.

It was all too familiar—just like Eric, dodging my questions about his late nights, whispered phone calls, and locked phone and laptop. Jax faced the looming threat of fallout with a calm that was wrong. It wasn't the calm of someone in control. It was the calm of a man with secrets.

Button disappeared back into the tent, mumbling something about her phone charger.

"You knew this was coming, didn't you?" I asked.

For a split second, his hands stilled, then he plunged them back into his seabag, pulling out a flashlight and a bundle of rope.

"Jax. Please... look at me."

He hesitated, fingers curling around the rope until his knuckles turned white. Then he straightened, his expression tightening. The set of his jaw, the flicker of tension in his face—Jax was holding something back, and it was written all over him.

"I didn't know for sure. There were... whispers. Nothing concrete. Just things I picked up here and there. Nothing to act on—until now."

The dread in my stomach, heavy as concrete since the blast, sank deeper—cold and consuming. "Rumors about what?"

Jax sighed and ran a hand through his hair. "About potential strikes."

"So, you knew this was a possibility?" My voice came out harsher than I intended, frustration snapping through. "You should've warned us."

"Are you serious?" Jax's expression tightened. "I didn't know, not for sure. Wasn't about to scare the hell out of you two over rumors I heard months back. But right now, we need to think about survival, yeah?"

My frustration simmered, a low burn I couldn't extinguish. Jax's calm authority grated at me, but questioning it now was like stepping off a cliff without knowing how far I'd fall. He had answers—or at least sounded like he did—and that was more than I could claim. For the time being, I'd have to let it go.

I exhaled, trying to steady the storm in my head. Jax was right—this wasn't the time for blame or anger, no matter how much mistrust gnawed at me. Survival came first. But the "whispers" he'd mentioned stuck in my mind like thorns. *What kind of SEAL hears rumors like that? Was he high enough up the chain to get intel civilians couldn't imagine?* My only SEAL reference was Hollywood—the loud, explosive caricature of guns and glory. That couldn't be all there was to the job, could it?

Not now. Survival, I reminded myself. *Focus.*

I let my doubts hang, unasked and unanswered, like a radio tuned to static—persistent, distracting, but offering nothing clear. Jax seemed sure, and that had to be enough for now. Survival didn't leave room for second guessing—not yet.

"We should maybe try to get organized," I said. "Let's see what we've got. Work out a plan?"

Jax reached into his bag and took out a flashlight, two packets of Mountain House meals—just add water—a handful of Clif Bars, and a vacuum-sealed pack of turkey jerky. "I think I've got enough here for a couple of days. More if I ration."

He fished out a black device from the bottom of his seabag, then sighed. "I had to leave the cabin fast. Grabbed my go-bag but left the full kit behind. No KI, no chelating agents. Figures, right?"

I tilted my head, at first thinking the device was a radio. But no—it was definitely a Geiger counter—like the one I'd seen in my disaster training—with a small digital display and a slim probe. And a chelating agent was for treating radiation exposure. The abbreviation, though, didn't register. "KI?"

"Potassium iodide," Jax said. "Helps block radioactive iodine from getting into the thyroid. Not perfect, but better than nothing."

I frowned. "And you didn't bring them because...?"

He sighed, running a hand over his cheek. His mouth formed a wide O as if to release the tension locked in his jaw. "Left my full kit behind when I grabbed the go-bag. Didn't exactly have time to double-check the packing list."

The go-bag? Isn't that something out of a bank robbery movie? The stash hidden under the floorboards for when the FBI rolls up the driveway?

Before the thought could settle, before I could think of the right question to ask, before I panicked about shacking up in a trailer with who—a man on FBI's Most Wanted?—Button eased out of the Explorer, her legs unsteady, a slight sway in her stance.

"I got some water bottles... granola bars..." she said, words trailing off as if she didn't trust them. She lifted a can with a shrug. "And... bug spray."

I brushed past her to grab my backpack from the SUV. Back at the picnic table, I emptied it and surveyed the meager pile: a package of organic nuts, leftover veggies, oatmeal, powdered milk. Hardly the week's feast that Button had bragged about to Jax. Not much, but it would have to do. We needed to figure out how to stretch it—and what to do when it ran out.

Somewhere nearby, a mockingbird called out. Its cry wasn't the usual melodic mimicry but an eerie wail—a rising and falling whoop-whoop-whoop that raised the hairs on my arms.

Mockingbirds weren't supposed to sing at night. I knew that much. It was a springtime show put on by lonely males. But this one hadn't gotten the memo.

The usual swamp sounds were still there—the buzz of insects, the occasional croak of a leopard frog—but they were muffled, like a coffin lid creaking shut.

4 Duct Tape and a Prayer

With our supplies laid out and a tentative plan stitched together, I turned toward Maggie's trailer—a fragile promise of shelter against the looming threat outside. It was our only real chance to shield ourselves from the fallout, slim as it might be.

My fingers twitched against the strap of my pack. "We should head over."

Jax and I exchanged brief nods and stepped onto the path, swallowed by the darkness pressing in from all sides. Maggie's Airstream glimmered ahead, a lone oasis in the void, its string lights spilling a pale halo onto the surrounding trees.

As we walked, a low rumble echoed in the distance—not thunder, but something stranger, as if the atmosphere had been disturbed. The wind picked up, carrying with it a dampness that clung to our skin. The clouds churned in unnatural patterns, dense and dark, as if responding to the explosion's violent disruption. A light drizzle fell, the raindrops cold and sparse, yet thick with the metallic tang.

Button glanced over her shoulder. "Did anyone else feel that?"

I said, "The blast... it must've kicked something up. Changed the pressure or the storm system." I wasn't sure if the explanation was for Button or myself, but it sounded reasonable. *Grounded in science. Not threatening. Just a storm kicking up, that's all.*

Each step was heavier, gravity seemed lighter, my movements unsteady. I told myself it was the panic creeping in and making me lightheaded. I forced myself to draw slow, deep breaths.

The drizzle wasn't rain so much as an afterthought of it, a misty, gray soup that clung to my skin and hair, more like walking through the ghost of a storm than a real one. Only the soft scuff of our shoes and the rustle of leaves broke the silence. I felt the tension in every step, my senses sharpening with each movement. Fallout was coming, and with every passing moment, the risk grew. *Is it already in the rain? Am I already toast?*

Button asked, "Is this such a good idea? Shouldn't we be heading for caves or something?"

She was smart, perhaps too smart for her own good, but she had the common sense of a sandbag. *Caves in the Okefenokee? We'd be lucky to find a deep ditch.*

Jax rolled his eyes. "Sure. Let's all hop in the car and head to the Florida Caverns. What is it... three hours west? And since we're there, let's swing by Publix for groceries. Grab a pizza and a six-pack while we're at it."

Button's face went slack, like someone had flipped off her power switch. She repositioned her bag on her shoulder, then walked the rest of the way in silence.

Maggie stepped out of the trailer, waving us in with a warm, open hand. Inside, the scent of sage lingered—calming on any other day, but in that moment it felt out of place, like the smell of roses in a cadaver lab. Draped fabrics and trinkets decorated every surface, giving it a laid-back, bohemian charm. Framed pictures of mountains and inspirational quotes hung on the walls. One, a cross-stitch, said "If there is righteousness in the heart, there will be beauty in the character. If there is beauty in the character, there will be harmony in the home."

"That's a nice quote, Maggie. Is it from the Bible?"

Maggie chuckled. "Heavens, no. That was from... hmmm. I've forgotten. Ghandi, I think."

I smiled, thinking that it didn't seem like something that Ghandi would say. "Thanks for this, Maggie. You didn't have to."

Maggie scoffed, her smile crooked and fleeting. "We've gotta look out for each other, dontcha think?" Her voice carried a note of resolve, but the unspoken question lingered in the air. Who knew how many others had made it?

A shudder worked up my back. I'd been so focused on my own survival that I hadn't even considered how many others might have been killed in the blasts. *Hundreds? Millions? Was my home still there? Did Mr. Hughes and the neighborhood kids make it?*

Jax's voice cut through my thoughts. "Maggie, do you have supplies to seal the gaps? Windows, doors?"

Maggie nodded, her hands already moving toward a cupboard. "Duct tape, blankets. It ain't perfect, but it's better than nothing." She paused, glancing at Jax with a smirk. "Unless you've got a fallout shelter tucked in that seabag."

"Everything but. Once we seal it all up, I'll check the radiation levels with my Geiger counter."

"Prepper, eh?" Maggie asked.

Jax chuckled and shook his head. "Let's just say I'm cautious."

I caught the rueful smile they shared—as if they wished it wasn't the time to use prepper stuff, as though they had hoped this day had never come—before it vanished. Tension settled back in, pulling my focus to the task ahead.

The trailer was the kind of place where every movement had a cost. A narrow aisle cut down the middle, leading to a tiny bedroom in the back, separated by a thin sliding door that rattled with every step. Beds were stacked wherever they'd fit—a fold-out couch here, a dinette that doubled as a bed there—leaving little room to maneuver. As we scrambled to sort blankets and divide tasks, elbows bumped and shoulders brushed—like plane passengers wrestling for an inch of space in coach.

Winter wandered through the cramped space, sniffing the corners like he was mapping out his territory. Maggie passed duct tape and blankets to me from the bedroom. Jax instructed Button on how to seal a window. Greg hovered near the side door, shifting his weight, staring into the darkness, like a man who didn't know where to begin.

I grabbed a pile of blankets from Maggie. *Why isn't Greg helping?* "Is he okay?"

Maggie sighed. "Greg's got a TBI—traumatic brain injury. He's never been the same since his accident. I'll tell ya more later."

A pang of guilt struck me for judging too quickly. "That's terrible. I'm so sorry."

Maggie gave a small, tight smile. "Thanks. He'll pitch in when he can. Right now, let's just keep moving, yup?"

As we made our way to the front of the Airstream, I kept glancing back at Maggie, wondering how someone could stay so composed. Maggie wasn't just calm; she was prepared and composed. Was that what survival looked like? Not panicking when everything inside you screamed to run like a ten-ton truck was barreling your way?

Maggie handed tape and blankets to Jax and Button, then handed a roll of tape to me.

"Ellena, come with me to the back, would ya? I could use an extra set of hands."

Maggie led the way back to the bedroom and slid the thin, rattling door shut behind us. "So Greg don't catch wind of it," she whispered.

Even with the door closed, the muted sounds of Jax and Button working up front filtered through.

Maggie climbed onto the bed with a grunt. "We'll get the ceiling vent first, eh?"

I nodded and tore off a strip of tape. Watching Maggie work didn't quiet the noise in my head, but it gave me something to latch onto. There was something calming about the way she worked, like she was hanging paper chains for Christmas instead of sealing herself up in a crypt.

"You and Jax a couple?" Maggie asked, smoothing tape around the vent edges. Her bracelets jingled with each movement.

I blinked, surprised. "No. No, no. I just met him. This afternoon."

"Aww, I can see it in your eyes. Don't blame you, mind you. He's got a nice aura."

Nice aura? Nope, I wasn't touching that. But now Maggie had put it out there, I couldn't stop the thought. Jax gave off *that* vibe. But so had Eric. And look where that got me.

I cleared my throat, shifting gears. "What happened to Greg?"

Maggie paused, the tape in her hand suspended midair. She exhaled, her gaze distant. "He got the brain injury years ago, on his honeymoon, of all times. Him and his wife were on a cruise ship, and he was taking a tender to shore. One of those docking poles came loose, hit him bang in the head."

I winced, my EMT instincts kicking in. I knew all too well how devastating a TBI could be. It wasn't just the initial injury—it was the ripple effects that never went away. "That must've been... life-changing."

"It sure was. He was in a coma for two weeks. When he came to, he wasn't the same. His memory was shot, his emotions all over the place. He'd get frustrated over nothing or just... shut down. Couldn't go back to work—not full time, anyway. And his wife..." Maggie's lips tightened. "She couldn't deal. Walked out on him six months later."

I thought of how Eric behaved after his arrest, the way he'd retreated into his guilt until it hardened into something unmovable. When I'd been sick with the flu last January, he'd not so much as brewed me a cup of tea. The people you needed most had a way of turning into shadows when you needed them. "That's awful."

"Yup. But what could I do? Let him fall apart? Not on my watch, I'll tell ya that." Maggie let out a slow breath and resumed taping the vent. "I think about it all the time, ya know. I bought that cruise for them—my gift. Greg couldn't afford it, not working at the animal shelter. Scraping by, doing what he loved. If I hadn't pushed them to go, he wouldn't have been on that boat."

I opened my mouth to say something, then closed it again, rubbing a finger on my temple as I searched for the right words. "You couldn't have known, Maggie. It's not your fault."

"I hear ya. But it's hard not to go there sometimes. That guilt—it creeps in, slow at first, and then before ya know—it's all you can think about."

Maggie held out a hand for another strip of tape, then pressed it into place along the edge of the vent, smoothing it down with her thumb. "So, what's your story? You've got that haunted look. And don't tell me it's because a bomb went off. Us broken souls, we know our own, eh?"

"My ex, he got sent to prison for embezzling..." I faltered, swallowing hard. "Gambled our house away." *Then I lost the baby.* "It's not an excuse, I know, but... but... I got distracted on the job. A woman died. But if I'd been paying attention... maybe..."

My voice cracked, and I didn't finish the sentence. I was aware of Maggie watching me, but I kept my gaze fixed on the ceiling vent, willing myself to hold it together.

Maggie's hand settled on my shoulder. "Ellena, didn't ya just tell me I shouldn't blame myself for things I couldn't control? Sounds like you might need to hear your own advice."

A single tear slipped free and traced a path down my cheek. "But I could have controlled it. I was an EMT, I'm trained not to panic."

"Grief does strange things to us, ya know. If we could control it, then we'd be sipping Margaritas on a beach the day after, now wouldn't we? We make the best decisions we can with what we've got in the moment. And if it turns out it wasn't the best call, then you gotta forgive yourself and keep going."

I looked up toward Maggie and brushed the dampness from my cheek with the back of my hand. "You're right. I know you're right. It's just..." *Impossible.* "Hard."

"It is. But you're stronger than ya think. That spark in your eyes? You still got it, I tell ya."

The warmth in Maggie's words stirred something in me, something absent from my life for a long time. Hope, perhaps. Or a flicker of self-forgiveness. I wasn't sure if I could hold on to that feeling, but for the first time in what felt like forever, I thought I could try.

* * *

When Maggie and I returned to the front of the trailer, Jax was crouched by the vent near the floor, pressing tape over its edges. He smoothed each strip with slow, meticulous strokes. Button perched on the edge of the dinette, one leg tucked under her, the other swinging in a halting cadence. Her fingers picked at a loose seam on the blanket on her lap.

Winter scratched his paw in the trailer's corner, as if he was digging up a treat. *Sorry, bud. Treats are going to be in short supply from now on.*

Greg hovered at the kitchen sink, the sputtering faucet coughing out more air than water. His hands shook as he filled a pan, splashing water over the counter. "This... this doesn't feel like enough," he said. "Why does it feel like it's never enough?"

No one answered, but he didn't seem to care. "Radiation isn't something you can just block out with blankets and tape!" His voice rose into a falsetto. "It's invisible—it gets inside you—"

"Greg," Maggie said, stepping forward and resting a hand on his arm. Her voice was a gentle balm. "Love, listen. You're right—it's not perfect. But it's better than doing nothing."

Greg shook her off with a snap of his arm. "I'm not crazy, okay? I've read about this. You all think this is enough, but it's not." He grabbed another saucepan, slammed it on the counter with a thwack, and started filling it.

Maggie turned to me and Jax, her lips forming a silent "Sorry."

Button slid off the dinette and grabbed a blanket. "Maggie, what made you so ready for this?"

Maggie paused, her hand resting on the edge of the storage compartment door. She stared past the trailer walls, lost in thought. "My grandma lived through the Blizzard of '49 down in Nebraska. Used to say, 'You can never be too ready for when the world decides to go to hell.'"

Greg spun around, agitated. "But what if it's not enough? What if we're just sitting ducks in this tin can?"

Maggie said, "Greg, that's enough now, hey? You're spooking the dog."

Winter's hackles stiffened and bristled. His ears pitched forward like radar dishes, eyes locked on Greg. He barked once, loud and piercing.

Greg's hands clenched and unclenched before he turned back to the sink, mumbling under his breath.

I sat down on the couch and drained the last dreg of whiskey from my flask. *No more hot toddies on this lovely little holiday. Maybe not ever.*

Button joined me, slumping in the corner like she'd just finished a hard day's work on the farm. "Ellena, I'm so sorry. I feel like this is all my fault."

I gave her a pointed glare. *Was it her fault? Could Button have whispered something to Eric? Maybe not... but why else would he have needed to embezzle? Did he need the money for what—a fancy city apartment for his mistress? Diamonds? A vacation in Italy?*

Button's expression fell, as if she could read my mind. "This... camping trip. That's why we're here." She swept a hand around the trailer like Vanna White revealing the answer.

"That's..." *Such a dumbass thing to say.* "Not true. If we'd have stayed home, we'd be in the fen wi' no way oot."

"Huh?" Button asked, her brow furrowing, like I had just switched to speaking in Urdu.

"Up shit creek." I sighed, irritated that I had to explain Gran's idioms. Button had never warmed to Gran the way I had growing up. Or was it that Gran hadn't warmed to Button? Either way, it was a stupid thing to get worked up over, considering the circumstances, and I chastised myself. *Get a grip, Ellena.*

"But I dragged you into this!" Button's voice cracked, her eyes brimming with tears. "What if we don't make it? What if we're stuck here and... and—"

"Stop." My voice was too sharp, and I took a deep breath to pull it back. "We'll get through this. We will. We've got supplies, and... a plan."

Button wiped her eyes, nodding, though her pupils were blown wide with fear. "I can't stop thinking about everything that could go wrong... and I only packed the one lipstick... It's so stupid, but... I don't know... I don't even have gloss."

I bit back a retort. *Seriously?* The thought flared, sudden and unbidden, but I swallowed it down. *Focus, Ellena. You can't start snapping now.*

Jax, crouched by the vent, turned toward us with his Geiger counter in hand. "Radiation levels look good right now. Got this baby online—fifty bucks on Amazon. Not the best, but it works."

His attempt to break the tension, if that's what it was, fell flat. The walls felt closer, the narrow aisle tighter, the air less oxygenated. *Can I handle days of this? Weeks?* One minute at a time, I told myself. Just get through this one godawful minute.

* * *

Later that evening, the cramped quarters felt smaller with every passing minute. The stale air grew heavier with each exhale, and the scent of sage changed to the smell of duct tape, musty blankets, and damp dog. The windows were dark, their blanketed barriers blocking out the night, leaving only the dim glow of battery-operated lanterns to cast long shadows along the aluminum walls. Five people and a dog crammed into a space meant for two—it wasn't just claustrophobic; it was crushing.

Greg paced near the door. "Mom and I will take the bed." He glared at each person in turn, as if daring someone to object.

Maggie gave a small nod. I recognized the unspoken compromise in the gesture—it wasn't about comfort, but about keeping Greg from completely freaking out.

Button dropped her bag near the pull-out couch like a kid at summer camp racing to claim the top bunk. "Ellena and I can share this."

I, exhausted and not giving two hoots about where I slept, nodded and sank onto the worn plaid couch. The fabric scratched against my skin, and I wondered how many restless bodies had slept there before.

That left Jax. He stood near the door, gripping the Geiger counter like it would run away if he let it go. "I'll take the dinette then."

Winter let out a low whine and scratched the floor near the side door.

"Come on, Winter," Jax said, guiding the dog to the narrow bathroom. He grabbed a newspaper from the kitchenette counter, unfolded it, and placed it on the shower floor. "Go potty."

Winter paused, his ears twitching as if questioning the command. The silence stretched for a heartbeat, and then he moved forward, tail dropping as he stepped into the cramped space.

Button wrinkled her nose, leaning back against the couch. "So, the bathroom's a dog toilet now? Great."

Jax said, "Got a lamppost in that handbag of yours? Or how about some doggy diapers?"

Button gave him a look that could have dissolved a drain clog.

Score one for Jax. Guess that little flirtation is over.

Maggie folded the dinette cushions down to make a mattress, then spread a fresh sheet over the bed, topping it with a crocheted quilt, emblazoned with flowers in 1970s colors of avocado green, mustard yellow, and burned orange. It reminded me of the quilts my grandmother used to make while sitting in her rocking chair listening to golden oldies on the radio.

Winter came out of the bathroom and padded over to Jax, his soft movements a stark contrast to the tension thrumming in the room. He nudged Jax's leg, then flopped down at his feet with a sigh.

Silence wrapped around us, broken only by the soft click of Jax adjusting the Geiger counter.

I headed for the bathroom, brushing past him. Our arms grazed, and my breath hitched. We exchanged a fleeting glance, and something flared in his expression before it vanished. I swallowed hard, focusing on the bathroom door as warmth crept into my cheeks. Jax was evasive, aloof, and yet... something about him tugged at my thoughts. *Get a grip, Ellena. What the hell is wrong with you?*

I tugged the bathroom door open, and the smell of dog urine erased any romantic notions I might have had about Jax Mercer.

* * *

When I returned from the bathroom, Maggie was pulling a plastic jug from a kitchen compartment.

"Now, 'bout the water. We've got maybe fifty gallons. That's ten days if we conserve. Hands'll have to get cleaned with sanitizer."

Jax said, "No showers. The groundwater could already be contaminated."

Button wrinkled her nose, touching her face like she could already feel the grime. "What about a quick rinse in the campground showers? Just to clean up a bit?"

"No one goes outside. Not until I say it's safe," he said.

"Fine," Button said, slumping against the couch. "This just gets better every minute."

I felt my teeth clench, frustration simmering in every muscle. Part of it was Button, who was more worried about her beauty routine than our safety. But mostly, it was Jax—how quickly he'd taken control, and how easily we had let him.

"And who put you in charge, Jax?" I asked, surprised by my own nerve.

Jax said, "It's not about being in charge. It's about keeping us alive."

"That's what we're all trying to do. But we're not in the military. We aren't going to blindly follow orders. We decide as a group," I said.

Jax's stare lingered before he gave a curt nod. "Fine. We'll decide together. Does everyone agree we should stay inside until I can check the levels?"

Of course, no one disagreed. It was a rhetorical question, and we all knew it. Once again, I'd opened my mouth and regretted it. If only I could speak with authority, find the right words. But saying the wrong thing? That was my forte.

Winter's soft whine broke the tension. I glanced at him, a flicker of gratitude sparking for his grounding presence. He had a sixth sense for communicating the right thing. If only I could figure out how to do the same.

"We'll check the levels again in a few hours," Jax said, without taking his eyes from me.

Was he being nice? Cute? Sarcastic? I couldn't tell.

Greg emerged from the bedroom. "I can't stay in here. This isn't safe. What if the radiation gets bad?"

"Greg, love. We're safer in here, dontcha know," Maggie said.

Raw fear sparked off Greg like electricity from a plasma globe. "Sitting here ain't a plan, Mom! I need air!"

Maggie patted his arm. "Love, it's going to be okay. We're safe in here."

But before anyone could stop him, he lunged for the door.

* * *

I jumped in front of Greg, but he shoved past me, his expression wild with desperation.

Jax was there in an instant, blocking the door. "You're not going out there."

"You can't keep me in here," Greg said, boxer-stepping back and forth as Jax mirrored his movements. "I need air. I need space."

Greg lunged to the left, swiping for the handle. Jax grabbed his arm, then Greg wrenched free. His elbow slammed into Jax's temple, sending him staggering into the wall with a muttered, "Shit."

Winter barked at Greg, lunging for his ankles and snapping at his pant seams.

Button let out a startled gasp. "Someone control that dog!"

Jax glared at Button, and the expression in his eyes was an icy knife, sliding in and twisting. "He's not going to bite."

"Could have fooled me," Button said, as Winter grabbed the hem of Greg's pants and gave it a sharp tug.

Greg's hand yanked at the door handle, over and over, the metal clattering against its frame like teeth chattering in the cold. He shook his leg, trying to dislodge Winter. "Get off me, you damn varmint!"

41

Maggie clasped her hands above her head. "For criminy's sake Greg, listen to me. Please, love, I'm begging ya, just stop."

Greg ignored Maggie's pleas, twisting the lock with one hand and pushing on the door with the other.

"Winter, stop!" Jax said, his hand still pressed to his forehead, blood streaking through his fingers.

Winter released Greg's pants and stepped back a foot. He kept his eyes fixed on his target, tense and on guard.

I needed to anchor Greg, and I needed to do it fast. I stepped forward and cupped a hand over his trembling fingers. "Your mom is here, and she needs you. She can't do this without you."

He froze, chest heaving, the fight draining out of him like air from a punctured tire. His fingers twitched beneath my hand and then his shoulders sagged. His face crumpled. The tears came, slow and silent, pooling in his eyes until they spilled over.

I kept my voice steady, though fear surged through my veins. "I get it, okay? It feels like we're trapped. Like we're running out of air. You're scared—I'm scared too—but running out there isn't going to help. You know that."

Part of me wanted to run, too. I could see the temptation—an open door, the promise of escape. Run like hell. Away from that trailer, away from everything. I'd felt the same way 36 hours into labor, when the back labor had become unbearable—why, oh why hadn't I opted for the epidural?—and I'd wanted to walk out of the hospital, to stop being pregnant altogether. I'd wanted to scream, *I changed my mind! I don't want to be pregnant!* But what good would that have done? The baby would still have been inside me, just as surely as the fallout would be inside me if I bolted out of the trailer now.

"I can't—" Greg choked on the words, his voice cracking. "It's too much. I can't do this."

I moved in closer, placing my other hand at the small of his back. "It is too much. It's overwhelming, and it feels impossible. But you don't have to handle it alone. Your mom is here. We're here."

As the words tumbled out, I realized how trite they sounded—words I'd recited a thousand times on the job, like "stay with me" or "take deep breaths, I've got you." I braced myself, certain he wasn't listening, certain that all 300 pounds of him would panic, bowl someone over, and barrel out the door into a haze of swirling fallout.

Instead, he stumbled to the back room, his frame bumping off the narrow walls of the hallway. He slammed the sliding door shut behind him, and a muffled sob escaped through the door.

I let out my breath. My knees buckled like a Temu camping chair, but I didn't have time to collapse.

Jax teetered on the edge of the dinette bed, his posture unsteady. Blood dripped through his fingers, streamed down his cheek, and pooled on his collar.

I grabbed a folded towel from the kitchenette counter and poured water over it from a jug. The towel was printed with twenty philosophy quotes for happiness.

"Let me see your head," I said.

He stared at me for a second, shrugged and then dropped his hand, revealing a three-inch jagged gash above his eyebrow.

I crouched in front of him, close enough to catch a hint of citrus deodorant. It smelled familiar—but not like Eric. No, it was Gran's garden in winter, when oranges and limes dropped from the trees by the hundreds. The memory lingered, bright and fleeting, before the pressing reality of the moment pulled me back. My hands moved quickly, tearing thin strips from the towel and cleaning the cut. My cheeks flushed under the heat of his stare.

"You've done this before," he said.

"You could say that. Just don't expect stitches—I'm fresh out of sutures."

For a moment, our eyes met, and something fluttered in my chest—a relic of an emotion I hadn't felt in years. It was inappropriate, at the end of the world, to feel anything close to affection. But there was something about Jax... something that made me feel steady, like I'd known him forever.

You don't know him, Ellena. You don't know him at all.

I shook off the thought and secured the strip of rag with two small pieces of duct tape. "You'll live," I said, then winced. *Dumb comment. None of us might live through the next few days.*

Jax gave a small nod. "Thanks, Ellena."

And there it was. My face was inches from his. He had softened—like Von Rothbart at the curtain call, shedding the villain as soon as the lights dimmed. The moment dragged, teetering on the edge of something it shouldn't be, like it needed a swell of romantic music. *No. No, no. Stop this.*

I looked toward the back room, where Greg's muffled sobs filtered through the thin door.

"I'm so sorry," Maggie said.

I said, "It's not your fault. It's no one's fault, it's..." I shook my head. *This damn horror movie we're all living in.* "Everything. We're all on edge."

"Greg... he's been like this since the accident. When he gets too worked up, he just... needs a minute to reset, ya know."

Reset. Wouldn't that be nice. If only I could rewind to yesterday, when my biggest worry was another call from a bill collector. When my worst fear was the repo man's stealth truck crawling up my street in the dead of night. When my deepest dread was the Sherrif posting the eviction notice.

If I could just erase this nightmare—go back to that moment at the mailbox, take the sliding door on the left and head to the park instead of picking up Button. Sit with peppermint tea. Watch the ducks. Get a job—any job—Wendy's, Burger King, Walmart. Life might have gone on.

But normal wasn't coming back. My stomach sank as a bitter truth settled in. *Normal* was about to be erased from the dictionary, tossed in the archaic word archives—along with words like happy, romantic, and safe. In their place? Core crazy. Fallout fever. Geiger clear.

* * *

The next morning, Winter's bark split the silence like a razor, insistent and cutting.

I froze on the pull-out couch in the trailer's cramped front room. Button was asleep next to me, earbuds in—*bet she drifted off to* Party in the USA.

The thin paneling quivered with the sounds outside: rustling, the harsh crack of snapping branches, low grunts and snarls. The noises yanked me out of the fragile calm I'd fought to find after Greg's breakdown, replacing it with a dread that knotted deep in my gut.

Jax stood near the door, tense as a coiled spring. He reached for the Geiger counter, its green glow reflecting off his hands as he brought the sensor closer to the taped-up window. He looked at me, nodded, then peeled up a corner of blanket and looked outside.

"There's a bear out there," he said. His head tilted as he took in the motion. "More than one... and they're moving fast."

He placed a hand on Winter's head, a silent signal of praise. The dog let out a low, rumbling growl before falling silent, ears pricked, golden eyes locked on the door, body taut with awareness.

"Bears?" I repeated, the word scraping past my dry, cracked lips. It was one thing to brace for fallout and the slow creep of radiation, but the thought of wild, unpredictable muscle and claw charging through the campground sent a chill up my spine.

"Something's spooked them. The blast, I bet. I hope to God it's not a tornado. Those storm clouds last night didn't look good." He scanned the scene, his fingers brushing his lips as he chewed over the thought. "They're not alone either—looks like deer, or raccoons?"

A tornado? *That'd be the wolf at the door*, Gran would have said.

Losing our roof in the middle of fallout rain would be the ultimate irony—like that old song. What was it? *Ironic*? No, it was worse than that. It was like that Led Zeppelin song about the false security of levees, only to face disaster when they failed. No, it was worse than that. It was the stars aligning for annihilation. Just when I thought it couldn't get worse, it always did.

A sudden thud struck the roof of the trailer, loud and jarring. I flinched, my body stiffening as I looked up to the roof for answers. Then another hit—a series of dull, wet thumps—followed by a sickening, splattering sound like guts hitting an abattoir pail.

Winter barked again, rising to his feet, his ears pinned back.

Greg let out a panicked gasp from the back room, opened the sliding door and peered out. "What is that? S-s-somebody tell me what is that?"

Not now, Greg. Not now. I had hardly slept, and something—wet hailstones? Mud balls?—was pelting the trailer. There could even be a tornado brewing. Babysitting a grown man's meltdown wasn't high on my list of priorities.

Jax peeled the blanket farther back. I scurried over and joined him, my breath hitching as I caught sight of the surreal scene under the trailer lights: fish—large, small, some missing their heads or tails—were raining down around the trailer. They slapped against the walls and littered the ground, their once silvery scales coated in black slime.

"A fish storm. I've heard of this happening, but..." Another loud thump struck the roof, the vibration rattling the trailer's walls.

"It's not real," Greg stammered, his voice an octave higher. "This can't be real. Fish don't just... fall from the sky!"

Jax said, "It's real. The blast must've triggered something—an updraft, or winds pulling them from the swamp. Either way, they're here."

The sound grew more intense, the *thwump* of fish striking the trailer merging with an eerie hiss of wind that encircled us. The trailer's confinement deepened as the storm intensified. A thick tang seeped into the trailer, despite our attempts at hermetic sealing. It was like the smell of a burning house, an awful mix of plastic, chemicals, wood, and something worse—something that could only be burning bodies.

Maggie emerged from the bedroom. "Did I hear you say fish storm? Nature's going haywire, I tell ya."

Button emerged from a pile of blankets and shook her head like she was throwing off a hallucination.

And then the sound shifted—quieter, but no less ominous. The falling fish tapered off, then ceased altogether, leaving only the steady pitter-patter of slashing rain pressing in on us.

Outside, near the door, a series of abrupt hisses erupted, like air escaping from tires.

"What's that?" Button asked.

Jax leaned toward the window again. "Alligators."

"Alligators?" Button and Greg said in unison.

"Jinx," Button added, giggling like she'd just told the world's best joke.

Jax shot her a puzzled look, then glanced at me, as if to say—*should we add her to the crazy list too?*

I pressed my fingers to my temple, where the first pulse of a headache was hammering out a beat. I couldn't take Button losing it on top of Greg's near-meltdown and Maggie's shell-shocked stare, like she too was one step away from crumbling. Jax was the only one keeping his cool, but even he looked like he was holding it together with duct tape and a prayer. And myself? Compared to Maggie, Greg, and Button, I was the picture of stability—a total joke, considering I was one stray push away from going over the edge.

"They're everywhere," Jax said.

"What do you mean, *everywhere?*" I asked, edging closer, though I stopped short of looking outside. As if not seeing it could somehow make it not real. Like when I'd clamped my hands over my eyes on the Big Mouse rollercoaster, just as Eric and I had creaked to the top of that first drop—back when fear was a welcome thrill and not the monster lurking behind every damn corner.

"They're as far as I can see in this light. Looks to be about forty, fifty of them." His tone was matter of fact, like he was tallying up bullets in a clip, but he chewed his lip after he spoke.

Maggie gasped, covering her mouth with one hand. Button whimpered, eyes locked on the sealed door as if expecting it to bust open. Greg retreated to the back room, sliding the door closed with a thwack.

I watched Jax's calculating stare, waiting for him to say more. *How in blue blazes do we get rid of them, Jax?*

He chewed his lip, clearly uncertain how to handle this fresh development. A shiver ran down my spine as I realized I was looking to Jax for answers, even though he likely knew as much about animal behavior after a nuclear bomb as I did—precisely nothing.

"Hopefully, the animals will have cleared out by the time we leave in three days," Jax said.

"Why three days?" I asked. The number seemed arbitrary, like he'd drawn it out of a hat.

"That's the minimum for the fallout to settle enough to move safely."

"Oh," I said, searching—and failing—for something intelligent to say. I knew that, right? From training? But if I did, I'd forgotten it.

So much for that five-minute nuclear disaster class. Thanks, FEMA.

* * *

By evening, the rain eased, and the tornado we'd feared never materialized. The low, guttural grunts and hisses of the alligators carried through the night, a haunting symphony that curdled my stomach and kept me drenched in cold sweat for most of the night. The noises ebbed and swelled, fading to a murmur before surging again with startling intensity. Every snap of a branch or rustle of movement set my nerves on edge.

Every so often, Button let out a small, stifled cry, her body trembling next to me on the couch bed. She tried to muffle her cries with her hands, but the fear leaked through in soft, hiccupping sobs every so often.

"Why won't they stop?"

Winter paced until the small hours, his claws scraping against the linoleum, stopping now and then to plant himself near the side door, his body coiled like a spring. A short time later, his ears would prick, he would whine, and then the pacing would restart.

I lay on the edge of the mattress, my body stiff as a board, unable to relax. Every time my eyes fluttered shut, a sudden thump or a wet squelch of movement outside jolted me awake. My chest tightened each time I thought I heard the scrape of alligator claws against the trailer, mingling with bellows and hisses. It was a constant reminder of just how thin the trailer walls were. Or how thin my sanity was.

Button let out another soft sob, her knees pulled to her chest. "They're going to break through."

"They won't," Jax said. He sat up in bed, shoulders squared, the Geiger counter resting beside him.

Has he been awake the whole night? Watching? Guarding?

"They don't want us—they want the fish. As long as we stay quiet and keep the door shut, they'll move on."

"Do you think they'll leave in a few days?" I asked.

"Once the fish are gone, yeah."

I swallowed hard, trying to draw comfort from his assurances, but the persistent grunts, snaps, and hisses outside made it impossible.

I thought of the alligator farm down in Saint Augustine, where you could zipline over the enclosures. Eric had taken me there once, swearing it wasn't scary at all—that there were safety nets and everything. He'd lied. It was the most terrifying thing I'd ever done. My legs had dangled inches above those snapping jaws, and I'd screamed the whole way across. On the other side, I'd playfully smacked him for lying to me, though in truth, I was glad he had. I never would have gone if I'd known how terrifying it was, but afterward, I could pretend I'd been brave enough to take the ride.

That's what the Airstream reminded me of: a zipline harness keeping us safe, for the moment. I just hoped the trailer would hold, and that the ride would end as planned—with us getting the hell out of there.

Winter let out a whine, his body stiffening near the door. I beckoned him over, reached out to touch his head, my fingers brushing over his fur in an attempt to soothe us both. "It's okay, boy," I whispered, although it obviously wasn't. He cocked his head back and forth, his ears pricked, as though he was questioning my bullshit.

Hours passed in fragmented moments of shallow sleep and tense wakefulness. Button fell into an uneasy doze, her breathing ragged and punctuated by soft murmurs, the *rumpumpump* of a pop song leaking through her earbuds. Winter's pacing slowed but didn't stop, and each time I stirred, his golden-eyed gaze caught mine in the dim light, full of quiet vigilance.

By the time the first hints of dawn bled through the blankets on the windows, the world had fallen silent, broken by the occasional splash or wet snap—proof the predators still lingered.

Jax leaned against the door, his eyes heavy-lidded but still watchful. He glanced toward me, his voice soft. "We made it through the night."

I nodded but knew the next two nights would be no easier.

"We'll get through this," Jax added.

Is he trying to soothe me? Is he worrying about my mental state too? How did I look right now? I hadn't glanced in the mirror or even put on deodorant since the emergency alert.

Gran would have chastised me. *"Even if the whole house is in a state, you should always keep your front door shining,"* she used to say.

I glanced down at my fingernails, grungy with grime, and at the brown mud streaks on my T-shirt. *When Button wakes up, I'll borrow her compact and clean myself up a bit.*

"Two more nights and we can move on," Jax said.

The trailer's walls quivered like a drum skin. Was it the alligators brushing against the sides? The weight of the trailer shifting into the soft, wet earth? Or just the wind playing tricks on my frayed nerves? I didn't know, and I wasn't sure I wanted to find out.

Jax's words stayed with me, laden with risk but laced with a sliver of hope. Two more nights in this shiny cage, built for weekend warriors chasing sunsets, not five half-crazed strangers trying to survive whatever hell this was.

5 Biology Lessons

The morning dragged on in fragments: tight breaths, strained silences, and the occasional snap of a branch or distant rumble of thunder. We all waited—for what, exactly, I couldn't say. Alligators? Bears? The next unthinkable horror?

I changed into clean sweatpants and a t-shirt, freshening up with wet wipes. The "Rose Garden" scent did little to mask the lingering combination of sweat and grime. That stink filled my nostrils like a toxic fog, stubborn and heavy, calling up memories of my grandfather in his final days. He'd sat in that recliner, wasting away until the end. The smell clung to my nose even after I knew it had faded from the air. I understood the science of it—how odors could get trapped in the nasal passages—and prayed the stench lived only in my mind, and not on my skin.

By the time afternoon crept in, the tension inside the trailer was alive, thrumming with every creak of the floor and shift of the walls. Outside, the wind had picked up, rattling the trailer with a low, mournful howl that seeped through every crack like whispers from the undead.

The Geiger counter in Jax's hand clicked faster now, its tone sharp and insistent like a digital locust. Just two days ago, nature's comforting chorus of cicadas, frogs, and crickets surrounded me. That harmony was gone, replaced by a mechanical harbinger of death.

My stomach turned as realization settled in. The quickening clicks could mean only one thing. I didn't need to ask, didn't want to ask—but Greg filled the silence.

"What's that sound?" he asked, his voice thin and taut with unease.

Jax moved the Geiger counter closer to the dinette wall, studying the machine's screen with intensity. "Radiation's increasing. It's getting worse out there."

Greg's head snapped toward Maggie. "We're... we're sealed in, right? We're safe, right? Mom? You said we're safe!"

Maggie reached over and patted Greg's knee as though they were waiting for a doctor to deliver grim news. "Yes, love, we're safe."

"We're safe for now," Jax added, his tone measured and firm. "But this trailer—as insulated as it is—wasn't built for radiation shielding. We'll need to stay as far from the exterior walls as possible."

Greg stared down at his shoes, his breaths quickening. "Too thin. So, it's getting in?"

Jax said, "Not much. But if the wind shifts, or if a stronger wave comes through..."

He didn't finish. He didn't need to.

Greg's breathing turned shallow, his knuckles whitening as he clawed at his chin. "What happens if it does? What if this place isn't enough?"

"We'll deal with it," Jax said, his eyes on Greg. "For now, we stick to the center of the trailer."

Greg shook his head, his voice trembling. "This can't be happening. We're trapped in here, and you're saying even this might not be enough? What are we supposed to do?"

"Greg," I said, crouching in front of him. My voice was gentle reassurance, a quiet strength in the storm. "I know this is hard. But panicking isn't going to help. I mean..." I caught myself, softening. "What I'm trying to say is, we need to focus on staying as safe as we can."

Greg's wide, frightened eyes met mine. "But what if we can't stay safe? What if—"

"We *can*," I said. "We've got a plan. Two more nights. That's it. We let the worst of the fallout settle, then we move. Jax has a cabin with better shielding," *I hope*, "and... and that's where we'll go. But we can't leave until it's safe."

Greg blinked, my words settling in like paper in water. "Two nights?"

I nodded. "Two nights. We can do this, Greg. One step at a time."

Maggie, standing in the kitchenette, added, "She's right. We've made it this far, eh? We'll get through this too."

Greg let out a shuddering breath, his shoulders loosening. "Okay. Two nights."

Button snapped her compact mirror shut with a decisive click and groaned, muttering about how this was "...worse than a frat house." She didn't press the issue, though, and I figured that was as close to cooperation as we'd get from her.

I asked, "What else can we do to make this space safer?"

Jax tapped the side of the Geiger counter, his brow furrowed in thought. "Reinforce the center of the trailer—cushions and blankets to put more distance between us and the walls. Anything reflective over the weak points might help. Maggie, do you have aluminum foil to put over the windows? And I'll keep checking the counter every few hours."

"Got it," I said, already pulling cushions from the couch. I began stacking them in the middle of the room. "Maggie, can you grab the blankets?"

"You betcha," Maggie said. Her steady voice belied the worry that pinched her eyes shut.

The group fell into a tense flow. Greg shifted cushions into random places, but at least he was trying to help. Maggie layered blankets and pillows against the walls, her movements methodical, like a nurse dressing a wound.

Button grumbled under her breath as she tossed a couple of pillows onto the improvised barrier. For all her muttering, she didn't argue. *It takes a fire to temper steel*, Gran would have said. Perhaps the fallout had forced my stepsister to confront herself, though only time would tell if the change would last.

As we worked, the trailer grew quieter, the frantic edge of our fear dulled by the steady motion of our hands. The activity gave me something to focus on—something to push back against the darkness gathering at the edges of my mind. It wasn't much, but it was something.

Winter settled in the center of the room, his keen eyes tracking our every move. I couldn't help but marvel at his calm demeanor. Weren't dogs supposed to sense their owners' fear? He should have been pacing, barking, or clawing at the door.

An image of Gran's Scottie dog, Nessie, flashed through my mind. When my grandpa had died, that poor dog had unraveled right along with the family. It hid under the couch for weeks, emerging only when dragged out for potty breaks or lured with steak. Even then, it was like feeding a monster from *Alien*—jaws snapping from the shadows to grab the treat before retreating to its lair.

But Winter? Not a flicker of stress. If he were human, he'd be Yoda, calm and wise. I could almost hear Winter's voice: *Too frantic, you are.*

As the group settled into the quiet, Jax straightened from his work and surveyed the trailer. "It's not perfect. But it's the best we've got for now. Stay in the center, away from the walls."

I met his gaze. "Two nights. We can do this." I forced conviction into my words, but inside, doubt churned. The tension in the room was brittle, like sugar glass. One wrong move, and it would shatter.

Jax gave me a small nod, his expression softening just enough to hint at reassurance. "We will."

But as the storm's rumble grew louder, blending with the percussive beat of the Geiger counter, I couldn't shake the gnawing certainty that our hardest test was still ahead.

* * *

By early evening, every creak of the walls reverberated in the cramped space. I swore I could hear my heartbeat pounding in time with the tick... tick... tick... of the wall clock. It wasn't loud, but it was unignorable, a reminder of time grinding on like coarse sand through an hourglass, each tick scraping against my nerves in our fragile shelter.

Greg huddled in the corner of the couch, his knees drawn to his chest. He stared at the clock like it held the secret to salvation, his hand clamped over his mouth as though stifling a desperate plea. Maggie knelt beside him, her hand rubbing his back. Her lips moved—whispering reassurances, I assumed.

Jax stood near the door—his usual spot. Why it was always the door, I didn't know. Was it a SEAL thing? Always on edge, ready for the unexpected? *Should I be doing the same? What—guard the vent? Stand sentry by the toilet for snakes?* I pushed the absurd thought away.

Jax's fingers tapped an erratic drumbeat against his thighs, his shoulders rigid, his stance braced like a spring wound too tight. His eyes flicked between the Geiger counter and the window, tension carved into every line of his face. He wasn't just standing there; he was waiting, ready for the next strike in a battle none of us were equipped to fight.

Winter pressed against my leg, a low whine slipping from his throat. It wasn't a treat or a potty break whine—I knew that much. This was a *pet me* whine, clear from the soulful, puppy-dog eyes he gave me. I scratched behind his ears, and for a split second, everything felt homey—like Gran was in the kitchen, making tea.

Jax said, "We should inventory what we've got. Whether we leave in two days or not, we need to know where we stand."

I nodded, giving Winter one more pat on the head before I stood up. "Okay. Let's do it." I welcomed the distraction—anything to keep my mind occupied.

Jax and I moved through the trailer, sorting cans and bottles into neat piles. Button stayed on the couch, silent, her earbuds in, but her stare lingered on Greg. On any other day, it might have drawn a sarcastic quip: *I can tell an attention seeker when I see one.* Or, *How come no one's noticed my broken nail?*

I turned my attention to the kitchen. Each shuffle of supplies had a purpose—a minor effort to impose order on the madhouse. Jax didn't just stack items—he made them shipshape: labels facing the same direction, large items in the back, small in front, every can aligned *just so.*

He opened the last storage compartment, his brows knitting together. "I didn't see a first aid kit, Maggie. Do you have one?"

Maggie said, "Yup, I do. But... Oh, Lord. I had a blister from getting kindling when we got here—took the kit out to the picnic bench to deal with it."

"Where's the kit now?" Jax asked.

"Out there," Maggie said, jabbing a finger toward the door. "Now it's covered in fallout, for Pete's sake."

I could picture it perfectly: the kit sitting forgotten on the picnic bench, buried under a layer of ashen dust.

I opened my mouth to mention my EMT kit in the car but hesitated, my thoughts tangling. Was this the right moment to tell them I'd been an EMT? Could I even say it without sounding like a braggart? And did it even matter anymore? I was state-certified to apply Band-Aids and administer CPR—skills any random Joe could pick up from YouTube. All my certification meant was that I got to apply those skills in my work. And I didn't even know if I still *had* that profession.

The letter from the State of Florida in the glove box held the answer, but as long as it stayed unopened, I could pretend. If a bad-news letter stays sealed, does the bad news even exist?

Before I could sort through the mess in my head, Button's brittle sarcasm cut through the air.

"Oh, great. Radiation, alligators, and now not even a Band-Aid. Isn't this just the dream vacation?"

Greg let out a low, strangled sound—a mix between a groan and a whimper—and hunched further into himself. His hands twisted together in his lap as he rocked, like he was trying to tune everyone else out.

Maggie rose slowly, as though one wrong move might shatter the fragile moment. "His brain injury..." Her voice faltered, and she glanced at Greg, who now had his face buried in his hands. She dropped her tone to a whisper. "It messed up the part that handles stress. The something cortex, they called it, dontcha know. He can't deal with things like this— his emotions just... take over."

"That makes sense," Jax said, his voice quieter now, edged with guilt or understanding—perhaps both. He glanced at Greg, whose body seemed to fold further in on itself. "We'll keep things as calm as we can."

I nodded, my voice soft but firm. "Maggie, you're doing everything right. We'll get through this."

Greg whimpered again, a raw sound as if someone had torn it from him.

Maggie crouched in front of him, her expression tender. "You should take a nap, love."

He nodded—an unsteady motion, like a spinning top on its last spin—and let her guide him toward the back room. The bedroom door rattled shut with a soft click.

Jax finished stacking cans into precise piles. "We ration everything. Every bite, every drop of water. Nothing wasted."

I eased onto the dinette seat, my body tense. Winter padded over and settled at my feet.

Jax glanced at the dog, a flicker of approval—or amusement— crossing his face. "He likes you. He's a one-person dog, usually. I might get jealous."

Despite everything, I couldn't help but smile. "He's got good taste."

Jax returned my smile, faint but warm. For a moment, the trailer was a little less suffocating. But Button eyed us, and the moment dissolved before it could bloom.

Jax excused himself to the bathroom, and the air in the room shifted. Button's voice broke the silence, low and hesitant. "I need to tell you something."

"Now is not the time." I didn't want to hear it, not now, maybe never, but especially not now. Whatever Button was about to spill, I knew it had to do with that damn letter—a tiny bomb waiting to blow what was left of our family apart. And now? In the middle of this shitstorm? *Not the time.*

Button's words tumbled out anyway, scattering like marbles spilled across the floor. "It's not what you think. Eric—we ran into each other at the Taproom on King Street. Lunchtime, a couple of years ago. I didn't plan it. I didn't even know he'd be there. But then he started talking, and one thing led to another... I didn't tell you because you two weren't getting along, and I thought—God, I don't know what I thought."

My breath hitched, ragged and uneven. My hands curled into fists at my sides, my nails digging into the skin of my palms as my mind recalled Eric's stupid pet name. *Lizzy. No. God, no.*

The thought of Eric and Button—my husband, my stepsister—made my skin crawl and my stomach twist—barbed wire coiling tighter with every word. *Had they hooked up during lunch hour at the credit union? Had Button taken a break from coding to mess with my husband? Had he wandered from the mailroom to "test her system" instead?*

The betrayal yawned wide, vast and all-consuming, leaving no room for words, no air to breathe.

But before I could process it, a deep, reverberating scream ripped through the air from the back room, abrupt and piercing, breaking the moment apart.

From the back room, Maggie said, "Don't you dare open that window!"

"I need air!" Greg's voice was high and frantic, just before the sound of breaking glass echoed through the trailer.

Jax lunged out of the bathroom as I bolted to the back room. Greg stood by the window, shards of glass scattered around him. A shard stuck out of a gash in his wrist, and blood streamed down his shirt sleeve, dripping onto the carpet.

"Jesus," I said, dropping to my knees beside him. "We need medical supplies. Now."

Maggie hovered in the doorway, her hands covering her mouth. "We don't—"

"It's in my SUV," I said, cutting her off as I bent to scan the wound. "There's a med kit in the trunk."

Jax crouched beside me, lifting an eyebrow. "You're a medic?"

"No. EMT. If I don't get that kit to sew him up..." My voice trailed off, aware that Greg was right in front of me.

"I'll go," Jax said.

"You don't have to risk yourself. I can handle it," I said, although the thought of going out *there* broke me into a cold sweat.

Jax didn't bother answering. He ducked into the wet bath and came back with the shower curtain, knotting one end as he spoke. "What do you know about alligators?"

I blinked. *A biology lesson? Is he serious?* "I know to stay clear of them."

Jax snorted, pulling the crinkling fabric tight. "They're ambush hunters. Two of us splits their focus—one distracts, the other moves."

Goosebumps rippled up my arms. I had forgotten for a split second about the noise outside. "It's a hundred feet," I said, as if the number mattered. It didn't. Not when the ground between the trailer and the Explorer might as well be a minefield.

"Yeah, a hundred feet where they're practically invisible." Jax slipped the shower-curtain poncho over his head. "They blend into the vegetation, they're fast, and they're stealthy. You need me to spot them while you focus on getting us to the car."

"Alligators ain't dangerous if you stay clear, my loves," Maggie said.

Jax said, "Sure. But last night there were hundreds out there. Still are hundreds, I bet."

"Fair point, eh," Maggie said, her hands fluttering for a moment before she stilled, looking like she wished she could say something more.

"Maggie, you got another shower curtain? Tarp? Anything?" Jax asked without looking up.

"I've got a tarp, yep," Maggie said, already moving. She pulled it from a closet and handed it over.

Jax gave it a cursory inspection, then gave her a nod of approval. "Ever been in a death roll, Ellena?" His tone was casual, like he was asking if I'd ever been to Disney World. He didn't wait for my answer. "I have. And unless you've got a knife and know exactly where to stick it, you're done."

I held up my hands, surrendering the argument. "Point taken. We go together."

Jax tossed me the tarp. "Poncho. Every inch of skin covered. Don't leave gaps." He spoke calmly, methodically, like a surgeon walking a patient through a procedure. He wrapped a scarf around his neck, tucking it under his jacket. "Face and head covered too. No exposure."

I pulled the tarp over my shoulders, fumbling with the knot as I tried to tie it. Jax leaned in, his fingers brushing mine as he tightened the fabric.

He stared into my eyes. "When we're back, everything comes off under the awning. Clothes, boots, all of it. No exceptions."

I froze for a beat and swallowed hard. "Got it."

Jax said, "Maggie, do you have any petroleum jelly?"

"Petroleum jelly? Uh, yup," Maggie said, disappearing into the bedroom. Moments later, she returned with a half-empty jar, its label peeling at the edges.

Jax popped the lid, scooped out a glob, and smeared it around his eyes. The jelly caught the light, giving his face an unnatural sheen. He looked like a prizefighter gearing up for the ring.

He held out the jar. "Here. Your turn."

I frowned, hesitating. "Okay, but why?"

Jax said, "Protects your exposed skin. Radiation clings to surfaces. This won't stop it, but it'll help. Better than nothing."

I dipped my fingers into the jar. The jelly was cold and slick against my skin. "Does this even work?"

Jax's lips twitched into a half smile. "Better than bare."

The subtext of that statement sent a rush of heat to my cheeks. I'd heard that phrase recently, and I was fairly sure it was a condom brand catchphrase. I glared at him, but if I could glare at myself, I would. *You're trusting this cocksure egotist to guide you through fallout?* But what choice did I have? No, the choice was simple. Trust him and save Greg. Or throw the stupid jar of jelly on the floor and hide in the bathroom—until Winter pawed at the door for a potty call.

I smeared the jelly around my eyes while Jax went into the bathroom and yanked the shower curtain rod free, the metal squealing in protest. He held it up like a spear. "Maggie, pliers?" he asked, his tone clipped, all business.

When she retrieved a pair from a kitchenette drawer, he squeezed the end of the rod until it bent into a crude, pointed tip. He gave it a quick test jab into the air. "We move slow, Ellena—real slow. No sudden moves, no noise. The gators are probably full from fish, but they're out there. You startle them, you're dinner. Stay calm, and they should leave us alone."

I nodded and took the gloves Maggie handed me. My chest tightened, like a band was cinching tighter with every breath. Jax's calm voice grated on my nerves, but I clung to the hope that he knew what he was doing—because I sure as hell didn't.

Jax said, "Stick close. Watch the ground, every step. If you see a gator, freeze. Running makes you a target. Back away slow."

"But didn't I hear once that you can outrun alligators? So can't I just run?"

"You could. But why risk it? They're fast enough to catch you if you panic. Your best shot is to stay calm, keep your distance, and back away slow, okay?"

"Understood," I said, but my gut knew better. The thought of standing there like a department store mannequin while an alligator slithered closer made my throat seize like an engine running dry. My mind kept flashing images of yellowed teeth, the kind that had been tearing flesh since the dinosaurs walked the earth.

Jax's expression softened, enough to let reassurance slip through the cracks in his commanding tone. "We'll be fine. Trust me."

I held down a scoff and glanced at the door. The world beyond felt like a living thing, crouched and waiting. A shiver crawled across my skin, despite the trailer's stale warmth. My hand tightened on the scarf around my neck as I drew a shaky breath. "Let's get this over with."

6 Soft Spot

The trailer door creaked open. Outside, a dark mist rolled through the cypress trees, black and shiny, like a crop duster had sprayed a fine coat of oil.

I stepped to the edge of the awning, and the silence hit me like a physical blow. No cardinals, no wrens, no warblers—just nothing. I hadn't expected a symphony, not after everything, but the absence of sound was stark and unnatural. Birds were sensitive to noise, I reminded myself. The sonic boom of the blast would have sent them scattering, just like when they built the I-10 extension last year. The birds had vanished then, too. Perhaps they were still out there somewhere, hunkered down like our group, waiting for the world to feel safe again. Or perhaps they were gone for good.

Jax went ahead, holding the shower curtain rod low, testing the ground ahead with each careful step.

"What are you looking for?" I asked, my voice barely cutting through the thick air.

"Soft spots on the ground. Gators like to stay hidden until they lunge. If they're there, I'll know it."

I followed him, my poncho shifting as I moved, every nerve in my body stretched taut.

The landscape crouched around us, distorted and grotesque. It was like it had swallowed the world we knew and spat out a scene from the banks of the Styx. Cypress knees jutted from the blackwater like broken fingers, and the air clung to my skin—damp, cloying, with the rancid taste of rust and spoiled butter. Now and then came a sound that was just wrong: a hiss of shifting water, a slick pop of something unseen breaking the surface. It didn't just seem different; it felt alien, its depths pulsing with an unknowable beat.

Fallout slicked the water with iridescence, its sheen interrupted by fish bodies scattered like grotesque confetti. Each step squelched, boots sinking into decay-slick mud.

"Slow. Watch the ground. Stick close." Jax probed the muck with the pole, tapping ahead and testing suspicious shapes. A mud mound here. A yawning hole there. A pile of leaves, blackened and slick, as though they'd been rotting for years. Each soft thud of the pole cut through the stillness, a steady reminder of the dangers lying just out of sight.

Alligators, spread around the perimeter, reflected the waning light in their eyes, glowing like tiny red lanterns among the reeds. Their still forms merged with the shadows, but the occasional ripple of water or twitch of a tail betrayed their watchfulness.

My breath slowed, each inhale shallow and careful, as though the alligators might hear. My pulse thudded in my ears, a constant drumbeat I couldn't silence. We moved in unison, steps precise as Jax tested the ground ahead. My attention shifted between the treacherous mud and the swamp's murky edges, searching for the slightest hint of danger.

A low hiss froze us in place. Jax held up a hand, his posture rigid. Ahead, ten feet away, an alligator emerged from the water, its massive body moving with deceptive grace. The creature paused, its head lifting as if testing the air, its dark, glittering eyes locking onto us.

I held my breath and I willed myself not to move. Jax stayed still as a stone, his pole angled toward the alligator. The moment stretched. The beast watched, calculated. Then the creature slunk away, its tail swiping through the water as it disappeared back into the depths.

Jax pointed forward with two fingers, his hand bobbing as if to coax me along. "Easy. We're okay."

I wanted to scream, *Easy? I'm not a horse,* but I bit it back and followed him, hanging a few feet behind.

The Explorer loomed ahead, its bulk a distant buoy. As we crept closer, I scanned the ground for movement, every muscle in my body trembling with the strain of self-control.

Jax reached the SUV first, circling it with careful steps, his pole testing for hidden alligators. Satisfied, he waved me forward. "Pop the door. Quick but quiet."

I fumbled with my glove-covered hands, feeling for the keypad on the driver's side door. The keyless entry on my 2020 Ford Explorer was a small blessing: even on a normal day I had trouble finding my keys, let alone in our game of reptile roulette. I punched in the code, and the doors unlocked. The door eased open, its creak slicing through the silence.

I slid into the Explorer, my trembling hands fumbling in the back seat. The kit slipped against my grip as panic clawed at me, each second stretching too long. When my fingers skittered over its familiar contours, I exhaled, then brought the kit up and clutched it to my chest. Its weight was a tangible reminder of the life I once had—chaotic, grueling, but one I understood. That life was impossibly distant now, swallowed by a world that refused to play by the rules.

"Got it," I said.

A guttural snarl jolted me so hard the kit slipped from my grasp.

Jax stumbled backward onto the hood of the Explorer. His knife flashed in the dim light. A monster of an alligator lunged at him, its jaws snapping with terrifying force, tearing a hole in his poncho.

"Jax!" The sound slipped from my lips, no stronger than a breath.

As the alligator thrashed, its enormous tail churned the rotting mire, releasing foul air that stung my nose and burned the back of my throat. Fallout dust rose in a gritty haze, falling to the hood like powdered glass, catching glimmers of light.

Muck streaked Jax's arm as he fought. The dust—silent and deadly— filled me with a dread that rivaled the snapping jaws of the alligator.

I froze in place, my thoughts looping like a scratched record. *No, no, no—not again. I can't freeze, not this time.* My mind lurched back to that moment when I froze on scene. A paramedic guided me to the ambulance, placed a blanket around me, and treated me like a patient when I should have been a savior.

But what could I do in the Explorer? There was nothing to fight an alligator with: no handgun in the glove box, no rifle stashed inside a case, no machete stuffed under the seat. If I left the SUV's safety, I'd only turn myself into one more target, one more body for the meat grinder to chew on.

Jax lunged to the side, avoiding the alligator's snapping jaws, and drove his knife downward. The blade glanced off the thick hide of its neck, skidding away. The alligator twisted, its enormous body slamming into Jax and sending him sprawling onto the ground.

"No." My throat tightened; my hands gripped the kit so hard it dug into my palms. I scanned the interior of the SUV, desperate for anything I could use. Hiking boots. An umbrella. An empty gas can...

Umbrella.

I grabbed it, yanking it free, hoping for a pointed tip I could weaponize. But no—a rounded cap. Just a useless, plastic, rounded cap. "Damn it!" I yelled, the frustration burning through me like a lit fuse.

Jax rolled aside as the alligator lunged again. Its teeth snapped inches from his exposed face. He shoved his arm out, driving his gloved hand against the creature's snout, trying to hold it back. The force of its attack pushed him down into the mud, the gritty surface clinging to him as the alligator's jaws thrashed, seeking a new target.

"Jax, get up! Get up, get up, get up!" I yelled, my voice raw with desperation.

His teeth clenched in a grimace of determination. The alligator roared, its jaws twisting as it snapped at him again. This time, Jax didn't dodge. He shifted his weight, grabbed the knife in the dirt with his free hand, and plunged it into the alligator's eye with a brutal thrust.

The beast convulsed, its massive body twisting and rolling, each movement sending tremors through the Explorer. The alligator let out a final, guttural bellow, then flopped onto the ground, its sides heaving with labored breaths. Its chest rose once, twice—and then it went still.

Jax lay sprawled on the ground, his chest rising and falling like broken bellows, eyes fixed on the gray, empty sky. Fallout dust clung to him, smudging his skin with a ghostly film that made him look half-dead already. His face was bare, his head exposed, one glove missing—the kind of little detail that screamed disaster louder than words ever could.

My legs refused to move at first, nerves locking me in place until sheer will forced me to exit the SUV, each step unsteady as if my legs had turned to tubes of sand. Although I understood the physiology of fight-or-flight—heightened senses and all—I also knew it triggered trembling and muscle quaking due to the adrenaline rush. I swung my legs out, willing them to move. Taking one step, then another, I clutched the EMT kit as I approached Jax.

He pushed himself up, his movements slow and exhausted. He glanced at the alligator's limp form, then at me, his expression unreadable beneath the streaks of crud and sweat.

"You okay?" I whispered. *Please be okay. Please, please be okay.* Did I care for him? I wasn't sure. What I knew was that I needed this man to keep us alive. He'd just fought an alligator with his bare hands—something no one else in the trailer could have done. Without Jax, the hell we were trapped in would only spiral further out of control—a radioactive disaster gathering momentum until it exploded, obliterating us all.

Jax raised his arms, turning them over as if inspecting them for damage. Satisfied, he pushed himself to his feet. "I'm good. Let's get the fuck out of here."

I wanted to argue, to insist he let me check him over, but the words caught in my throat. Standing out in the open was a stupid idea. I'd risk fallout exposure myself, and a proper inspection would take too long—time for radiation to seep into his cells and do its damage. And God only knew how many alligators might be lurking, ready to strike. Instead, I nodded and fell into step beside him, bracing myself for the slow, grueling journey back to the Airstream.

Each step felt heavier than the last. The swamp closed in around us, its dangers lurking just out of sight. I stole a glance at Jax, his shoulders slumped but his grip still firm on the knife at his side.

How much exposure had he received? Was that slick film on his skin enough to kill him? How were we supposed to get it off without making things worse? The questions swirled, a restless energy coursing through me, leaving my limbs weak with apprehension. But Jax didn't say a word. He didn't wince. He didn't stop. He just kept moving, as if quitting wasn't an option. My earlier doubts about him being a SEAL faded. He might have been cagey about some things, but at that moment, he looked the part.

The alligators were closer now, their shapes more menacing in the closing darkness.

My boot caught on a slick patch of mud, and I stumbled.

Jax's arm shot out, steadying me with a firm grip on my arm. "Careful. Almost there."

When we reached the awning, the tension didn't break—it tightened. Jax motioned for me to stop. "Strip. We leave everything here."

I hesitated, my mind snagging on the absurdity of it. Stripping under the awning should have made me blush, but now it felt as perfunctory as peeling off a blood-soaked uniform in a fire station locker room. I tugged off the tarp and gloves, unwound the scarf, and peeled away the layers of fabric, dropping them in a heap at the edge of the awning. Standing there in just my underwear, the chill biting at my skin, I didn't think about modesty or awkwardness—only about what needed to happen next.

Jax worked beside me, his movements brisk and methodical as he shed the remnants of his clothes. I glanced at his body. Miraculously, despite his shredded clothing, his skin remained unscathed except for black fallout smears.

When we stepped back into the trailer's relative safety, modesty was the furthest thing from my mind. I triaged the scene in my head: Greg's wound first, then Jax. But a cold thought clawed its way in—what if there was nothing I could do for Jax? What if all I could offer was to make him comfortable while he slipped away?

7 Classified

Maggie materialized at my side and thrust a robe into my hands. "Here, put this on. Not sure you wanna work in jus' your skivvies."

The fabric smelled of fresh linen but felt like layered starch.

I slipped into the stiff robe, pulled on nitrile gloves, and unwrapped a package of gauze. When I pressed it against Greg's wrist, blood soaked through, warm and sticky against the material. I tore open another sterile packet and layered fresh gauze on top. First, I needed to stop the bleeding and clean the wound. Stitches could wait. Closing it at then would only have trapped the filth.

Button's panicked voice rose in the background. "I don't know what to do, Ellena! Tell me what to do!" But I didn't respond. All that mattered was stopping the bleeding from Greg's wrist.

"Stay with me, Greg."

His face was the color of milk, his eyes wide and blank. The sour tang of stale sweat surrounded him, mixing with the copper smell of blood. His lips moved, but the sound that came out was a whisper. lost between breaths.

"You're not checking out on me. Not here. Not now," I said.

Maggie crouched beside me, passing gauze packets and antiseptic wipes from the kit. "Thanks, Ellena."

I'd done nothing to deserve thanks yet. Maggie had no idea how close Greg had come—or how close he still was—to a tipping point where blood loss or infection could finish him. My focus stayed locked on the task.

"Hold this in place," I said to Maggie, lifting my hand from the gauze.

Maggie didn't hesitate. She pressed down hard, her jaw set.

I grabbed bandages from the kit and waited for the bleeding to slow. "Okay. Lift your hands, just a little."

Maggie eased her grip, and I wrapped Greg's wrist with a bandage. I pulled it snug, securing the dressing before the bleeding could start again.

"He'll need antibiotics," I said. The glass was filthy with grime that could turn a cut into a death sentence without antibiotics. Greg wasn't out of the woods—not by a long shot.

Maggie's eyes welled with tears. "Then we'll find some, you betcha." Her hand patted Greg's shoulder, as if reassuring herself he was still alive under her touch.

Jax stood by the door, wiping himself down, tossing the filthy rags outside one by one. Button hovered in front of him, clutching a fresh pile of rags. Her face was slack, like her brain had stalled somewhere between panic and action.

Jax flicked his fingers in a "gimme" motion. "Button, rag."

She blinked, then handed him one without a word.

"Maggie, keep pressure here," I said, nodding toward Greg's bandaged wrist. "I'm going to help Jax."

Maggie nodded back, but her forehead creased with concern.

I stepped into the narrow hallway and averted my eyes from Jax, standing there in nothing but his pristine white boxers. Gran's old saying popped into my head: "*Always mind yer knickers are clean, in case ye get hit by a bus.*" I smothered a nervous laugh. Good thing Jax listened to folk wisdom—or perhaps decent underwear was standard Navy kit. I thanked heaven I hadn't been wearing my period panties—the old baggy ones Gran would've called "practical."

"What do I do?" Button said.

Wet wipes were out of the question—I was down to my last two or three. By the looks of Jax, I'd need a case of them to clean him up, so rags would have to do.

I grabbed the jug from the counter and filled a bowl with water. I squeezed a generous dollop of dish soap into the water, and stirred it with my hand until it foamed. Outside, rain pattered against the trailer. I shivered at the thought of what would have happened if the fallout-laced rain had started on our way to the Explorer—soaking us to the bone with ionizing radiation.

I turned, holding the bowl out to Button. "Start with Jax's back. Anywhere he can't reach." I remembered watching the *Chernobyl* miniseries on HBO, how they'd warned against scrubbing radioactive ash because it could grind into the skin. My stomach turned like it was full of sour milk.

"Don't scrub—just wipe. Fallout sticks like glue, and we don't need it grinding into his skin."

Jax nodded once, his lips forming the silent shape of "thanks." I smiled at him and handed the bowl to Button.

She dipped the rag into the water, wrung it out too fast, and spattered droplets onto the floor. It was like she wanted the whole thing done before it had even started.

I said, "Get it all. Every speck."

Button wiped Jax's back, then dunked the cloth back into the bowl. The water darkened, swirling with black grit.

"Stop!" I snapped, freezing Button in place. "You've just tainted the water."

She stared at the bowl, her face blank, the rag limp in her hand like she'd forgotten what it was for. I exhaled hard through my nose, tamping down my frustration. I grabbed the bowl, stepped outside, and dumped it into the muck. The blackened water splattered onto the ground.

I said, "Dip a rag. Wipe. Then toss it in a pile by the door. Got it?"

Button nodded, her hands trembling as she took the bowl.

"You okay, Jax?" I asked, glancing up at him as I wiped the back of his thigh. "You're not saying much."

"Just thinking about the killer sunburn I'm waking up to tomorrow."

I chuckled, the sound feeling out of place. "Guess you'll have a bikini tan then. You want me to check... you know, down there?"

The words hung in the air, directionless and awkward. The heat rushed to my cheeks as fast as the words had spilled out. Had I really said that? I glanced at Button, who shot me a wide-eyed look that said, *What the hell?*

"I was just—" I started, the blush crawling up my neck. "Just keeping things light."

Jax grinned, the smile crinkling the corners of his eyes. "Make sure you get everywhere. But I think we're safe skipping the man-bits."

Maggie emerged from the back room with a shirt and pants tucked under one arm, rescuing me from further banter. She slid the door shut with her free hand. "He's sleeping. Told me he loved me before he drifted off, so I reckon he's fine for now."

Once Jax's skin was visibly clean, Maggie handed him a towel and the clothes: a faded chambray shirt and a pair of drawstring pants. "They're not Men's Wearhouse, but they should fit ya."

Button hovered near the kitchenette, her fingers twitching like she needed something to do.

Maggie nodded toward a neat pile of towels. "Rip those up into squares, Button. You never know when we might need more rags, eh?"

Button jumped at the sound of her name, then grabbed the towels and retreated to the couch.

While Jax got dressed, I went into the kitchen to pour myself a glass of water. The narrow space smelled of must and burned coffee, the type of stale air that clung to old trailers and bad days. My hands trembled, and I clasped them together, willing them still. Greg was stable—for now. And Jax was clean. I sent up a brief prayer—just in case someone was listening.

Maggie tapped me on the arm and nodded toward the top drawer. "Got something for ya."

She rummaged through the drawer, muttering, "Where the heck is this thing?" A moment later, she pulled out a weathered notebook with a rugged, olive-green cover.

The cover had scuffs and creases, and its spiral binding was bent at the edges. Maggie held it for a moment, her fingers brushing over an embossed *Aqua Scribe* logo in the corner, then flipped it open. Neatly written notes and detailed sketches covered the grid-lined pages.

Maggie's fingers traced the edges of a page. "Been adding to this field notebook for years. Figured it might be handy someday, though never imagined..." She tapped a drawing of a plant—slender leaves with tiny purple blossoms. "This here is skullcap, eh. It's a swamp herb. Grows wild near shallow water. If we can find it, it could work as an antibiotic."

"But if the plants are contaminated—"

"We'll cross that bridge when we come to it. What matters right now's knowing what to try, not worrying ourselves into a hole over what we can't fix."

I nodded, but the thought gnawed at me—something as basic as an edible plant felt like a gamble, a risk I hadn't even considered before.

"Here's another thing, eh. Purifying water when the bottled stuff's gone," Maggie said, pointing to a diagram of a solar still. "Slow, but does the trick."

I studied the diagram, brushing my fingers over the page. The surface was smooth and wax-like, resistant to my touch. "This... is wonderful."

"It's not just about having the tools. It's about knowing you can find a way, even when the odds are stacked against ya. This place may be hostile, but it's full of good stuff if you know where to look."

Maggie closed the notebook and handed it to me. "Take it. Let it remind you that you can do this."

I hesitated, holding the notebook like it might crumble in my hands. "I can't take this Maggie—"

"No arguments. These hands ain't much good for stripping wood or hunting anymore. This is yours now. It's your turn to shine."

For a moment, we stood in silence. Then Maggie reached out and rested a hand on my shoulder. "You're stronger than you think, Ellena. You've already kept Greg alive. And you probably saved Jax's life too." She leaned in close as if to whisper a secret. "I imagine Jax wouldn't fare too well in the morning if Button had been the only one to do the job, ya know?

My lips curved into a small, tired smile. I clutched the notebook to my chest, its worn leather oddly warm, like it had been waiting for me all along. "Thank you."

The rough sound of fabric tearing drew my attention to Button, who sat on the couch next to a pile of shredded towels. Button had turned out to be about as useful as a hairdryer in a bathtub. No surprise there. Despite everything, Button was still my hopeless little sis. The one who needed looking after, no matter how independent she pretended she was.

Could I forgive her for Eric? For whatever betrayal had unraveled between them? Maybe not right then. The wound was still too raw, the betrayal too fresh. But a strange certainty crept in—I could take care of Button, at least for a while. My stepsister had lost everything too. Her house. Her life. Her third limb—her smartphone. No endless Spotify playlists blaring Taylor Swift and Ed Sheeran anymore.

Maggie's grip on my shoulder pulled me back to the moment. "You'll be okay. Just remember—you don't have to do it all at once. Just take the next step, love."

* * *

By midnight, the trailer was silent, except for the crackle of the dying fire in the wood stove. Shadows flickered along the walls, swaying with the unsteady flames. Outside, the usual nocturnal chorus was absent.

I wondered if my mind was playing tricks on me. Was nature really on pause, or was I failing to notice what was right in front of me, like a train wreck victim oblivious to the carnage around them? *Was this shock? Would I even know if it were?* I tried to recall the signs of shock I'd seen in patients over the years, but the information was buried somewhere under the wreckage of the day.

I sat cross-legged on the floor and opened Maggie's survival notebook. Sleep was a distant memory, an impossible luxury. What horrors might creep in while I slept? Someone needed to stay awake—just in case. Better me than anyone else. My gaze lingered on the hand-drawn diagrams of plants with antimicrobial properties—goldenseal, yarrow, and calendula—each plant rendered with Maggie's characteristic precision, accompanied by labeled notes. I traced the edge of the page with my fingers, letting the practical wisdom of it anchor me, a thin thread pulling me away from the storm in my mind.

As I flicked through the pages, a soft murmur came from the back room—Greg and Maggie whispering in low, uneven tones. I couldn't make out the words through the closed door, only the gentle rise and fall of their voices. Then the thin strip of light beneath the door blinked out, replaced by black.

The whispering stopped, and minutes later, the snores began. At first, slow and staggered, until an uneven rhythm emerged: deep and loud, like a puttering boat—Greg's snores, most likely—and high-pitched whistles, like a toy train passing a station. Once the image of toy trains and boats popped into my head, I couldn't let it go. Every whistle and chug sent me into a fit of giggles.

Stop! Oh, hell. I'm in shock. I need to ground myself.

I'd seen it before—a trauma victim laughing after a car accident that had maimed his spouse, a mom giggling while her child lay in the ambulance with a possible broken neck. *Okay, senses. Grounding technique for high stress.*

What do I see? Jax, asleep, his face twisted, covered in sweat like he's trapped in a night terror. Lips mouthing something. A girlfriend's name?

What do I feel? The pages of Maggie's notebook resting in my lap, rough paper, edges curling. Familiar. Safe.

What do I taste? Staleness. Wish I had toothpaste. Or a hot toddy.

What do I hear? A train whistle: distant, like a toy train chugging around a circular track.

I didn't giggle. *Good. Grounded.*

Jax stirred on the dinette bed, sat up, and switched on a lantern. The glow sharpened his silhouette, highlighting his drawn, weary face.

"Couldn't sleep?" I whispered, careful not to wake Button.

Jax rubbed the back of his neck, leaning forward with his elbows on his knees. "Looks like I'm not the only one."

Winter—sprawled next to Jax—cracked one eye open, sighed, and went back to sleep.

I set the notebook aside and shifted to face Jax. He rested his hand on his chin and stared into space.

"Penny for your thoughts?" I cringed at the question, bracing for a sarcastic reply: *Oh, you know, bad day in the swamp, couple of nukes, rabid gator, the usual stuff.*

Jax glanced at me, his eyes shadowed but searching, like he was deciding what to say—or what to hold back. "You don't want to hear what I'm thinking."

"Try me," I said, rising and stepping over to the dinette. I sat at the foot of Jax's bed. "We're all stuck here. Might as well get to know each other." *Oh God, did that come out right? I hope he doesn't think I'm flirting. Wait—did I just sit on his bed? Oh, no. Worse.*

Jax's fingers tapped on his knee. "I was just thinking about before."

And there you have it. The Before. It's got a name now. So, what was this now? The After?

"What about before?"

Jax took a long breath. "I think it's worse out there than we can even imagine."

Worse? How could it possibly be worse?

I struggled to find the right question, then thought of my Gran's words. "*Sometimes the quiet's like the rain, lass—it gives the wee seeds their chance tae grow.*"

Jax's brow tightened, as if he were picking the right words to land a punch.

Then it came to me—a nudge of intuition. "You found something out? With the SEALs?"

He shrugged—Maybe so, maybe not—then let out a soft, humorless laugh. "I was assigned to one of the military's more... creative programs."

"Creative? Like...?" I groped for an idea, but the words felt slippery. What did "creative" even mean in a military context? Finger painting with grenades? Interpretive dance with land mines? The whole concept didn't compute, and my mind hit a blank wall.

I frowned, trying again. "Creative doesn't scream 'military' to me."

Jax's lips twitched, a ghost of amusement breaking through his weariness. "Trust me, it doesn't. Not in the way you're thinking, anyway."

He leaned forward, staring at the floor, fingers tapping his knees. "I was in Jamaica—Cockpit Country. Stunning place, if you can forget why we were there." He paused again, gripping his knee like it might steady his thoughts. "Thing is, they were asking us to do things that weren't exactly... above board."

My stomach tightened, my mind flashing to the black-ops photos the world had once wished it could unsee. Part of me didn't want to know Jax's definition of *creative*. Ignorance might be safer, but I was stuck in this trailer with him for who knew how long. After a tense pause, I asked the question I'd been suppressing.

"Like what?"

Jax blew out a breath. "Experiments. Effed up mind games. I thought about blowing the whistle—WikiLeaks or something. Wish I had. Guess I was too scared of court-martial, which is ironic since..." He trailed off, his lips twisting into a smile-grimace that made him look like a man trying to laugh at his own funeral. "Well, I went AWOL anyway. Court-martial's still on the table if they ever find me."

I narrowed my eyes. He hadn't answered the question I really wanted answered—what part he played in creative—but his words led me down a different path. "You were a SEAL, and you went AWOL?"

Jax met my eyes and held them, then glanced away.

I stared at him, his silence enough of an answer. He was holding something back—not a dirty little secret like Eric's, but something personal. Something eating at him. If he'd walked away from black-ops torture, or worse, maybe he wasn't the type of guy I'd feared he might be. Maybe he was one of the good ones.

An image of Jax came to mind: him standing back at the campsite, staring into the darkness.

"Oh, is that what you were doing here? Hiding out?"

Jax rubbed the stubble on his chin, as if sorting through what to say. "Vasquez—my friend at NAS Jax—called me to warn me the M.A.s were on my trail. As soon as she called, I jumped into the canoe with Winter and headed here."

"M.A.s?"

"Master-at-Arms. Navy cops."

"How did they know where you were?"

"Ah, stupidity. It was my dad's cabin. Registered with the state. Still can't figure out what I was thinking. I should have gone to Mongolia."

"Wait... Mongolia? Isn't that part of China?" A shiver ran down my spine. Was he a spy?

Jax laughed and waved a hand, as if brushing away my thoughts. "No, nothing like that. It's bordered by China. Great stargazing and no extradition treaty. If this hadn't happened," he said, waving his hand in the air, "I would have hightailed it to their embassy in Chicago, spilled the beans, and asked for asylum."

"Oh, like Julian Assange?"

"Exactly."

"I still don't understand. You said you thought it was worse out there. Why do you think that?"

He paused for a long time before answering. "Vasquez. She warned me. Told me that they'd upped to Defcon 1."

"Oh, I see," I said. But I didn't. Not really. I was pretty sure that Defcon 1 meant finger on the big red button, but if Jax had known the country was on the brink of nuclear warfare, why had he chosen to stay in the Okefenokee? Why not head for the hills? I wanted to ask more, probe deeper, but my head throbbed, and the seeds of a headache bloomed in my temple. At least Jax was opening up to me. That was something, I supposed.

Button stirred, and Jax held up a hand, signaling me to lower my voice. His attention shifted to Button before returning to me. "Thousands of missiles aimed at every square inch of Russia, North Korea...you name it, we have missiles covering it. No one walks away."

I scrunched my brow. This Vasquez, whoever she was, knew a lot about missiles. Was she high up in his chain of command? Why had she confided in him? Every time Jax spoke, it opened up ten more questions. "What are you saying, Jax?"

"I'm saying the world's probably gone. What we're doing now? It's surviving the long goodbye."

"But... but we don't know that for sure..."

"Think about what we saw. King's Bay to the east—military. But that bomb to the west? The one I said could be Tallahassee? There's no military there, just state government. And honestly, it could've been closer. Lake City, even. We won't know for sure until we get radio contact."

I sat back, my mind racing with the implications. I thought of Gran's words—about the quiet being like rain, coaxing growth—but how could anything grow in a world reduced to ash and silence?

Jax broke the stillness, his voice tight. "I was part of it, Ellena. I was part of that machine for too long. I should've sent it all to WikiLeaks. Then maybe we wouldn't be here."

I blinked, taken aback. It hit me: Jax wasn't just carrying the present. He was drowning in guilt for the past—guilt for something no one could have stopped. It reminded me of the man from the previous summer's I-95 pileup. His car had been crushed between two semis, both tailgating when traffic stopped. His entire family had died. "It's my fault," he'd sobbed. "If I hadn't insisted on taking I-10 because it was faster..."

Jax's guilt felt the same. Misplaced. He blamed himself for being a cog in the machine, for being part of something no one person could stop. What could a SEAL have done? Sure, WikiLeaks might've exposed the experiments, but even if those experiments had something to do with US nuclear warfare, then...

"These weren't our nukes that hit us, Jax. They were someone else's. It couldn't possibly be your fault."

He shook his head, paused, then said, "You could be right. But it sure as hell doesn't feel like it."

The silence stretched, thick with unspoken truths. I broke it, my voice quiet but firm. "You're not them, Jax. You left it behind. That counts for something."

His voice softened to a whisper. "I'm trying to believe that."

"You're here. That's what's important." But a tiny voice in the back of my mind whispered: *What is he not telling me?*

But before I could probe further, Jax changed the subject, catching me off guard.

"What's up with you and Button?"

I paused for a moment. I wasn't ready to unravel it all—not there, not then—but Jax had just opened the door wide, and it was wrong to leave him standing there alone. "I think she had an affair with my husband."

Jax's eyebrows shot up. "Your husband?"

"Ex-husband now. They worked together at the credit union."

I shrugged, like it was no big deal—and it wasn't anymore. Not after everything that had happened. The word *affair* drifted in my mind, with no purpose and no meaning. I should've been angry, should've screamed or cried. But then? In the After? It was nothing—just someone bumping into me in the hallway. *Sorry. No problem.* The empty emotion scared me more than the thought of betrayal.

Jax let the revelation hang in the air, his head tilting. "But... she's your sister."

I nodded. "Eric had his secrets, so I shouldn't be surprised. But Button?" My voice wavered, and I pressed my lips together, swallowing hard. "I don't get it."

Jax shifted closer. "If you need to let it out, do it. If not, fine. But don't let her take up rent in your head if she doesn't deserve it."

I looked at him, grateful for the unspoken permission to feel grief, anger, or whatever was bubbling up inside me. My mind was as blank as an unboxed Etch A Sketch, but each breath was getting harder to take. "I just don't have the energy to care anymore. I lost my..."

My breath hitched. *Baby.*

"...my marriage, and then the job that made me feel like I had a purpose. Thought I could outrun it all out here, but..." My laugh was hollow. "Turns out, you can't outrun life, not really."

Jax's silence was a comfort, a kindness I didn't deserve. But none of my problems mattered anymore, not in that moment. Like the leaking bathroom faucet that would never get fixed, the broken TV stand that would never get replaced, the loose door handle that would never get screwed back in. None of it mattered. None of it.

Jax said, "It's okay to grieve what you've lost, Ellena."

For the first time in what felt like forever, I looked him in the eyes. I saw no pity or judgment there—only a quiet understanding that settled in my chest like a dull ache. In that fragile moment, telling the story out loud didn't feel like it would crush me. It didn't result in hysterical sobs and waves of regret. Yet I could feel the threat of tears well up in my eyes and I willed them to hold back.

Jax shifted closer and wrapped his arms around me. The hug wasn't hesitant or awkward; it was warm and secure. I let out my breath and before I could second-guess myself, sank into him. The tears came next, hot and silent, soaking into his shoulder.

He didn't say a word, just held me as I cried, one hand resting on my back.

When I pulled back, my face flushed and my throat tight, his hand lingered before falling away. I searched his face, hyperaware of how close we were. He met my eyes, and for a moment, the air between us shifted, charged with something I couldn't name.

"You guys are awake?" Button asked, her words like a cold shower.

"Barely," I said, my voice cracking just enough to betray the spell of the last few minutes.

Jax glared at Button, but she didn't seem to notice—or didn't care—as she shuffled to the bathroom, her hair a wild mess and her face slack with exhaustion.

I stood, brushing myself off like I could dust away the last two minutes and start anew. *I said too much.* Opened my mouth—again. "I'll check the fire."

The silence between Jax and me stretched like an unspoken invitation, full of promise and fear. It pulled me back to him, even as I forced myself to move into the kitchenette, my heart pounding louder than the clatter of pans in the sink. Behind me, Jax's presence lingered, unspoken but impossible to ignore.

8 Not a Log

Breakfast was steeped in silence, not the easy kind, but the sort that kept conversation at bay. The hot air sat dead in the trailer, thick with the syrupy-sweet smell of canned peaches and stale coffee. It reeked like a dumpster in a heat wave.

Maggie ate in short, distracted bites, her eyes flicking toward the emergency radio on the counter. Jax sat across from her, rolling the last peach slice around the edge of his bowl with a spoon. My focus stayed on my lap, my fingers twisting the hem of my shirt.

When the bowls were empty, Maggie wiped her hands on her jeans, got up, and turned to the emergency radio. "Let's see what this thing has to say."

She hunched over it, fingers tightening on the dials. A crease formed between her brows as she squinted at the flickering display. She leaned in closer, as if the signal might clear up if she listened hard enough.

"You hear that?" She bent closer, pressing her ear to the speaker. "It's voices—faint, but voices dontcha know. Could be military?"

The static warbled and hissed, punctuated by occasional bursts of garbled sound. Was it words crackling through the static? A fragmented broadcast? It was impossible to tell.

"You sure about that?" Jax asked, cocking his head to the side as he stared at the radio.

Maggie's face flushed. "Yup. I heard something. Makes sense, don't it? Broadcast on open frequencies?"

I shifted, my fingers pressing into my thighs. I'd heard static like that once on my ambulance's two-way radio, the hiss and crackle shaping itself into quasi voices. My brain had filled in the gaps, twisting the noise into something it thought made sense. "Or it could be static?"

Maggie raised an eyebrow, her eyes dropping to the radio for a moment before flicking back to me. She let out a soft hum, neither agreement nor denial, but enough to make me wince, realizing how my tone might've come across. "I just mean... it could be."

Stop digging the hole deeper, lass, before you cannae crawl yourself oot. It was my Gran's voice, the same tone she'd used when I lied about calling Button a useless drama queen—first claiming Button misheard, then insisting Button had started it, and finally accusing her of always trying to stir up trouble.

But before I could say something else to disappoint Maggie, Jax cut in. "We don't even know if anyone out there is still operational."

Button said, "Still operational? You're talkin' like it's all over. What if it's not? What if there's people out there who can help us?"

Jax's hand tightened on the counter, his lips scrunching as if he were chewing the inside of his cheek. "Let's keep scanning. But we shouldn't get our hopes up too high. Even if there was a signal, it could be automated, which means there might be no one on the end of the line."

The hours stretched on, each burst of static a cruel tease. Hope sparked and died with every hiss, leaving the air heavier each time.

Jax leaned back, rubbing a hand over his face. "That's enough. No use burning energy chasing ghosts." He stood, grabbed a washrag, and went into the bathroom.

A split second later, he came back out, his face like stone. "Why is there water in there? Who used the shower?"

"I did," Button said, crossing her arms. "What's the big deal? I didn't drink it!"

Jax said, "The *big deal*, is that the water's probably contaminated. If so, you just spread radioactive particles everywhere."

He returned to the bathroom with the Geiger counter, reappearing moments later.

The gadget buzzed as Jax ran it over Button's body. He frowned at the readout. "Two hundred CPM. Not catastrophic, but not good either. Did you breathe it in?"

"What? Did I breathe in the water? Of course not!" Button's voice was indignant, like Jax had just asked her if she'd licked the toilet bowl.

He swept the device around the room. "And now there's radioactive particles on the floor. Fantastic." He looked at Button, then at me. "Everyone who used that bathroom needs to clean off and change their clothes. Wipe off, gently, with damp rags. Toss the dirty stuff outside."

Button stormed to the back of the trailer, snatching a towel and a bottle of water. Muttering under her breath, she yanked the sliding door shut with a thud.

Jax gathered rags from the counter. "I need to clean the bathroom."

Maggie fished a pair of work gloves out of a drawer and handed them to Jax. "What about us? We used the bathroom this morning too, eh, Greg?"

Greg nodded, but said nothing. He flipped through a *National Geographic*, turning the pages too quickly for me to believe he was actually reading. I didn't blame him. The last time I'd touched one of those magazines—two years ago at the oral surgeon's office—I'd only stared at the pictures. Vibrant, otherworldly photos that made the dense black and white text feel about as inviting as homework.

My front tooth throbbed, like the thought of dental work had irritated the nerve. I should've had the cavity filled months ago, but an extra three hundred bucks hadn't magically materialized in my bank account. I'd kept putting the procedure off, telling myself there was time. Now, with the world falling apart, I wondered if I'd ever see a dentist again. *Awesome. Nothing like rotting teeth to drill home the whole 'civilization is over' theme.*

"Ellena," Jax said, snapping me out of it. He wiped Winter's fur in slow, deliberate strokes, the damp rag pressing against the coat. "Change clothes. Same with Maggie and Greg. We can't afford more slip-ups."

One by one, we shuffled into the bedroom to change. Maggie hovered near Greg, her voice low, until he swatted at her like she was a fly buzzing too close. "Fine," he said, dragging himself off the couch and letting her steer him toward the back.

When we finished changing, Jax grabbed the pile of dirty rags, cracked the trailer door open just enough to hurl the mess outside, then slammed it shut.

Button said, "Look, I'm sorry y'all, I really am."

What the fuck, Button? Could you get any more clueless? What's next—Sorry, y'all, I didn't know tap water was a no-go for oatmeal or Oops, sorry guys, I thought we could wash our undies in the sink?

"No, seriously guys, I was tired of feeling grungy. It was quick. Real quick—"

Jax thrust a hand in the air, palm out, and closed his eyes. He bit his bottom lip like he was clamping down on the words I was already thinking. "Stop talking. Not another word."

A warning—firm and final—from a man on the verge of losing his cool, or worse.

And the conversation stopped, snuffed out like a candle at lights out. No one said another word all evening.

* * *

The next morning, I stirred, my senses prickling like the remnants of a half-remembered fever dream. The tang of dampness lingered in the air, a dank musk that clung to my skin like sweat. A thin draft threaded through the trailer, its bite raising goosebumps.

Swinging out of bed, I followed the draft to its source: the trailer door hung open a crack, its hinges creaking as the morning breeze teased it wider. I clicked it shut. Winter's head shot up, his nose twitching, and he let out a low whine.

Jax stirred on the dinette bed. "What's going on?" His voice was thick with sleep.

Winter whined again, cocking his head toward the door.

"Door was open," I said.

I moved to the back room. Easing the door open, I peered inside. Maggie was bundled under a duvet, her breathing steady. But Greg's side of the bed was empty, the blankets piled at the foot of the bed. Frowning, I checked the bathroom. Empty. No Greg.

I stepped back into the main room. "Greg's gone."

Jax sat up fast, his feet hitting the floor with a thud. "Gone? What do you mean, *gone?*"

"I mean he's not here. He must've slipped out."

Maggie emerged from the back, rubbing her eyes. "What's going on, eh?"

"I can't find Greg," I said. The words were trivial, like saying I'd misplaced my phone. Greg wasn't under the bed or hiding in the bathroom. He was gone. "He must've left in the night."

Maggie frowned. "You sure?"

I nodded. "I woke up, and the door was open."

Maggie's brows knit together. "You sure? Did you check the bathroom? I bet he's..." Her voice trailed off as she glanced toward the open bathroom door, the emptiness inside confirming what I already knew.

Maggie pulled her robe off the wall and slid her feet into slippers. Her calm felt surreal, like she hadn't grasped it yet. Greg wasn't out picking flowers—he was wandering around Lord knew where in an irradiated swamp.

"He could be in serious trouble," I said.

"I know what's out there, you betcha," she said, shuffling to the kitchen and grabbing the counter.

Button stirred on the couch. "What are you guys talking about?"

"Greg left," I said, the words grating against my nerves. "In the middle of the night."

Button blinked at me, confused. "What do you mean, *left?*"

I sighed, pressing my hands against my face.

Deep breaths, Ellena, deep breaths.

I jabbed a finger at the door. "He's out there."

Button sat bolt upright. "Why?"

I said, "Because he had enough, that's why. Maybe, if we weren't cleaning up after your little shower stunt, we'd have seen the signs. He was struggling, and we missed it."

"How is this my fault? Jax should've been sleeping by the door like he said he would!"

The jab hit its mark, but I wasn't letting it slide. *Oh, here we go.* "It's always someone else's fault. You've been doing this since we were kids. Every broken vase, every mess you made—it was always me who got blamed. You never take responsibility. Just once, Button. Say sorry. Just once."

Button's face flushed, and she crossed her arms. "Perhaps if you weren't so busy playing drill sergeant, Greg wouldn't have wanted to escape."

The anger came on so strong I couldn't contain it. "Drill sergeant? Where the hell did that come from? I've been busting my ass trying to keep us alive, and what have you been doing? Manicuring your nails between—" The words snapped off in my mouth.

Stop talking, Ellena. Stop before you say something you can't take back.

For a moment, I wasn't sure who I was more furious with—Button or myself.

"That's enough."

Maggie's voice dropped like a lead weight, heavy and final. The argument died in the air between us, replaced by the soft tick of the wall clock marking off seconds Greg didn't have. She stood there in a faded cotton dress, arms crossed tight against her chest. "Both of you need to shut it down right now. Greg's out there somewhere and fighting like cats in a bag ain't gonna bring him home any faster."

Gran's voice flitted through my memory, reminding me to *take a wee step back when the fire burns too hot*. I exhaled and nodded. "You're right, Maggie, sorry."

Button glared at me. Her face twisted in that sour, pinched expression I knew all too well. The last time I'd seen it was after Eric's arrest. Button had shown up the next day, rapping on the door like she had urgent news. When I opened it, she launched into a ramble about needing money, about how the credit union wasn't paying her enough. I had stood there, torn between slamming the door in her face or tearing into her for being so self-centered.

I'd chosen the latter. They had just hauled my husband off in cuffs, and all Button could do was whine about her paycheck. And when I snapped—when I laid it all out, naked and ugly—Button had just stood there, staring at me like I'd grown a second head. Like I was the one who was unhinged.

Embarrassment had come later, curling around me like smoke, dissipating the last of my anger. Button's insensitivity didn't excuse losing control. That sharp-edged guilt had lingered, and now it was back, gnawing at my bones like a January wind through a cracked window. I'd lost my shit again. In front of Maggie. In front of Jax.

Maggie said, "Blaming each other doesn't help, eh. What matters is figuring out what to do next."

Jax glanced at the clock. "How long has he been gone?"

"I was up and about around six. Bathroom run. He was still asleep then," Maggie said.

"So, a couple of hours at most. If he's not back soon..."

I didn't need him to finish the thought. *Radiation exposure.*

I sank down by the stove, my gaze settling on the survival notebook still open on the table. Maggie had said it was mine and told me to use it to shine. But what had I done to shine so far? Aside from stitching up Greg, nothing. Nothing but piss everyone off and make a fool of myself.

I needed to do something useful, something to prove Maggie hadn't been wrong about me. What if Maggie was rethinking that gift now? What if she was wondering if she'd made a mistake, if she'd put her trust in someone who couldn't even keep herself together, let alone anyone else?

I stood up. "I'll go. I'll find Greg and bring him back."

* * *

83

Dawn's gray fog still cloaked the morning as I finished knotting a fresh sheet into a poncho. My gloved hands trembled as I pulled the scarf across my face. *What kind of craziness had made me volunteer for this?* One word summed up everything I knew about radiation and alligators: jackshit.

The temptation to back out flashed through my mind. I could hear myself saying it—*This is a bad idea. Someone else should go.* But I couldn't. Wouldn't. Admitting fear wasn't the same as weakness—but it was close.

Is this stupid? Probably. Could I live with myself if someone else got hurt because I was too chickenshit to do the job? *Not a chance.*

The Geiger counter dangled from my neck. Each staccato click cut through the silence like a cold, mechanical heartbeat, driving home the stakes. My EMT kit hung over my shoulder, crammed with extra supplies: six bottles of water, bear spray, and a whistle in case I needed help. Jax stood by the trailer door, arms locked across his chest, his face etched with the grim focus of a paramedic rolling a battered and bloodied patient into the ER.

"This is a bad idea," he said, as if he'd read my mind. His eyes searched mine, perhaps looking for a sign I might back out. "You don't even know how far he's gone."

"I don't need to know. I just need to try." I didn't bother saying the rest: that doing nothing was what had gotten me into this mess in the first place. Not this radioactive mess—that wasn't my fault—but the old one, the slow collapse of my life before all this. I wasn't going to sit around like Button, checking my reflection in the mirror while the world fell apart.

"I should go," Jax said, a ghost of conviction behind the words. He already knew he couldn't. We both did. He'd been through too much already—the alligator attack, the radiation clinging to his clothes, his skin, his lungs. Another trip out there could seal his fate, and we all knew it.

I shook my head. "You know you can't."

Jax gave a curt nod, like it hurt to agree. His eyes stayed locked on mine—not worry, but something deeper, harder to define.

It was the same look Eric had worn that night in the delivery room when the nurses rushed in, their voices clipped and urgent, their movements frantic. Machines beeped; nurses scurried. The baby was in trouble—we all knew it. I could see it in Eric's face, the way his fear bled through his attempts at calm.

Jax had that same look now. That same fear, raw and unspoken, etched into every line of his face. "You've got 60 minutes, max." He held up Maggie's old wristwatch, its timer already set. "No heroics, Ellena. If you're not back by then—"

"You'll assume the worst," I finished for him, snatching the watch and strapping it over my sleeve. My attention shifted to Maggie, who stood nearby, her face lined with concern. "I'll do everything I can to bring him back."

Maggie placed a hand on my shoulder. "Be careful, love. Remember—you can't save anyone if you don't save y'self first."

I nodded, adjusted the watch strap, and stepped outside. The damp air curled around my exposed eyes. I picked up the shower curtain pole, the cold metal unfamiliar but reassuring in its stability. It was a reminder I wasn't completely defenseless, even if the sharpened tip was a toy weapon against the lurking dangers.

Gray mist curled around the trees like smoke from a damp brush fire. It didn't drift or scatter; it clung, as though something ancient and patient had exhaled poison into the air.

The clicks of the Geiger counter punctuated the silence like a cardiac monitor counting down to a flatline. I gripped the pole, prodding the ground ahead of me. The mud clung to my boots, each step a struggle against the sucking earth. I kept my eyes low and sweeping, scanning the ground for any sign of Greg's path.

Unease settled low in my stomach. Greg could've gone anywhere, swallowed whole by the maze of trees and muck. But then I spotted boot imprints pressed into the thin layer of ash blanketing the ground. Relief flooded me, enough to propel me forward toward the shadow of a chance it was Greg. The prints led toward the road. He wanted out, and he probably thought that the road was the fastest way to escape. Although where he thought he was escaping to was anyone's guess.

I glanced toward a darker path edged with reeds and broken reflections of the sky rippling in blackwater. The path twisted deeper into the park. One misstep there, and we'd both disappear into the hungry mire for good.

My pace quickened as I moved along the trail to the road.

"Greg?" The sound hung in the thick air for a moment. The response came—not from Greg, but from a low grunt that rumbled up from the shadowed water. My lungs seized like a motor throwing its belt—sudden, jarring, locking tight before I could even suck in a breath, let alone scream.

Alligator.

The grunts multiplied, a warning reverberating across the water. I gripped the pole in my hands like a spear.

Stupid, stupid. Stay quiet, Ellena.

I couldn't risk calling out again. Not unless I wanted to invite every alligator in the vicinity to dinner. Had they gorged themselves on fish, or had the desolate landscape left them starving, their instincts honed for the next kill? The attack on Jax flashed in my mind. Was it a fluke, or a preview of what came next? My thoughts swirled as the silence pressed in. I'd stepped into their feeding grounds, crossing my fingers and hoping it wasn't dessert time. *Got to stay focused. Keep moving.*

I cut my eyes to the roadside ditch, searching for the smallest ripple, anything that might betray a lurking shape beneath the surface. The Geiger counter's clicks punctured the silence, each one ratcheting up the pressure in my chest.

Instinct screamed at me to run back to the trailer and slam the door on this hellscape. My boots shifted, my legs tensed, ready to launch—but I forced myself still. Greg was out here, somewhere, alone and vulnerable in a place that consumed anything not equipped to survive. If I panicked now, this mutated wasteland would swallow Greg whole, leaving no trace.

And Maggie? She'd look at me with that empty, broken expression I had seen too often in grieving families. What would Jax see then? A coward who ran at the first sight of the trenches?

Fear rose in my belly, bitter and acidic, like I'd swallowed a cup of bile. I steadied my grip on the spear, my fingers slick against the damp fabric of my gloves. I rounded a dense thicket of reeds, each step careful, measured. The Geiger counter spiked, its frantic clicks shattering the swamp's hush. My heart hammered as I stepped forward, my breath shallow, my senses hyperaware.

Something shifted in the water ahead. I locked onto a log that stirred—slowly, intentionally.

Not a log.

An alligator's head broke the surface, its ridged snout gleaming in the light. It locked onto me, its stare dark and ancient, as if remembering its last prey. The creature glided forward through the water. I took a step back, gripping the pole, the muscles in my arms taut.

The alligator lunged. Its tail whipped the water into a frenzy, jaws snapping close enough for me to see the jagged edges of its teeth.

I let out a startled cry, my pulse spiking as I jabbed the pole forward. The crude point glanced off the creature's thick hide, sending a jolt up my arms. It twisted with a hiss and lunged again, faster this time. I stumbled back, my heel catching on a root. The ground slammed into me, the Geiger counter pressing hard against my chest as its clicks reached a frantic tempo. My backpack hit the mud, spilling its contents in a scattered mess.

The alligator advanced, mud spraying from its powerful movements. I swung the pole again, catching it across the snout. The beast recoiled with a guttural hiss, the sound vibrating through my ribs like a shockwave.

The reprieve was fleeting. It surged again, jaws snapping, body lunging with savage intensity. The pole flew from my hands and landed in the roadside ditch with a splash.

No no no. No no no.

I scrambled back, my hands groping for something—anything. A rock? My palm landed on my half-open EMT kit. Fingers fumbling, I searched until they brushed against a scalpel wrapper. The sharp crinkle jolted me into action. I ripped the packaging open, revealing the blade inside—gleaming, cold, and clean. My breaths came fast and shallow as I gripped it tight.

The animal lunged again, a coil of pure muscle and fury. My grip on the scalpel tightened. In a flash of desperate clarity, I raised the blade high. My focus narrowed to a single point: the predator's eye.

Please, God, let me have Jax's aim.

I drove the scalpel down, and it sank deep. The resistance was sickening, like cutting through the tough, slick tissue of a mangled leg, the way flesh and tendons fought the blade before giving way.

The alligator reared back with a guttural bellow. The sound rolled through the trees like distant thunder. Its tail whipped the water into a churning froth, waves crashing against the bank, sending cold spray lashing across my face. The beast writhed, its agony sending ripples racing outward, warping the reflection of the branches overhead.

I scrambled to my feet, the scalpel in one hand, my breaths ragged and burning my chest like I was breathing in flecks of hot embers.

The creature sank into the murk, its scaly bulk disappearing beneath the surface. I stood there, legs trembling, staring at the ripples until they faded into the gloom.

My hands tightened on the scalpel, slick with a grotesque mix of mud, fallout, and what had to be vitreous humor from the alligator's eye.

The Geiger counter clicked faster, its panicked clicks drilling at my ears: a warning I couldn't outrun.

I shoved the spilled water bottles and bandages back into my backpack and staggered down the road. The billboard loomed ahead, barely recognizable under a crust of black dust. Once, it had promised "Stargazing Tonight," bright and hopeful. Now the words were buried, smeared, meaningless—a ghost of something better left forgotten.

My steps dragged and my legs burned. Each movement was a fight through the mist that clung to me like damp gauze. Time stretched thin, a slow grind that wore down my resolve. Doubt crept in, whispering with every click of the counter. There was no sign of Greg, no guarantee I'd find him. The thought of turning back slithered into my mind again, its coils tightening with every step. I pressed on.

Thirty minutes, maybe more. The timer on my wrist had long since told me I was out of time, but my feet kept moving, driven by something I couldn't rationalize—a mix of desperation and stubbornness.

Then I saw it: a flash of orange against the bleak, dust-choked landscape.

A hunter's jacket, crumpled at the base of a tree.

"Greg?" My raspy voice cracked through the silence. I didn't care who—or what—might hear. Saving Greg was the only thing that made sense, tethering me to something larger than sitting in that trailer, waiting for despair to swallow me whole.

A groan broke through the fog ahead. I turned toward the sound, and there he was—slumped against the base of a tree, like gravity and rot had negotiated his fate and were now sealing the deal.

Relief surged through me, a force so sudden it buckled my knees. I stumbled forward, the scalpel slipping from my hand as I crouched beside him.

"Greg, it's me," I said, gripping his arm. My gloves smeared the thin gray dust clinging to his skin. His bare arms stuck out from the sleeves of a Detroit Red Wings T-shirt. His matching baseball cap lay on the ground, leaving his head exposed to the fallout. *Not good. Not good at all.*

His eyes opened, glassy and unfocused, his lips parting to release nothing more than a shallow breath.

"We have to go," I said, picking up the scalpel. "Now."

I hooked my arms under his and hauled him to his feet, draping his arm over my shoulder. He groaned, his weight threatening to pull us both down, but I tightened my hold. My muscles screamed with effort. *No, Greg. You don't get to quit. Not now. Not when we're this close.*

"Move!"

Greg's legs dragged like they were attached to a ball and chain as he stumbled forward.

I dug in, my feet slipping but holding just enough to keep us upright. I struggled for breath through the damp and smothering scarf, my lungs burning from exertion.

A crack sounded behind us. I froze, pivoting toward the noise. The dark water between the cypress roots rippled, but nothing else moved.

"Keep quiet," I whispered. Greg groaned in response, and I jostled him. "I mean it, Greg. You want to attract a—" I cut myself off. Saying it would make it real. *Pack of alligators? Sloth of bears? Nest of cottonmouths?*

I pressed forward, every step a battle against the thick mud and my screaming legs. Stopping wasn't an option. Stopping meant the lurking monsters in the reeds—or the ones slithering on the road behind us, real or imagined—would pounce, dragging us down like frenzied zombies.

"*Those late-night horror films'll gie ye death dreams,*" Gran had once said. What I wouldn't give to be sitting in her garden right now, drinking tea. *If I pinch my leg, will I wake up from this monster movie?* The thought was absurd, but the temptation was real, and I pinched my leg anyway—just in case. *Still here. Great.*

My grip on the scalpel tightened at the sound of a splash to our left. A vivid image seared my mind: an alligator with jaws as powerful and crushing as a grapple claw, poised to drag us both under. My breath caught in my throat, but I forced myself forward, one trembling step at a time.

"Don't stop," I muttered, unsure if I was talking to Greg or myself. "Just keep moving."

The swamp breathed around me, each sound hammering against my skull. A frog's croak hit like a train horn. Leaves crackled like brittle bones. Every nerve in my body screamed, bending like laurel oaks in a storm, ready to snap.

The sagging awning of the trailer came into view, ghostly through the mist.

Greg mumbled something, his voice slurred and thick.

I tightened my grip, forcing him to stay upright. "Save it. Talk when we're inside."

The last few steps felt like wading through molasses, the trailer looming closer but never close enough. My legs protested, every muscle a burning ache, my breath rasping in shallow bursts. Still, I kept moving.

By the time we reached the trailer, my hands were trembling so badly I nearly dropped Greg while adjusting his sagging body. The door swung open, and there was Jax, his face a mix of worry and relief. I registered him only in a haze, my mind buzzing with exhaustion, my nerves strung out like frayed wire. I'd made it, but this was only the start—the first section hike on an apocalyptic trail that stretched endlessly ahead. This wasn't over. Perhaps it never would be.

Jax's expression tightened as he stared at me—soaked, trembling, and streaked with gore—and Greg, wobbling like a marionette. "What the hell happened? Are you okay? You're not hurt, are you?"

"Not me," I said, then hesitated, my words faltering. The precision of my EMT training was a distant memory. Before all this, I'd have rattled off something useful—vitals, symptoms, details the ER could use to assess and treat. But standing there, my mind dulled by exhaustion and static, all I could manage was, "He's not good."

Jax stepped back, keeping his distance but leaving the door ajar. "Greg, strip down right there. Ellena, you're going to have to help him."

Greg swayed, his eyes glassy and unfocused. He looked at me, then at Jax, his confusion as exposed as a man waking up in a jail cell after drinking himself blind.

"Greg, now!" My voice cracked, desperation cutting through my exhaustion. He stared at me, dazed, his hands fumbling at his jacket. I yanked at his sleeve, my movements clumsy but insistent. "If you don't strip down, you'll die."

Jax watched from the doorway, his face unreadable. Had I been too slow? Should I have cleaned Greg up first? His expression gnawed at me— was he angry I'd lost the pole?

My tone jolted Greg enough that he fumbled at his jacket, his hands shaking as he peeled away the layers. I didn't wait; I yanked off my poncho and gloves, my movements efficient despite the way my hands trembled. Every piece of clothing felt as heavy as lead. Each piece was slick with grime and blood. I threw it all to the side, where it landed on the mud with a splat.

"The backpack. It spilled on the ground. We'll need to wipe it all down," I said.

Jax nodded. "I'll take care of it. Don't miss anything. Boots, socks— everything. Leave it out here."

Greg hesitated, his body trembling. "Ellena, I can't—"

"Do it! Do it, or we don't go inside. Your life depends on it," I said.

Greg's resistance crumbled, and with my help, he stripped down to his underwear.

Jax said, "Greg, come on in, sit on the edge of the shower. Don't touch anything."

I peeled off my mud-caked socks and tossed them onto the pile. My whole body trembled—not just from the chill creeping through my damp clothes, but from the adrenaline still thrumming in my veins. It was the aftershock of too much danger too fast.

When I was down to my base layers, Jax stepped forward, his expression shifting as he squinted at me. "Wait. Ellena..."

"What?" I asked, my breath catching at the sudden concern in his tone.

Jax moved closer, his gloved hands hovering but not touching me. The sight of him—steady, focused—calmed me for a moment, even as my body wavered. He pointed at my arm. "You're bleeding."

I blinked, my mind struggling to catch up. Bleeding? I stared down at myself, trying to locate the source. Panic and confusion collided as my legs trembled anew, my vision narrowing. "Where?"

He pointed at my left arm, but I couldn't feel a thing. Come to think of it, I was numb all over. I couldn't even feel the ground under my feet. That had to mean—*Shock? Or worse.*

"Get inside. Bedroom. Now." Jax's tone was firm, but his eyes softened, like he was channeling Gran, ready to slap a Band-Aid on my scrape.

The realization slammed into me, twisting deep.

Not good. This is not good.

I swayed, the edges of my vision swimming, narrowing to a tunnel of white light that flickered like a bad bulb. The ground tilted. The rapid clicks of the Geiger counter faded into a high-pitched whine. Before everything went black, one thought pushed through the haze.

Jax will fix this. He has to.

9 Fool's Lottery

I came to. The world returned in hazy fragments that pushed through my fog. A dull ache pulsed in my arm, each throb dragging me closer to consciousness. I held my fingers to my temple as if willing my mind to hurry and reboot. The trailer's dim interior came slowly into focus. Clean white bandages mummified my forearm, wrapped so tightly it felt like a cast.

Jax knelt beside me, peeling off nitrile gloves and tossing them into a wicker garbage can.

I shifted and a twinge shot up my arm, forcing a hiss from my lips. "What happened?"

"You were out cold," Jax said, jerking his chin toward the suture kit splayed open on the counter, its sterile packaging torn open. "Didn't have time to wait around for you to bleed out."

"Bleed out?" The comment made no sense, like he'd just told me the steaks were on the grill and the champagne was chilling.

"Looks like a talon got you. Pretty deep."

I frowned, my thoughts sluggish, remnants of a scaly phantom clawing through the haze. "I don't understand how..."

"You mumbled something about an alligator. Close call, huh?"

An alligator? It was unreal, like a fever dream. The memory was fuzzy, disjointed. *Did I really kill it?*

The pain in my arm, though, was all too real. It burned like a fresh paper cut, radiating from my wrist to my elbow. "You could say that. I didn't realize it... did anything."

How could I not have realized an alligator attack might leave me injured? I should have checked myself right after. An icy chill seeped into my bones as my mind spiraled with what-ifs: lying in a pool of blood, or face down in stagnant water, ooze clogging my lungs as I exhaled muck bubbles and fought for air.

I drew a deep, calming breath, then exhaled and counted to ten. "Where'd you learn to suture?"

"Hunting. Gut enough deer, patch up a dog that hit barbed wire... you figure it out. Didn't think I'd be using those skills to stitch up someone like you." He glanced away, as if the words had slipped out unplanned.

The words hung between us, carrying a resonance I couldn't place. For a moment, the ache in my arm faded and a fleeting thought crossed my mind—what if I could trust him? But just as fast, I reminded myself of how little I knew about Jax Mercer.

My Gran's voice echoed in my mind, a lesson delivered long ago when I had a ridiculous elementary school crush on Jasper Tewkes. He'd been in the eighth grade, I in the sixth, and he reminded me of Jax—similar coloring, the same easy confidence that made everything seem effortless. But the infatuation fizzled after I discovered Jasper was a stoner who spent his nights glued to video games and his days sleeping like the dead. Our single, disastrous date ended with me coming home, mascara smudged and tears streaking my face. Gran had been waiting, arms open, ready with a hug and a nugget of advice: *"Dinnae give your heart to a stranger, lass. That's playing the fool's lottery with your heart."*

Am I being a fool now? The thought hit me like a shot of electricity—the kind that jolts EMTs into action when seconds mattered—but I pushed back against it. Of course, I wasn't thinking straight—I'd left my logic somewhere back on the trail. My amygdala was in charge, flooding me with instinct and emotion while my rational mind stayed out of reach. Textbook trauma response.

"You'll live. But you owe me some fishing line," Jax said.

"Huh?" Did he say I was out of line?

He held up a roll of Berkley Trilene XL. "Fishing line. Took a fair bit to stitch you up."

I smiled as my fog lifted. "Sure. I'll run out to the bait shop as soon as I'm up."

Jax chuckled, letting the humor hang for a moment. "We'll talk about payment later."

My stomach fluttered as Jax's eyes lingered on me. *Am I imagining this?* I shoved the thought aside and forced my focus elsewhere. "How's Greg?"

Jax shook his head slowly, like a doctor about to break bad news. "He was out there too long. Looks like he's got a nasty sunburn on his face, neck, and hands, and it's starting to blister."

I bit my lip, searching for something useful to say and finding nothing. My body had awakened, but my mind hadn't caught up. "Where is he?"

Jax jerked his thumb toward the open bedroom door. "Bathroom. Puking his guts out again."

"Oh, no." The words tumbled out, small and useless, dissolving into the air. I hated myself for them—for how hollow they sounded.

I'd trained for nuclear disaster, back when it was theoretical. Hurricanes, floods, tornadoes—we'd spent days on those. Nuclear fallout? Half a lecture, glossed over like it wouldn't happen. I'd tried to fill the gaps myself—watching *The China syndrome, Chernobyl,* and *Silkwood,* then forgetting most of the details. Except for the scene where they shot the dogs at Chernobyl—that image stayed with me.

Now it was here, staring me in the eye. But I wasn't thinking about morphine or pain relief. The word that jumped into my head was expectant. And despite the fogginess in my mind, I could hear the disaster prep instructor's voice like a cheesy jingle I couldn't forget: "Expectant means Jane Doe isn't screaming because she's giving birth—she's screaming because she's about to know what being roasted alive feels like."

Was Greg expectant? "When did he start vomiting?"

"As soon as he walked in the door, pretty much."

A single truth blazed into my skull. Not an inchoate thought, but an explosion: *Lethal dose.*

It was as if a monstrous, exploding mechanism gripped me; its detonator compressing fissile material with machinelike precision, unleashing a chain reaction so intense that it could vaporize me in a zeptosecond—obliterating flesh, bone, and thought—simply because I was alive. The sense of doom was so overwhelming that for a moment, I thought I might faint. In that instant, a vision of Greg flashed through my mind with sickening, brutal clarity—writhing in agony, his flesh blackened and peeling away in grotesque ribbons.

In any ordinary situation, I would have found the right words to express my fears in a calm and collected tone. But this wasn't an ordinary situation. This was a charnel house of suffering, raw and unforgiving, and I had nothing. No comforting phrases, no professional detachment—just a sickening loop in my head of, *He's toast,* and, *Shit, he's going to suffer.* I was supposed to be the expert, the one who kept her cool in the face of disaster. Instead, I was as much use as an empty saline bag.

As if on cue, Greg emerged from the bathroom, his steps unsteady, each one thudding against the floor like a drunk testing unfamiliar ground. He shuffled and staggered toward the front of the trailer, a wheeze rattling with each breath.

A second later, Button scurried to the bathroom door, waving a hand in front of her nose before slipping inside. The door clicked shut a second later.

Maggie appeared in the doorway, leaning in close. "You two up for taking a look see at something? While Button's in the bathroom."

I swung myself out of bed, my legs protesting the effort. Weakness tugged at me, but Maggie's tone carried a pull I couldn't resist; She sounded eager and cheerful, like she was about to show off a prize turkey at a county fair. I couldn't lay the truth out—not now. I wasn't about to say, *Oh, by the way, Greg's going to die.* But the truth pressed against me, insistent and heavy, daring me to keep it contained. My training had taught me to tread lightly, to avoid delivering the thick, unvarnished truth when it might send someone spiraling into hysteria. And so had Gran: *Best say a good nowt than a bad owt, hen.*

"I don't know about everyone else in here," Maggie whispered, "but I know who I trust with this, you betcha." She nodded toward the bathroom, her expression flat, eyes unreadable.

Jax glanced at me, one brow lifting. He gestured to the front of the trailer with an outswept hand. After you.

"Lift this up, Jax would ya," Maggie said, pointing at the bench seat.

Jax stepped forward and hefted the seat aside with a grunt. Beneath it was a scuffed wooden panel, its edges softened from years of wear, a hint at secrets hidden below. Maggie crouched down and pried it open.

Jax and I crowded in, a mix of curiosity and unease hanging between us.

Maggie reached in and pulled out a revolver, gleaming and menacing. The light hit it just right, throwing a cold shine across the room. It didn't just sit there—it demanded attention, a promise wrapped in polished steel.

Maggie's hands moved again, emerging with a compact crossbow, its frame immaculate, followed by a machete with a leather-wrapped handle. She set them down beside a small box of ammunition.

Jax broke the silence first. "You've been holding out on us, Maggie." His fingers curled around the revolver, testing its balance like it was a tool he'd known all his life. "What else you got stashed in here? A grenade launcher?"

Maggie didn't flinch. "You don't get to my age without preparing for a rainy day, I tell ya."

Jax nodded, setting the revolver down on the table.

Maggie glanced at my bandaged arm. "I'm so sorry I shoulda shown this stuff to you before. If you'd had a real weapon, then..."

I said, "It's okay. You didn't know us." I wouldn't have trusted us with this stash yesterday, either.

Sure, I'd pulled Greg back from the brink—twice—but could anyone trust a woman on the edge with a gun? And then there was Jax. He was an unknown, with secrets like shadows I couldn't see through. But despite my doubts, the weapons were in front of me and having them felt like we'd crossed a line—from campers under the stars to a ragtag group straight out of a *Predator* movie.

Button stepped out of the bathroom a second later, like she'd just done a quick mirror check.

Maggie sighed and shook her head in resignation.

So much for keeping this secret from Button.

But then again, there were only so many secrets five people could keep in 200 square feet of space.

Button eyed the revolver on the table with disgust, one corner of her mouth twisting as she gritted her teeth, as though trying to keep the object from entering her mouth. "You're kidding. What's that supposed to be used for?"

The question was so dumb, so utterly influencer-level Blonde. The jab came out before I could stop it. "It's a fancy hairdryer. Want to give it a go?"

Button's lips pursed. Quick retorts weren't her forte, and I knew it. But I also knew I'd pay for that little dig later.

Jax picked up the crossbow, testing its weight and pulling back the bow's string. His brow furrowed. "I think we need rules. No one carries the gun unless there's an immediate threat. Same with the crossbow. And no one goes swinging that machete around unless it's absolutely necessary."

Maggie nodded in agreement. "That's fair. And the gun stays unloaded unless we need it, eh? Agreed?"

"Agreed," Jax said, not missing a beat.

Button said, "Fantastic. Now we're, what? Going out there like vigilantes?"

My jaw clenched. Button had her smarts—sure, she could code circles around most software developers, fix a laptop in her sleep—but when it came to survival, she was as clueless as a toad in a tornado. The world out there wasn't just dangerous—it was a question mark with teeth. I didn't have the energy to break it down for her, not now, not like she was a kid who needed mollifying when the closet was too dark.

Alligators, for starters—big, mean, and developing a taste for human flesh. And if the animals weren't bad enough, the people might be worse. I'd seen enough post-apocalyptic movies to know how fast things could spiral when the rules went out the window. Somewhere out there, a pack of savages could already be waiting to strip us clean. And Button—with her blonde hair and magazine-cover skin—would be the first thing they'd grab. Hell, they wouldn't think twice.

I opened my mouth to try to put it all into words, but Maggie beat me to the punch.

"Button," Maggie said, her tone cutting through the room like a cleaver. "This ain't about violence—it's about preparation. Survival doesn't wait for perfect answers."

Button huffed, folding her arms. "Fine. You decide. Whatever."

Maggie picked up the revolver, handling it like it might snap at her, before tucking it back into the compartment. The unspoken doubt hung between us: not just about the weapons, but the group itself—whether we could hold together or were already unraveling, the thread of sanity and survival tearing straight through, leaving only a jagged, irreparable hole.

* * *

The trailer was quiet during dinner, except for the hum of the emergency radio scanning for signals in vain. I sat on the edge of the dinette, my bandaged arm resting across my lap. Jax stood near the window, one hand braced against the frame, his gaze fixed on the swamp outside. Greg lay slumped on the couch, pale and shivering, his breathing shallow. From the bathroom, a muffled retching sound cut through the silence.

I winced. Button had disappeared into the bathroom twenty minutes ago. My first thought was our diet—canned beans and crackers were far from gourmet, and Button had always been the type to prefer kale smoothies over anything processed. But as the dry heaves dragged on, a more ominous thought crept in. *Surely that shower hadn't...?*

"We can't stay here," Jax said, breaking me from my thoughts. "Between the fallout and the... other risks..." His glance shifted to me, a silent nod to the alligator attacks. "Not a good idea."

Button emerged from the bathroom. "No kidding." Her voice sounded thick with sickness, like she had a brutal hangover.

I studied my stepsister for a moment. She looked fine. Or maybe she didn't. 'Fine' was relative after three days holed up in a creaking metal tomb. Didn't we all look washed out? The kind of sickly sheen a good day outdoors might fix—if the world outside wasn't trying to kill us.

I leaned forward, my arm flaring with a biting twang of pain that I ignored. "We need a plan. Greg needs real help, and we're running out of supplies."

What Greg needs is morphine. A bucket load. Yesterday.

"I agree," Jax said.

Greg stirred on the couch, his voice thin and brittle, like paper crumpling. "The Braves played yesterday. Might get a hot dog after the game."

A hollow ache settled into my chest. Neurological symptoms— confusion, lethargy. His body was shutting down, cell by cell. His organs were failing. I had to say something to Maggie. I had to prepare her. But what could I say?

As an EMT, I had no training in how to tell a relative their loved one wouldn't make it. That was left to the cops and ER docs. As a human being, I knew I had to tell her something, but considering the situation we were in, I wasn't sure we could handle a grieving mother in addition to her dying son.

Jax said, "We've got another day, tops, before this place goes from refuge to death trap."

And by then, Greg will be in cardiac and respiratory collapse.

Jax straightened, his arms crossing over his chest. His voice dropped into a low, decisive cadence. "My cabin. It's up north, twenty miles. Stocked with firewood, tools, supplies."

I let the words settle. My mind raced through the risks and odds. The cabin was a gamble, but staying in the trailer would seal our fate. In a more equipped space, I could make Greg comfortable.

With what? Tylenol and Band-Aids?

I said, "How do we even know north is safe? We don't know where the fallout's drifting."

Jax said, "East is where the bomb went off. Same for the west. South takes us to the Gulf Coast, where we'll be locked in. North is our best shot. My cabin gives us a waypoint. From there, we can figure out where to go next. Atlanta's a possibility since it's not a primary target, but..."

I did not like the "but" in that sentence. Not one tiny little bit.

Maggie held a finger in the air and waggled it in a circle, as if summoning a thought from a higher power. "We could take my truck. But it's only a single cab, so two of you'd have to ride in t'back. But with all that dust flying about, I don't reckon it'd be the smartest idea."

Button retched into her hand before speaking. "Won't we all fit in the Explorer?"

Bad food, that's all it is. Some bad canned food. Maybe a touch of salmonella? Listeria? Did we even check the expiration dates? Spoilage-related toxins. That's it. She ate spoiled peaches, along with the rest of us. Any moment now, we're all going to be fighting over the bathroom.

I said, "We could make it work. It seats five. Winter could sit in the trunk?"

Winter whined at the mention of his name, his tail giving a half-hearted thump against the floor, as if protesting his demotion to cargo.

Jax rubbed the back of his neck, then scratched his chin. "Honestly? They're both probably dead. EMP from the blast likely fried the electronics."

"EMP?" Button asked, frowning.

"Electromagnetic pulse. It knocks out anything with a circuit—electronics, vehicles, anything not shielded. But with fallout settling, even if the vehicle starts..." He paused, letting the nebulous hope dangle a moment before cutting it loose. "...it might be too contaminated to use. But we'll check anyway. If it doesn't work, we take my canoe."

Button said, "Canoe? Uh, uh. I can't swim. What happens if it tips over?"

Jax ran his hand along the side of his head, staring into space, his jaw tight. "Five people and a dog. Canoe's rated for, um, 800 pounds? So we're not sinking it. Long as nobody does anything stupid, it shouldn't tip either. Just sit steady, spread the weight... and we'll be fine."

I didn't like the hesitation in that explanation. Greg might weigh 300 pounds on his own. But Jax knew what he was talking about, didn't he?

Maggie said, "What 'bout the radiation? How long d'ya think we can be out there?"

Jax gestured to the Geiger counter on the counter. "We'll use it to guide us. We'll aim for clear water routes—fallout settles heavier in stagnant areas. Flowing channels should be safer."

Button scoffed. "Oh, perfect. Let's just play Marco Polo with a Geiger counter and a banana boat. What could possibly go wrong?"

And she's back. Spoiled food then, that's all.

Jax rolled his eyes and covered his mouth as if to stifle his first words of choice. "If you've got a better idea, let's hear it."

Button glared, her lips pressed thin and white as paper.

Touche.

But Button *wasn't* back to herself. Had I ever seen my stepsister without war paint? Not once. Not ever. Her porcelain skin, stripped bare, had a vampiric sheen to it—like years of foundation had hidden it from the light. And was that redness on her neck? In the dim light, I couldn't tell. It could have been a shadow.

"Let me look at your neck, Button," I said.

"Pfft," Button said, wafting her hand up and down, swatting me away. "It's nothing. I think I'm allergic to that cheap soap in there. It's too harsh on my skin."

That made sense. Button's botanical cleansers came from Goop with a $30 price tag. Maggie's two-dollar Good4U soap bottles probably felt like battery acid to Button's gently cleansed and exfoliated complexion. At least, that's what I tried to think. But a vision floated into my mind, of Button in the shower, lathering everywhere except her face.

I asked, "Are you red anywhere else?"

"Give it a rest. I just said I was fine."

Maggie stepped forward, her hands resting on her hips. "Ladies, please. Now's not the time for bickering. I say we do it. Staying here's just waiting to die. At least out there, we're trying, eh?"

"Then it's settled. We head out at dawn," Jax said.

The choice was like a balancing act on a knife's edge—one step forward might save us or send us straight to the ground.

I said, "What do we need to take with us?"

"Pack everything we can carry. Food, water, flashlights, batteries."

So we had a plan. It wasn't perfect, but it was something. Right then, something had to be good enough. "What about Winter? Are we putting booties on him?"

Winter's ears flicked at my voice, his head bobbing from left to right as if trying to decipher the message.

Jax shook his head. "Too risky. If he sniffs around, he'll end up breathing the dust—or licking it off his fur. I'll carry him on my back. I'll rig a pack from what we've got."

Jax stepped to the door. He peeled back the window covering and lingered there, staring out at the swamp. I joined him, glancing out into the inky black.

When Jax spoke, it was quiet, meant only for me. "You know what's out there. Think we've got a shot?"

"We keep moving. That's all we can do."

Jax's eyes didn't leave the window. "Yeah. Until we can't."

Neither of us spoke again that evening. There wasn't anything left to say.

* * *

At first light, Jax eased the trailer door open. The outside greeted us with a choking gust of air, acrid as burning plastic. Fallout clung to everything. The mist, hanging low and dense, had turned the world into a smudged gray smear where outlines vanished.

"Let's move," Jax said.

The group shuffled out, Jax leading with the Geiger counter in one hand and a spear improvised from a broken broomstick in the other.

Winter, nestled in Jax's backpack and swaddled in one of Jax's gray hoodies, let out a soft whine that echoed our collective unease.

Maggie and I helped Greg into a fold-up wheelchair. His head lolled as Maggie adjusted the blanket draped over his head and lap. He resembled a ghost from a fifth-grade play—two eyeholes cut out, though in his half aware state, I wasn't sure if he was seeing anything at all.

The wheels creaked against the damp ground as I gripped the handles, pushing Greg with steady determination. Maggie and Button followed behind, their silence thick, moving with the solemn tread of mourners trailing a casket.

We made it halfway to the Explorer when a loud growl froze us in place. Jax raised a fist. *Don't move.*

"What is it?" Maggie asked.

"Bear," Jax said, fixated on the hulking black shape emerging from the mist. Mud streaked its matted fur, and its dark eyes glinted with primal intent.

Button gasped. "Oh, God."

Jax said, "Stand tall. Don't run. If it comes closer, yell."

I adjusted my grip on the wheelchair. But wouldn't that attract alligators? *He knows what he's doing, girl. Trust him.*

The bear stopped, ears flicking. For a moment, it hesitated, as if it teetered between retreat and attack.

Then Button screamed—a high, panicked cry that shattered the tense silence. She stumbled back, catching her foot on a root, and hit the muddy ground with a thud. Her scarf slipped down as she fell, leaving her face exposed. She landed face-first in the dirt, fallout clinging to her clothes and streaking her fair skin. Coughing and gagging, she clawed at the ground, struggling to push herself upright.

"Button, stop moving!" I said, my heart pounding as I bent to grab her. "And quit touching your face—you're spreading it!"

The bear roared and took a step closer.

Jax waved his arms high in the air, stick in one hand. "Hey! Back off!"

I hauled Button upright, dragging her to the side of Greg's wheelchair.

"Move. Explorer. Now!" Jax said, waving the stick at the bear. "I'll be right behind you."

I pushed the wheelchair forward. When I reached the SUV, I yanked the door handle and slid into the driver's seat.

The ignition clicked like a dying man's teeth.

And then, nothing.

10 Predator's Lair

"EMP! Head for the canoe!" Jax yelled.

We abandoned the Explorer and headed toward the boat launch. The air reeked of rot and metal, a smell that clawed at the back of my throat, grasping for purchase. Sludge covered the path, storm clouds bloated the sky, and the trees appeared to be dying—or about to shed their leaves for the long nuclear winter.

It was a monster's den, and we were trespassing.

I pushed Greg's wheelchair, each step a battle, as if I were dragging it through quicksand. Beside me, Button lurched forward, her body sluggish and unsteady.

Maggie trailed behind, pointing out landmarks with a steady voice, her monotone like a tour guide trying too hard to keep her group calm. "The water's black as tar. Look at the reeds—life's been drained right out of 'em. But the mistflowers are still blue; must be the trees shaded 'em."

I realized it wasn't detachment; it was distraction, a desperate way to keep from spiraling. Survivors often grasped for the ordinary in the face of the unimaginable. Car crash victims counted ambulances instead of staring at the wreckage. Hurricane refugees fixated on notices taped to school gym walls:

Wrestling match tonight!

Sign up for volleyball!

Practice canceled this week!

And now, a mother distracted herself from the thought of her son's decaying body by narrating the landscape.

Ahead, the vague outline of the boat ramp emerged through the swirling haze. In the morning, the sun should have burned the mist away. But this mist curled in defiant tendrils as dense as wet cotton, covering the world in a milky void.

The overturned canoe sat by the water's edge. Even from a distance, the outline made one thing clear: five people and a dog would be stuffed inside like hot dogs in a vacuum-sealed pack—squished so tight we'd lose our shape.

Jax raised his fist, signaling us to stop, and crouched low.

But it was Winter's growl that froze me in an instant.

"Quiet, bud," Jax said, as he scanned the haze.

A low rumble rippled through the air. From the shadows, a black bear emerged, its matted fur streaked with mud. Its body trembled with rage, sickness—or both.

Winter's bark snapped through the silence. Jax adjusted the revolver, his movements slow and steady, as if trying not to disturb Winter's position on his back. He held out his left hand, palm open. "Maggie, bullets."

"Oh, uh—yes," Maggie said, fumbling forward to hand him the box.

Jax popped the revolver's cylinder open and slid in the bullets one by one, each *click, click, click* cutting through the stillness like a metronome.

The bear stepped closer, its paws squelching into the mud, muscles rippling beneath its filthy fur. Blood smeared its muzzle, and ropes of saliva swung from its jaws, swaying like grotesque pendulums.

Radiation? Possibly. I tried to suppress the other thought—the one more terrifying than a bear driven mad by air changes and fallout. Radiation was something I could measure, something I could apply science to, something we might outlive. But the other possibility...

"Rabies," Jax said, as if reading my mind. He stretched out his arms, creating a barrier between the rest of the group and the bear. "Everyone, step back. Slowly."

I might have lost my mind right then and there, might have forgotten Greg and the wheelchair, forgotten the canoe, forgotten myself, turned tail and run. But before my hypothalamus had time to execute the flee command, Button let out a ragged screech, her arms flailing as she stumbled and fell to the ground. The oily dust clung to her gloves and sleeves as she scrambled to get up.

I let go of the wheelchair. My boots slipped on the muck as I rushed to Button's side and dropped to my knees.

My stepsister's frantic movements and wide, crazed eyes spoke of untamed terror.

Button—clumsy? The thought flickered, a moment of cognitive dissonance.

Button wasn't clumsy. That wasn't like her. Stumbling and tripping? That was my territory—my cursed genes. My brain spun out of control, overwhelming me with panic when I needed to act. *Is my mind playing tricks on me? Likely.*

Which meant Button wasn't running on all cylinders either. Stress? Panic? *Yes, that has to be it.* Button couldn't handle the magnitude of the situation. I struggled to handle it myself—and this was something I'd trained for. No wonder she was struggling to hold it together.

I need to do better by her, I—

Jax raised his gun and fired into the air. The crack of the shot echoed, snapping me back to reality. Winter yelped, twisting in the backpack as if trying to escape the sound.

The bear froze. Then, it reared up on its hind legs and roared—a sound so primal it made my stomach lurch.

I rose to my knees, gripped Button's arms, and shook her. "Get up, now!"

Another growl rumbled from behind one of the shifting walls of mist. Then, a smaller but equally threatening bear appeared, its fur on end as it smelled the air.

The smaller bear stepped closer. Its attention shifted to Greg, who lay motionless under the blanket, his body heavy and unresponsive. "Bearsh," he rasped.

Jax raised the gun again, the barrel hovering between targets like he couldn't commit.

My mind screamed in panic, a soundless wail like I was dangling from a cliff, my grip slipping. *Why isn't he shooting?*

Jax fired another shot skyward, the cracking sound splitting the air. The bear flinched but didn't retreat.

Maggie yanked the crossbow from her back. Her gaze locked on the bear, the way a raptor's might fixate on a mouse. She steadied her aim, exhaled, and fired.

The bolt sank into the chest of the larger bear as it lunged toward Button. It roared in pain, stumbling and collapsing into the mud with a wet thud.

Winter barked at the water, the piercing sound drawing everyone's attention. The surface exploded as an alligator lunged from the reeds, its body a blur of motion. Its jaws clamped shut in the air with a bone-jarring snap.

The smaller bear shifted its stance, tension rippling through its frame, ready for either fight or flight. It growled low, attention flicking between the group and the new threat.

"Get to the canoe!" Jax yelled.

I held Button, hands on shoulders, giving her a light shake. "You good?"

Button's eyes were vacant for a moment. Then she nodded and picked up her pack from the ground.

I hauled Greg's wheelchair forward. Button stumbled beside me, clutching an armrest for balance.

If I hadn't been so fixated on Button's erratic steps, if I'd taken just one second to look around, I might have seen the movement from the ditch.

A second alligator punched through the surface like a torpedo wrapped in leather. Its jaws clamped onto Button's ankle. The scream that ripped out of her wasn't human. It was the sound prey makes when it knows it's about to die. Fallout and filth caked her hands as she struggled against the alligator's ruthless pull. Its tail whipped, sending water churning into a turbulent froth as it dragged her closer to the water's edge.

I dropped my grip on the wheelchair and rushed toward Button, fear roaring in my mind but smothered by the instinct to save my stepsister. Seizing her wrist, I dropped to the ground behind her head, four or five feet from the alligator. I didn't stop. I didn't think. I couldn't afford to.

My vision blurred at the edges, narrowing to one terrible focus: Button's bloodless face, streaked with mud, her eyes wide with terror. The alligator's jaws gripped her lower leg, its teeth embedded deep in her flesh. Blood seeped from the wound, staining the muck in widening, dark streaks.

My breath stopped dead in my chest. The alligator's beady black eyes gleamed like wet stones, cold and calculating, as it held still. It didn't flinch, didn't acknowledge me—it was as if I wasn't even there. Yet I felt its purpose in my bones—ancient, unyielding, poised to twist into a death roll.

I hadn't thought about the danger to myself. If I had, I wouldn't have left the safety of the wheelchair. It was a flimsy metal barrier, but a barrier nonetheless, between me and the alligator. I would've frozen, screamed, begged someone else to do what I was doing now. This was biology at its worst—an instinct older than fear. It wasn't bravery, wasn't logic, wasn't anything human. It was stupid. It was suicidal.

The realization hit me hard: I wasn't saving Button. I was offering myself up as the next course.

Maggie said, "Shoot it, Jax! For God's sake, shoot it!"

Button's leg wrenched at a sickening angle as the alligator twisted, its powerful jaws grinding deeper into flesh. The alligator thrashed, flipping her onto her stomach. Its body churned the mud, coiling for the death roll. Her scream exploded like a twelve-gauge blast, ricocheting off the trees that dotted the hammock.

Jax hovered next to us, revolver raised. The barrel wavered, but he didn't fire. "Hold her still!"

Seriously? Hold still? Is he fucking crazy?

"Just shoot it!" I screamed, watching Jax's revolver hover back and forth. He didn't aim the weapon at the alligator; he pointed it at the sky, waving it around like he was hunting pheasants.

"Jax, shoot, for fuck's sake! Shoot!" I yelled.

Maggie stepped forward in front of Jax. She gripped the crossbow, her eyes narrowing as she lined up the shot. The bolt streaked forward before slamming into the alligator's skull just behind its eye.

The beast bellowed, its jaws slackening as the bolt sank deep. It released Button's leg and thrashed backward into the water, snapping at the air before disappearing beneath the murky surface.

Button's face twisted in agony, her leg a mangled ruin of torn flesh and blood-soaked fabric.

"What the fuck, Jax, why didn't you just shoot?" I asked.

He stood there, head drooping like a scolded child. *SEAL? This is the guy who's supposed to protect us? Who the fuck is he, really?*

My hands trembled as I hovered over the mangled mess of Button's leg. Bright red blood poured from the torn flesh, soaking the shredded remains of her pants. *Did it hit an artery?*

Button's breaths came in panicked gasps, each more ragged than the last.

"Please, I can't die like this," she said, her voice thin and edged with hysteria.

It was a plea I had heard too many times before in too many voices. The words landed with the weight of a wet tissue, lost in the flood of all the others I'd heard before. No one wanted to die. That wasn't the kind of thing you needed to say, but everyone said it in one way or another when their time came.

"You're not dying," I said, pressing down on the wound to stem the bleeding. "Stay with me, Button. You're gonna be fine."

I'd said those words to strangers before—whispered them as I handed them off to more strangers in an anonymous hospital.

But I never knew how many of those people I'd told the truth to. How many had made it through the night? Those with a leg injury like Button's? All of them, most likely. But if they'd been left in the field to battle infection, sepsis, and shock—like soldiers left in no-man's-land in World War I? None of them would have made it home.

But this was Button. My family. She had to make it.

Had to.

Yet that mangled, bloody leg told a different story.

11 Is there a Doctor Left?

A week ago, I would have triaged Button's wound as a Yellow Tag—serious, but fixable. But now? With no ER, no antibiotics, no clean ambulance stretcher to work my magic, was it survivable? I didn't know. And the thought struck more terror into me than any alligator or bear attack ever could.

"You're going to be okay," I said, more for myself than for Button. "I just need to fix you up."

Jax grabbed a T-shirt from his pack, a blue one with NAVY printed in gold letters, and tore it into strips, the cloth ripping with a low purring sound.

I glared at him. I wanted to slap him. Wring his neck.

But this wasn't his fault. It was mine.

I could have carried the gun. I *should* have carried the gun. Button was my responsibility, and I fucked up.

I blew out a deep breath, forcing myself to focus. The anger receded, enough to tend to Button's wound with supple hands instead of clenched fists.

Jax wrapped a tourniquet around Button's leg. His eyes glistened for a moment, and I thought I saw tears threatening to spill.

He's scared shitless, too.

I'd been expecting him to act like Rambo, and that was unfair. We were all in this together. He shouldn't have had the responsibility of protecting a pack of strangers all on his own.

"We've got to move. There's more out there," he said.

As if summoned by his words, the second bear let out a deep growl, a sound that rumbled through the humid air like distant thunder. Its attention snapped to the group, muscles coiling as it threatened to lunge. But then the water exploded again. Another alligator surged forward, its jaws gaping wide, slamming into the bear in a chaotic blur of teeth and claws.

My breath caught, stealing the air from my lungs. This was beyond survival—it was absurdity. Like nature had rewritten its rules, gone rogue in a way that defied logic. A disquieting thought struck me: What if the fallout wasn't just radiation? What if it was something worse? A dirty bomb laced with something vile. Something that could twist life itself, bend minds. Maybe we weren't just running from the swamp. Maybe the madness was already in us, crawling just beneath the surface.

"Get into the canoe!" Jax yelled, ripping me from my thoughts.

We hauled Button to her feet. She slumped on me, her injured leg dragging like dead weight, while Jax supported her other side.

Maggie stayed close, pushing Greg's wheelchair through the uneven ground, the wheels creaking with every lurch. The group reached the canoe in a breathless scramble.

Jax flipped the canoe over onto its hull. "Get in!"

He knelt to secure a dog-sized life jacket on Winter, tightening the straps over his hoodie with a quick pull.

Then Jax grabbed the only human-sized life jacket on the canoe. He glanced at everyone, then stared down at the life jacket, as if trying to figure out how to split it into five. He shoved it into Button's arms. "You can't swim, right? Put this on."

Button shook her head. Her gaze fixed on the canoe like she was staring down a tsunami. "I can't do this," she said, pointing a trembling finger. "I can't get in that... that toy boat."

Button had never so much as dunked her head underwater. When we were younger, I used to tease her about being afraid to get her hair wet and messed up. But even then, I'd known the truth: water was Button's kryptonite—she was terrified of it. And now, she was terrified of water monsters too.

The water was so black it was easy to imagine thousands of alligators lurking just inches below the surface, waiting for the slightest rock of the boat to signal the dinner bell.

"Just get in," I said, grabbing the life jacket and pulling Button's arms through.

I tightened the straps, then shot a glance at Jax. Wordlessly, we worked together, lifting Button as carefully as we could—fast, but mindful of her mangled leg. Button sucked in a sharp breath, biting back a scream, and then we had her in the boat.

I said, "If you fall in, I'll save you. High school varsity swim team, remember?"

Jax offered Maggie a steadying hand as she climbed into the canoe. We then carried Greg into the rear, his shrouded body slumping like a sack of turnips onto the bench. With everyone in, I settled onto a bench seat, my breaths ragged from the effort.

Jax hopped in, grabbed the paddle, and pushed us off from the bank with a grunt. The wilds behind us boiled with sound—the bear's enraged roars, the cracking whip of the alligator's tail, the crash of bodies locked in mortal combat. The clamor faded into the mist as we floated further into the depths, but it lingered, heavy in the air, a reminder that death lurked close.

Maggie leaned against the side of the canoe. "Another fight down, eh? The swamp ain't through with us yet."

* * *

Jax sat in the stern, his paddle slicing through the blackwater. Each stroke sent pulsing ripples across the surface, making the waterway feel like a living, breathing thing.

The reeds swayed, though there was no breeze. The motion hinted at life, though my mind conjured images of rats and swarming cockroaches. I took a deep breath, hoping to steady my thoughts, but the air assaulted me with the cloying sweetness of decay—rotting and fetid, a festering mix that turned my stomach. It was the kind of smell that made me wish for a smear of mentholated ointment under my nose—the old trick for keeping nausea at bay in the morgue. But there wasn't any VapoRub out here, nothing to mask the odor of decomposition. I'd read there were millions of creatures in the Okefenokee. Now, I couldn't help but wonder how many had succumbed to the fallout—too many, surely.

My thoughts churned as the canoe glided forward. *Alligators. Bears. Jaws. Desolation. Blood. Fallout. Alligators. Bears.*

I focused on my breathing, shallow and uneven, my hands trembling as they clutched the gunwale. I forced myself to remember that, for now, we were safe. For now, the coast was clear.

I turned my attention to Button, slumped against the canoe's side, her face slick with sweat. Her breath hitched in ragged gasps, a stark contrast to her usual vibrant energy. Blood streamed from the jagged gash on her calf, where it had torn through the great saphenous vein—a major vessel running from the foot to the knee. If the vein was severed, Button could lose her leg without immediate surgical repair, and surgery was something I had never performed.

And amputations? I'd learned about them in paramedic training, but that knowledge drove home how unprepared I was for something like this. Amputations required sterilization, proper instruments, and absolute control over blood flow—none of which were available in the boonies. What if Button needed one to survive? Could I do it? I thought I could try. But then again, the jagged wound was already a breeding ground for infection—cellulitis, tetanus, or God knows what polymicrobial bacteria from the alligator's mouth.

My mind spun, every treatment option branching into more terrible outcomes. What if I picked the wrong one? What if my decision killed Button? I could feel my heart thudding, hammering against my ribcage as if it might burst free.

Then I remembered Gran's words from decades ago, when our cat, Smudge, went missing. I had spent the entire day searching the neighborhood—under houses, in backyard sheds, even crawling into a sewer. By nine that night, Gran had told me to stop. I had panicked, spewing what-ifs. "What if he's dead? What if he can't find his way home? What if he jumped into a delivery truck and he's halfway to California by now?"

Gran had taken me by the shoulders and said, "*Lass, you cannae worry about the what-ifs. Worry about the What's in front of you, not the Ifs you cannae see.*"

The words rang in my head, cutting through the haze of panic.

What's in front of me? Button's bleeding wound.

"Button. I need to fix you up. It's going to hurt, but I'll make it quick."

Button blinked, her eyes glassy. "I can't... I don't—"

I shoved a rolled-up strip of gauze into my stepsister's hand. "You can. Bite down on this. Focus on me, okay? Not the pain. Just me."

Button nodded, her fingers clutching the gauze like it was a stress ball.

I rummaged through the remains of my med kit, pulled out the Tylenol and pressed two pills into Button's palm. I helped Button sip water to swallow them down. It wasn't much, but it was better than nothing.

I left the tourniquet on while I inspected the wound. The injury was a gnarled mess of torn skin and muscle, the edges already puckered and angry. Blood pooled in the deep wound and trickled down Button's leg, remnants of the damage done before the tourniquet had stemmed most of the bleeding.

A vein was a small blessing. If those jaws had severed an artery, Button might have bled out on the boat ramp. Instead, I could tend to the wound, remove the tourniquet and return blood flow to the lower leg. I wished for something stronger—like a vial of lidocaine or even a numbing spray—but all I had was antiseptic, a needle, and Jax's fishing line.

"This is going to sting."

I dabbed the wound with the antiseptic.

Button hissed and jerked, and the canoe lurched to one side. Water sloshed over the edge, soaking my legs as the hull groaned with the strain.

Jax looked back over his shoulder, said nothing, then resumed paddling. What could he have said? *Hey, guys, tone down the party back there...*

I said to Button, "Stay still. If I don't clean this, you're looking at an infection—or worse."

"Maggie. Could you hold Button for me? Wrap your arms around her," I said.

Maggie fixed her vacant stare on the swamp. It was as if she was seeing something no one else could.

"Maggie?"

She blinked twice before nodding and wrapping her arms around Button's waist.

Button's teeth clenched, her breath hissing through them. Her eyelids fluttered as she stared at me—a silent plea for a reprieve.

I threaded the needle. The latex gloves clung to my skin, slick with sweat. Every movement felt awkward, my hands fumbling as the gloves stuck and shifted.

I lifted Button's face covering and moved Button's hand up so that the gauze wad was in front of her mouth. "Bite down."

Button's eyes widened, fixed on me like I'd just slapped her. But she did as instructed, as obediently as a patient swallowing a bitter pill on doctor's orders.

I said, "You're tough. This is going to hurt, but less than you're imagining."

I started stitching, each pull of the thread through skin drawing a gasp from Button. My eyes lingered on the patchy redness spreading around the gash—what my stepsister had described as an antibacterial soap "allergy" now looked like radiation exposure. The inflamed, dry skin looked like an overbaked turkey, its surface cracked and oozing fluid. But I couldn't make a definitive call. I ached for the certainty of Google and reverse image search. I would have had an answer in seconds.

For the next few minutes, the slap of Jax's paddle and Button's muffled cries blended into an eerie discordance. Swish. Grmppph. Swish. Grmmmmuph.

The stitching job was rough, but enough to stop the bleeding. When we stopped to rest, I'd have to take a second look.

"I know it hurts, Button. But you're going to make it. We're all going to make it." *And a herd of wild pigs is flappin' their wee wings right o'er our heads this very minute*, Gran's voice said. I didn't know who would survive, but a creeping certainty told me we wouldn't all make it out of the swamp.

I pressed fresh gauze over the stitched wound, securing it with tape from my kit. I loosened the tourniquet just enough to restore a trickle of blood flow, my heart pounding as I watched for signs of renewed bleeding. *Please hold.*

The wound oozed, a dark stain spreading across the bandage. I hoped, prayed, that it would clot soon. Later, I'd assess the damage. But the burn, that was another matter. I had nothing, not a salve, not a potion, to soothe the irradiated flesh.

Had Button received a lethal dose? I didn't think so. Surely one shower and a couple of tumbles in the muck weren't enough to kill someone? She and I had our problems, but she didn't deserve to go out like that. And I didn't want to lose my only family, even if the tie was a fraying thread.

Button slumped back, her breathing ragged but steadier. "Thanks."

I wiped my brow. Don't thank me yet. It's going to get a lot worse. "You're welcome."

Jax glanced over his shoulder and gave me a small nod. There was something in that gesture—respect, possibly—but he said nothing. He didn't have to.

The steady rhythm of his paddle continued, guiding us through the blackwater, deeper into the waiting unknown.

I tried to find a position that didn't send a jolt of pain up my arm. The wound beneath my bandage throbbed with a steady, maddening pulse, a stark reminder of how close I'd been to death. I leaned back and dug into my kit. My fingers brushed past gauze and scissors before finding the Tylenol. I popped the cap, and two pills spilled into my palm. They rattled softly before I tossed them back with tepid canteen water that tasted like old pennies.

I peeled back my arm bandage and inspected the wound. It wasn't pretty, but it wasn't alligator-bite bad, either. The puckered, pink flesh showed no yellow discharge or reddened edge. I dabbed at the edges with a sterile wipe, biting the inside of my cheek to keep from hissing as the alcohol stung.

Jax's voice drifted back, as steady as his paddle. "Everything okay?"

"It's fine," I said, pressing the bandage back into place. But it was a long way from fine. We needed actual doctors, people who knew how to stitch flesh and pump bodies full of clean blood. All I had were over-the-counter pain pills and hands that wouldn't stop shaking.

The water flowed like dark silk, lapping against the canoe's sides. I shivered as a shadow slipped beneath the surface.

Jax said, "Keep your elbows away from the water. Lots of alligators out here."

"Do you think they see a canoe and think 'food,' Jax?"

"Not usually. But with things stirred up, who knows what's normal anymore?"

* * *

The sun rose higher, its rays piercing through the canopy and reflecting off the water. As the mist thinned, the cypress trees became clearer, their gnarled knees jutting from the water like skeletal fingers. Spanish moss hung from branches, swaying in a breeze that I couldn't feel, my layers of clothing dulling the sensation.

The light brightened, the gray giving way to soft yellows as the sun broke through a gap in the thick clouds. We passed a patch of sickly green lily pads. Delicate and translucent, the flowers held a macabre beauty, their colors persisting despite an oily sheen coating the water's surface.

As morning turned into afternoon, the heat intensified. Sweat dripped from my brow, stinging my eyes. It was too warm for November. Another storm was on the horizon, for sure. I just hoped we would make it to Jax's place before it broke.

I tapped Jax on the shoulder. "Are we close to the shelter?"

Jax shifted in the stern, his paddle pausing mid-stroke. "Yeah. Minnie's Lake is ahead."

For a brief, stolen moment, it felt like a weekend trip, a carefree journey on a quiet lake. *I brought the champagne, honey. And those chocolate strawberries you like.* But the reality was far more sinister, a world teetering on the brink of destruction. And then there was the gun. Jax still had it in his belt. *Should I come out and ask for it now? Or when we stop? Do I even have the cojones to ask for it? How would I say it? Oh, hey, Jax, looks like you might not know how to handle that revolver. Me neither, but can I give it a shot?*

115

Minnie's island came into view a few minutes later. A wooden dock jutted out over the water, its edges warped and weathered by the elements. The sandy ground was clear of fallout and puckered with tufts of wiregrass. I wasn't sure why this island had been spared, but it gave me hope that more swaths of land remained untouched. Maybe Jax's cabin would be okay, too. Maybe, I allowed myself to hope, maybe even Atlanta.

Jax guided the canoe to the dock, peeled off Winter's life jacket and hoodie, clapped his hands, and pointed to the shore. "Off you go, bud."

Winter bounded out onto dry land, running a couple of fast laps around the wooden gazebo, frolicking after being cooped up in the canoe. A second later, he zipped over to a bush on the side of the dock, cocked his leg, and peed. The sound was so normal, so weirdly pleasant—as if Winter thought we were on a weekend trip, too.

Jax climbed out of the canoe and tied it off. "Take thirty. Then we keep moving."

"You're not worried about Winter wandering off?" I asked.

"Nah," Jax said. "He's got this invisible string thing. Stays close to his sheep."

I frowned, about to tell him to speak in plain English, when it clicked. *We're the sheep. He's protecting his flock.*

"I need to pee, like yesterday," Button said.

Maggie grabbed Button's elbow. "I'll take ya. Come on, lass."

I shook my head. *Lass?* That wasn't something Maggie would say. Ellena had only ever heard that word from Gran. Then slowly, my brain processed the phrase. *Let's.* Maggie had said, *"Come on, let's."*

Maggie and Button hobbled slowly down the dirt trail past the gazebo, moving like they were tortoises in a three-legged race. Step. Hop. Step. Hop. They vanished into the bushes.

Greg stayed in the canoe. Lifting him out would take two people, and what was the point? He'd just end up lying next to the canoe, getting eaten alive by fire ants.

I shuddered at the thought. Fire ants didn't mess around. They could survive floods by forming rafts with their bodies, floating through water like tiny, venomous armadas. If the world ended for people, I figured the fire ants—and definitely the roaches—would inherit the Earth. They'd almost certainly inherited the cremains of my home.

I walked over to the shelter and leaned against a wooden post. The structure was little more than four posts and a warped roof, and offered little respite from the heat. But I was relieved to be out of the canoe.

Unlike Button, I didn't need to pee, and it was a reminder that I needed to hydrate. I fished a water bottle from my pack, took a sip of lukewarm water, and grimaced at the plastic aftertaste.

I lowered myself onto the worn, weathered bench. My legs told me to stretch, but the thought of moving was too much. Instead, I stayed put, letting the fatigue win for now. My Gran would have said, *there's nothing that oxtail soup and a nap can't fix.*

But I couldn't nap—I was wired and tired—and sleep wouldn't fix anything anymore.

And besides, what the heck was oxtail soup, anyway? Did they even have oxen in Scotland to get tails from? Surely there weren't actual beasts of burden roaming the Highlands... were there?

Then it hit me, as clearly as the knowledge that a storm was on the way. Scotland might also be destroyed. The thought was as chilling as a polar plunge, as if Jax's earlier words were catching up and screaming in my ear. "The world's probably gone. What we're doing now? It's surviving the long goodbye."

Jax settled beside me on the bench, and I jerked, almost elbowing him in the side.

"Sorry. Didn't mean to startle you."

We sat in silence, staring out at the swamp as if answers to our unspoken questions might ripple up from the blackwater. My gaze wandered to the trail where Maggie and Button had disappeared. I wondered what was taking them so long when a weight dropped in my lap.

I looked down. The revolver.

"Why?" I asked.

He kept his focus forward, not looking at me. After a pause, he said, "Back there, I nearly got us all killed."

Startled at his honesty, I opened my mouth to disagree, then closed it without a word. He was right, but I didn't want to agree with him, not out loud.

Jax pinched his thumb and forefinger together, a fraction of an inch apart. "In Jamaica. I was this close to shooting someone. Someone innocent. It was... a split-second decision. One moment, I'm protecting my men. The next, I'm ordered to shoot one of them."

"What? One of your men? Jesus, Jax." I knew little about warfare, but wasn't shooting one of your own against the Geneva Convention or something? "Why were you ordered to shoot them?"

I watched his jaw tighten, his fingers curling into fists on his lap.

"For no goddamn reason at all. That's why." He leaned his elbows on his knees and covered his mouth with his hands, as if the action could stop him from saying more.

The pieces clicked into place. The mood swings, the tightly wound energy, the haunted look in his eyes—it all fit. He had PTSD. I recognized the signs, though I didn't know the details.

What had happened to him? Was he remembering it right? I'd gone to a callout once where a vet was holding his brother hostage, convinced his sibling was spying on him for the CIA. Was this the same thing? Had Jax experienced something so traumatic that he wasn't remembering it as clearly as he believed? After all, officers don't shoot subordinates, do they?

My mind was a storm of questions, all fighting for space, but I knew better than to push. Still, I couldn't stop one from slipping out. A neutral one, I thought—something unlikely to stress him any more. "You were an officer?"

He nodded. "O2."

He didn't offer any further information, and I took that to be an end to that conversation—for now.

Instead of probing further, I set the revolver on the bench between us and sighed. "Look, I'm sorry for yelling at you earlier. I don't normally..." I trailed off, embarrassed. "I don't swear much."

Jax turned to me, his lips quirking into a half-smile. "Ellena, I was in the Navy. I've heard everything. You should hear what sailors say on a bad day. Trust me, we're good."

Bad day—is that what this is?

I snorted, fighting the urge to laugh.

He looked at me—not a glare, but a quizzical expression, his head tilted and one eyebrow raised.

I said, "Bad day. You said, 'on a bad day.' Sums up the kind of day we're having, right?"

He chuckled, and relief flooded through me like summer rain washing away days of grime. The raw space I'd torn open at the campground dock was sealing itself, the way a cut closes under a butterfly bandage. My stomach warmed, and I felt a connection click back into place. It was one I'd been missing—like the way you miss breathing until a bad cold finally breaks.

I shook my head at the ridiculousness of it all. *Love in the Time of Cholera*—wasn't that what the book was called? I had no idea if it was about romance or cholera or if the title was a metaphor. I'd never read it.

But I could imagine it was. And wasn't that what was happening now? Love in the time of cholera—or whatever disease was next down the road—because all the damn water was polluted.

Still, like the question of whether fire ants could survive the apocalypse—something I would've Googled without a second thought four days ago—I had another. What the heck was *Love in the Time of Cholera* about? Would you go insane without Google to get instant answers? I might just find out.

"Ellena?"

I looked at Jax, certain he'd said something, but it hadn't registered. "Sorry. What did you say?"

He nudged the revolver closer to me. "I said about this. You should know how to use it."

"I don't know, Jax. The only thing I've shot is one of those little lady guns at a range once."

"Like a Smith & Wesson Bodyguard .380? Or a Ruger LCP?"

I shrugged and held my hands up as if to catch rain. "A Ruger? The name rings a bell."

"Then you can handle this." He picked up the revolver, his fingers brushing against my thigh as he grasped the grip. Holding it up like a prize specimen, he said, "This here's the safety. And this"—he slid bullets into the cylinder—"is how you load it. Simple enough. Now, you give it a go."

I gripped the revolver, surprised by its heft. I raised it, aiming at the distance, my wrist straining against the dense, concentrated weight—like a bag of sugar gone hard.

He guided my movements, his touch steadying mine. As he leaned in close, the butterflies started again in my stomach. Those absurd creatures didn't belong, and were fluttering like I was on a date, not facing the end of the world. *There should be scarab beetles in my stomach, not goddamn butterflies.*

I stood up abruptly, and the revolver clattered to the floor. "Sorry, this is just a lot." *Understatement of the fucking century.* "I just don't know if I can do this."

Jax said, "You've got this. Just remember, it's a tool. It's meant to protect you. Protect us."

"You hold onto it, okay?" I said. "If we need to use it... we'll cross that bridge."

Jax glanced at me for a moment, nodded, then shoved the revolver into his waistband.

I looked up, and our eyes locked. For a moment, the air between us shifted, laden with possibility. I was certain he was about to tell me something monumental, something that would change everything. But before he could speak, the sound of rustling broke the spell.

Maggie and Button emerged from the bushes. Button hopped on one foot, wincing with every step as Maggie supported her. She held a long staff in her hand, and I was willing to bet that Maggie had had a hand in securing it. Draped in blankets and rags, they looked like Siberian beggars searching for bread.

When they arrived at the gazebo, I said, "Why were you gone so long?"

"Oh, ya know. Had to help Button. Wasn't exactly easy for her to go on her own, eh."

"Y'all try getting all these layers off while standing on one leg. Houdini could do it, but not me."

Jax stood and brushed his hands off on his jeans. "Let's get back on the water."

Maggie and I each took one of Button's arms, steadying her as we guided her down the dock and into the canoe. Winter hopped in and Jax redressed him in the hoodie and life jacket. Greg appeared to be asleep, but I checked his vitals anyway: a thready pulse and labored breathing—both what I'd expected, but not what I'd hoped for.

I remembered the *Chernobyl* show—how some patients clawed their way back from the brink, only to spiral into agony days later. Was that Greg's future? I prayed we'd reach Jax's cabin before it got that far. But the thought was absurd. What difference would it make? Whether he died screaming in the wild or holed up in the cabin, the end would be the same: unbearable, grotesque, seared into our memories forever.

Still, the cabin clung to my mind like a thread of hope, an image plucked from a pastoral fantasy. Calm. Normal. As if that could make Greg's death easier to endure—for us, anyway. Not for Greg. There was no escaping the truth for him. No matter how I looked at it, his death would be torturous.

Jax placed a hand on my thigh and leaned in close. "We're in this together, right? You've got my six?" he whispered, looking into my eyes.

"Yes. And you have mine."

My face flushed, but I didn't look away, letting our gaze linger for a heartbeat too long before turning to adjust my pack. The warmth in my cheeks remained long after we pushed off, the canoe gliding through the inky water toward whatever waited ahead.

12 Spilling Secrets

By the time we reached Big Water Lake two hours later, the sun was sinking low on the treeline, turning the sky slate gray. The trees thinned out, giving way to an expanse of blackwater that stretched in all directions. Once close and oppressive, the swamp now felt vast and open, its stillness broken only by the splash of Jax's paddle.

The isolation was palpable. Claustrophobic waterways, clogged with twisted roots, had given way to something far more unnerving—a sense of exposure, as if we were alone in the world and at the complete mercy of nature.

I leaned in close to Jax. "Are we almost to the campground?"

"Yes. Fingers crossed it's clean enough to stay there."

I pointed at a shoal of floating dead fish. "See those?" Not good.

Jax nodded. "I didn't want to say anything earlier, but I saw a hog some way back, on the shore. It was stumbling around like it was drunk, legs giving out under it. Its skin looked... wrong. Blotchy, burned, like something had scalded it."

"Radiation?"

"Probably. But I've never seen anything like it. Not even in training."

Jax's words caught me off guard. I remembered watching a documentary about nuclear testing in Nevada. They had tied donkeys to poles, and when the test blasts went off, the animals flew around like grotesque piñatas. I didn't want to ask Jax what he'd seen in training. I didn't want to know. Or maybe it was better not to know. Still, the question of what exactly he did in training nagged at me. *Now is not the time. I'll ask him later, when we're settled at his cabin and away from this black gloom.*

Instead, I asked, "Why didn't you point out the hog when you saw it?"

Jax said, "No point in scaring everyone more than they already are. But I think we're heading into a hot area."

"Okay, but we can use the Geiger counter, right? To guide us. If it spikes, we go a different way?"

Jax stopped paddling and turned to me. "It broke, Ellena. Back before we got in the canoe."

"Broke?" The word was absurd, like him saying, *Sorry, the canoe is out of service.*

"So much for the Flash Sale."

"Shit." Hadn't I just told Jax that I didn't swear much? But if there was ever a time to swear, it was now—venturing into the irradiated wilderness blind.

"Exactly."

"So, we what? Canoe into the fallout and cross our fingers?"

Jax rubbed his mouth with a finger. "We should be okay. By day five, the radiation's dropped to survivable levels. But let's not take chances. We'll detour north in the morning and try to stay out of the worst of it."

I wondered if we could handle a detour to our already arduous journey. I turned to check on everyone. Greg's head lolled against one of the half-empty duffel bags. Its sagging shape did little to cushion him. His lips were parted, and his breath rattled in his chest, shallow and irregular.

Maggie sat next to him, wringing her hands. "Ellena? Is he... okay?"

I hesitated. "He's not good, Maggie. But let's get him to the cabin. I'll take a look then."

Maggie nodded, tugging at the edge of her face covering. She glanced at Greg, then away, tension stretching across her brow like an elastic band.

"We'll figure it out," I said, hoping the words carried more certainty than I felt. Deep down, I knew I was stalling, pushing answers and decisions to the future. But what if later never came?

As we paddled north, a lone limpkin wailed, its cry rising and falling in a haunting lament. The sound stirred a fragile sense of hope—a reminder that life, however tenuous, persisted.

That hope faded when we rounded a bend. The limpkin sat on the shore, wailing into the open water. Its mottled feathers clung together in slick, clumped patches, coated in a film that made it look like a bird stranded on an oil-slicked beach. Its dull black eyes stared without blinking.

The trees farther ahead were bare, their bark peeling. Bedraggled leaves sagged from the limbs, lifeless and limp. The water shimmered unnaturally, a dark rainbow sheen spreading across its surface as if it had absorbed the poison of the blast.

Winter sat alert at the bow, his ears pricked and twitching under the hoodie, like he was trying to flick off flies. His eyes fixed straight ahead, a low growl rumbling in his throat. His unease only added to the tension in the air.

Jax said, "Keep your hands inside the boat. Hot zone."

The canoe slid forward, the stillness around us thick as the shadows that stretched in every direction.

I turned and patted Button's hand. My stepsister looked ill, almost gray. She made sucking noises through her teeth like a dying radiator. She was clearly in a lot of pain. "We're nearly there."

But would it even matter? Jax's cabin wouldn't materialize in technicolor, like the Emerald City from Oz. More likely, it was a ramshackle hideout—not much better than the Airstream we'd abandoned.

I turned to Jax and whispered, "What if your cabin is in a hot zone?"

"Trust me, we'll be fine."

Trust him? I wasn't in the mood for platitudes or more riddles and puzzles. "How can you possibly know?"

"Because it was my dad's cabin, and he fixed it up right."

"But what does that mean?"

Jax stopped paddling and let the canoe drift as he turned to face me. "Look, Ellena. The cabin's not just a shack in the woods, okay? My dad built it to last—reinforced walls, a well for clean water, supplies stashed for emergencies. He knew what he was doing. It's why I brought us here. We'll be safe there. You've just got to trust me."

His brown eyes locked onto mine, unblinking. It was as if he were willing me to understand. Something raw in his expression hovered just short of desperation.

I closed my eyes and focused on the sensation in my gut—the one Gran had called a *wee feeling in her water*, the one that always warned me when I was walking into disaster. The one I should have listened to when Eric started staying late at work.

But that sensation wasn't there. No wee feeling. Just calm.

I opened my eyes and met his. "Okay. I trust you."

And I was fairly sure I meant it. What I was very sure of was that we would reach the cabin, and almost as sure that it would give us shelter.

Jax placed his hand on my arm and gave it a gentle squeeze. "Good?"

"Yes. Good."

I felt a tap on my shoulder and turned to find Button slouched against the side of the canoe. She looked out over the water. "It's so empty."

I glanced from Button to the water. "You mean the lake?"

"Everything. No birds. No fish jumping. Nothin'." Button's fingers hovered over her lower leg, trembling. She shifted, and I caught the brief wince that crossed her face, a flash of pain she smothered.

I twisted in my seat to face her. I placed a hand on her shoulder, steadying her against the sway of the canoe. "We'll be okay."

Though the gnawing doubt inside me made the words feel hollow. *Why do I keep saying that?* In an emergency, things were usually okay. Wounds patched up, patients stabilized. But that was before. Now, would anything ever be okay again?

Button drew a shallow breath. She leaned closer, her voice dropping to a whisper. "Ellena, I've got to tell you what happened... If I don't make it, I don't want you thinkin'..."

There was no need for Button to whisper. Jax was focused on paddling, his movements steady. Greg lay unconscious, slumped awkwardly in the back of the boat. Next to him, Maggie's head lolled with the boat's gentle sway, soft whistles escaping her nostrils as she snored.

The pain from my tooth flared up again, throbbing like an exposed nerve. I drew in air through my teeth.

"You okay?" Button asked.

"I'm fine," I lied. Fine as could be expected with a toothache at the worst possible time ever.

But wasn't that the way dental problems always happened? A loose bridge the day before a cruise. A chipped incisor before a first date. A raging toothache in the middle of a nuclear apocalypse.

I bit my lip hard, then said, "Okay. What happened?"

Did it even matter now—what Button had done or hadn't done? I didn't think so. If Button admitted the affair now, what good would it do? I realized with sudden clarity that I no longer cared about Eric or the affair. It was so insignificant compared to the situation we were in. Button had been through hell in the last few days—we all had—but she carried more scars than most. She'd been attacked by an alligator, exposed to an unknown amount of radiation from the shower and her falls, and now she sat here, struggling to hold herself upright. Crying over a splinter when the whole tree was about to come crashing down on top of you—what was the point?

But Button was distressed, and I could see how much she needed to let it out. Whether I cared or not about what Button had to say didn't matter. What mattered was that she needed to say it.

"Go on, then, tell me," I said.

Button hesitated, her voice trembling as much as her body. "We weren't havin' an affair. I helped him take the money."

I scrunched my face, taken aback by the confession. "I don't understand. How?"

"I wrote the code for him." She dropped her head like a dog caught peeing on the carpet.

I drew in a sharp breath. I already knew Eric had embezzled money. In retrospect, the plan was clever—perhaps *too* clever for Eric.

The scheme's simplicity was deceptive: a customer's refund request triggered code that generated a random amount between fifty cents and five dollars. The bank refunded the original fee, while the code diverted a random amount to a Cayman Islands account. It worked because the small additional refunds weren't easily trackable, a loophole the code exploited perfectly. By the time a sharp-eyed database analyst noticed the anomaly, Eric had funneled $20,000 into the offshore account.

I had never questioned the how, only the why. But the more I thought about it, the more it made sense that Eric couldn't have come up with the scheme on his own. Not the guy who lost at Monopoly every single time we played. Not the guy who couldn't balance his checkbook. I could picture him jabbing random buttons on the universal TV remote, trying to switch channels but only cranking up the volume—or turn on the ceiling fan because it shared the same frequency as one of the remote's settings.

Eric had been a people person—a genuine I-love-people kind of guy. Technical details? Not exactly his forte.

I'd always blamed Eric for the foreclosure on my Gran's house, dragging that anger behind me like Marley's chains in *A Christmas Carol*, each link forged from resentment. But now it seemed that anger had been misplaced—or at least, it should have been shared. Why hadn't I figured it out before? Because my anger had gotten in the way, that's why. I wanted Eric to be at fault for everything.

Had I been wrong all along?

I leaned back, gripping my temple with one hand, trying to quell my anger. The swish of the paddles stirred the pot, keeping the rage simmering just below the surface.

I placed my arm on my lap and clenched my hand into a fist. "Why? Why did you do it?"

"I *had to*. I owed money to a loan shark, okay? Some lady at work told me about her. I was fifty grand in debt, and she made it sound easy—quick loan, ten percent interest, no questions asked. How was I supposed to know the interest was ten percent a week?" She rubbed her hands together, her voice dropping to a whisper. "I didn't have a choice."

I held up a hand, palm out. "I can't do this now." *Just let me think, damn it. Let me breathe for a moment.*

Button's tears dripped from her eyes, each one carving a path through the grime on her skin. I watched, unmoved, as if I were standing outside my body, a spectator to grief I should have felt but didn't.

I would have preferred it if Button had admitted to an affair. That. I could handle. But this? This was worse. This, I didn't think I could forgive.

"But why 'Lizzy?'" *Why the pet name, Button?*

"What?" Her brow furrowed, and she tilted her head, lips pressing together before she spoke again. "That's what everyone at work calls me. I use my real name at work, not Gran's nickname..."

I hated that there was a simple answer for everything, as though *I* were the crazy one—as if I had caused all this to happen and was now making cliffs out of cairns.

And then, a sudden realization. Why hadn't I known that Button was called Lizzy at work? But I already knew the answer: I didn't know my stepsister at all. All those years of resentment, and I had never asked Button about her life, her work. Hell, I didn't even know anything about Lizard Guy—other than that he talked about lizards. I didn't even know his real name.

My emotions tangled together now, a blend of all the wrong things— anger, hate, fear, guilt, sadness. My mind splintered under the pressure, fragments of emotion stabbing at me from every direction. I wanted to scream, cry, lash out—anything to release the storm brewing inside me. But I just sat there, frozen, because if I let one thing spill over, I might not stop until the entire pot boiled dry.

I turned around to face front; it was all I could think to do. I couldn't slam a door shut or throw a dish against a wall in a canoe.

Button reached out and placed a hand on my arm. "Please, Ellena—,"

I shoved her arm away. "Just don't. I don't want to hear it. Not now." Not ever.

Then Button gagged and lurched forward, bumping into my back. "I'm going to throw up."

She leaned over the side of the boat and vomited, a stream of chunks hitting the water with a splat.

The boat listed to the side, and Winter whined. I turned to see him wobbling at the bow, his legs stiff as he scrambled for footing on the slippery wood.

"Ellena, I'm gonna—" Button yelled, but before she could finish, the boat swayed more violently.

Winter tumbled to the bottom of the canoe with a yelp.

I grabbed Jax's waist to steady myself.

"Help!" Maggie yelled.

Jax and I turned around at the same time. Greg had slumped to one side, his torso almost slipping over the edge. The canoe lurched left as Jax and I moved to counterbalance the canoe. All that did was send the vessel into a stomach-churning sway, like a rollercoaster teetering at the peak of a drop.

For a heart-stopping moment, it was like watching a slow-motion disaster—Maggie's arms flailed like a modern dancer caught in a chaotic routine, while Greg's limp body swayed left, then right, as the boat rocked once... twice... a third time, seeking its equilibrium. Together, they moved in an unsteady dance that might have passed for a bastardized ballet, their shifting weight sending lagging ripples across the swamp.

Winter let out a shrill cry, claws scrabbling for grip, as the canoe tipped one last time. Then, with sickening inevitability, it capsized, spilling us all into the cold blackwater.

13 Sink or Swim

The world flipped in an instant. One moment, I clutched the edge of the canoe. The next, the cold, clammy depths swallowed me whole. The water struck me like a slap, stealing my breath and shocking my senses. I clawed to the surface, my lungs burning, and broke through with a desperate gasp. The blackwater tasted earthy and foul, like rotten leaves steeped in bile. Every gulp coated my throat with a slick, brackish residue.

Above the chaotic noise of water sloshing, screams rang out—sharp and frantic, filling the air with their echoes.

"Help me!" Button's voice tore through the air—a shrill, panicked wail.

I whipped my head around, my eyes stinging from the gritty water as I scanned the scene.

Button thrashed, her arms flailing as though a shark was pulling her under. The bright orange of her life jacket jerked and dipped with every movement. She wasn't sinking—yet.

Winter's terrified yelps pierced the air as he spun in tight circles, his white fur soaked and clinging to his head like a second skin, making him look like a giant water rat. I didn't think he was drowning—his orange life jacket collar peeked above the water—but panic was contagious.

Maggie's head broke the surface, her face ashen as she treaded water. She wasn't screaming, just bobbing—her eyes scanning, searching.

For Greg?

Greg was nowhere to be seen. Neither was Jax. A cold knot of fear tightened in my stomach.

"Jax! Greg!" I shouted, my voice like sandpaper dragging across glass.

I looked around me, desperate for any sign of them. The surface rippled and gleamed like oil. But other than Maggie and Winter, there were no heads, no hands, no bodies.

Then Jax's head broke the surface, his mouth wide open as he gulped for air. His head dipped back below a second later.

"Hold on!" I said, kicking toward him. My muscles burned as I fought against the water, my breath coming in ragged bursts.

"Ellena!" Button's scream ripped through the air like a bandsaw hitting bone.

Ten years of working the night shift in that white box on wheels had built a triage machine in my head. Now, that machine kicked into gear and the EMT part of me—the part that could work a thoracic hemorrhage with steady hands while a drunk puked on my boots—took over. I counted the bodies in the water, each one a ticket in the lottery of who lived and who died.

Maggie. Arms cutting clean strokes through the water.

Button and Winter. Orange vests like traffic cones in the murk.

Jax. Just Jax. No vest. No air. No time.

My heart wanted Jax.

My training chose him too.

I reached him as his head broke the surface again. Grabbing his arm, I hauled him, half-dragging, half-kicking, toward the bank. My arms burned like lit gasoline in my muscles, every stroke a battle against the swamp's hungry grip. I shoved him onto the muddy shore and rolled him onto his side.

Water spilled from his mouth as he coughed violently, his body shuddering with effort.

"Breathe, damn it," I said.

Jax coughed, a raw, wrenching sound, and his chest heaved. Relief swept through me, but it was fleeting.

The others.

I raced back into the water's edge, focusing on Button's frantic movements. She was still thrashing, still screaming, with the capsized canoe listing nearby.

Maggie bobbed close by—her movements slower, weaker.

I swore under my breath and focused on Button.

"Hold on, I'm coming!"

I plunged back into the water, my breath catching as the cold punched through my skin. I forced myself not to think about what swam beneath— scaled bodies, teeth, claws. The dark water grabbed at my limbs with each stroke, dragging me down like a grave trying to claim me.

I reached Button, her arms beating the water in erratic bursts. Her panicked movements churned the water, making it harder for me to grab hold. I clenched my jaw and pushed forward, forcing my aching limbs to cooperate until I was at her side.

I grabbed her shoulders. "Button! Stop thrashing!"

Button's eyes were wide and wild, her pupils pinpricks of terror. She wrestled from my grip, in a full-blown panic, blind to the rescue right in front of her.

I had only ever slapped one person—a man whose foot had been torn off by a train. He'd yelled, "Get the fuck away from me!" and landed a punch square on my jaw.

The slap landed against Button's cheek with a wet smack. She froze, her scream cutting off in a choked gasp. For a heartbeat, the only sounds were our ragged breathing and the rippling blackwater around us.

I hooked an arm around Button. "I've got you. Hold on."

Kicking toward Maggie, I closed the distance.

Maggie bobbed in place, her face blank and eyes glassy, like a discarded doll.

I said, "I'll look for Greg from shore. We'll see him better from there." A therapeutic lie, justified by the situation. If Greg hadn't surfaced by now, he wasn't coming up—he was settled in the muddy bed below, tangled in roots and muck, a submerged snack for the local predators.

Maggie hesitated, turning her head slowly as she scanned the water. Then, she nodded.

I kicked hard, dragging Button alongside me as Maggie swam beside us. My lungs burned, my arms felt like rubber, but I didn't stop. I couldn't stop.

My feet hit the slimy, shifting mud of the bank, and I hauled Button ashore, collapsing onto the soaked earth. Rolling onto my back, I pulled in air that stank of rot and death, my chest heaving with each breath.

Button coughed up gray water as she clutched my arm, then she burst into tears.

Maggie emerged from the water, collapsed to her knees, and let out a wail.

She knows. She knows he's gone.

Even so, Maggie would have stayed out in the water until dark, searching for Greg, if I hadn't nudged her toward the shore. Because that's what mothers do. They don't stop to weigh the odds. They run back into burning buildings, even when there's nothing left to save. They leap from cliffs after their children, because there's no other choice. Maggie had lost her son, and perhaps she would always wonder if she could have saved him—if only she'd stayed longer.

"Where's Winter?" Jax asked. He slumped on the bank, his chest rising and falling in labored breaths.

I looked out at the blackwater. The swamp had fallen silent again, its surface still, as if satisfied.

There was no sign of Greg. And no sign of Winter.

* * *

We sat on the water's edge, staring at the water like it might rewind itself and spit Greg and Winter back out. I couldn't tell if we were on an island. The water was black, an inky nothing, snaking around the land on both sides. Behind us, the hammock loomed: trees gnarled with moss, bushes clawing at the edges, everything tangled and dripping with shadow.

The sky was a sickly gray, the sun buried beneath clouds that weren't just storm-dark but sooty and foul. The air smelled like a forest fire— sharp, smoky—but beneath that lurked something else. A chemical stench coated my tongue like melted battery acid—burning plastic, hot metal. It wasn't choking yet, but it carried a promise of worse to come. A warning: Get shelter. Fast.

No one moved though. No one spoke. No one suggested moving forward to shelter. How could they when we had just lost two of us?

We just sat, staring at the capsized canoe floating fifty feet from shore.

I clenched my fists at my sides, hard enough to make my arms shake. I should be out there searching for them. That was what I did, what I'd done a hundred times before. But I'd needed to get Jax, Button, and Maggie to shore first—to dry ground, to safety. *Safety. What a goddamn joke.*

If there weren't alligators nearby already, there would be soon. The noise, the thrashing—it had painted a target on that spot. I didn't know how far alligators could sense movement. Half a mile, easy. Maybe more. But they were fast swimmers, and if they weren't already closing in, they would be soon.

My fury bubbled up, swelling into the space where action should have been. I wanted to scream, to hit something, to move, but all I could do was sit there, soaked to the skin and empty-handed. No supplies. No medical kit. No plan. Greg was gone, and without basic first aid, Button wouldn't make it. I shoved the thoughts away like roadkill found rotting in summer heat.

My gaze snapped to Jax. *Navy SEAL, my ass.*

"You lied to us," I said, my voice low, shaking with restrained fury.

Jax turned to me, his face drawn and haggard, dark circles shadowing his eyes. "Ellena—"

"No." I cut him off, my voice sharper now, cracking like a whip. "Don't. Don't you dare make excuses." I leaned forward, my face inches from his. "You told us we'd be safe. You said we could trust you. And now look at us! Look at the canoe! Look at Greg! Tell me, Jax—what the fuck are we supposed to do now?"

Jax opened his mouth, but nothing came out. His jaw flapped, useless as a busted umbrella, and I wanted to scream at him for that too—for his silence, for his failure, for my own stupidity in believing him.

I let out a shuddering breath and dropped my face into my hands. A scream clawed its way up my throat, but I swallowed it, letting the tears come instead. Hot, furious tears that burned my cheeks and blurred my vision.

The silence stretched, heavy as the clouds above. Only Button's muffled sobs and Maggie's shallow breaths broke it. Maggie, of all people, was the calmest. Her shoulders were slumped, but she wasn't crying or shaking. She just stared at the water, her lips pressed so tightly together that her mouth was almost nonexistent.

I closed my eyes, trying to pull myself together, but the weight of it all pressed down harder. Greg. Winter. Button's leg. My throbbing arm. The nukes. All of it. I clenched my fists again. The anger was still there, simmering beneath the surface, waiting for its moment to boil over.

I forced in a deep breath.

What do I see? Blackwater rippling. Twisted branches clawing at the sky.

What do I hear? Rustling in the trees. The lap of water against the bank.

What do I taste? Metal. Plastic. Sourness.

What do I feel? Wet. Cold mud squelching under clothes. Fear curling in my gut, twisting and churning like a nest of snakes.

I exhaled slowly, grounding myself in the familiar routine. I brushed a sodden strand of hair from my face.

"Are you okay?" I asked Maggie, though my voice sounded foreign to my own ears.

Maggie didn't answer right away. She just stared, hollow-eyed, her face pale and streaked with grime. Then she nodded. "He's gone." Her voice was flat, as if she were confirming the weather. A simple fact and nothing more: her son was dead.

Perhaps Greg had been gone for a long time—years, even. Gone when the TBI struck, stealing the man Maggie had known and leaving her with someone who needed her for everything. Years of caregiving, years of grief and resentment, all leading to this. Not a slow goodbye. Not a gentle letting go. A radiation-laced bang and a final plunge into oblivion.

I looked back at the water, its surface smooth and indifferent, as if it hadn't swallowed him whole.

I tried to think. Tried to focus. Tried to triage my next move. What was the priority? What could I do? Anything? But every thought slid away, my mind circling back to the same brutal truth.

They were dead: Greg. Winter. Gone.

And there wasn't a damn thing I could do about it.

Then from across the water, a bark—clear, defiant, alive.

14 Fetch

I froze. A bark? I strained my ears, breath sticking in my throat like a rusted hinge. Had I imagined it? Was it wishful thinking playing tricks on me? Or maybe... a bear? *No.* A boar? A coyote? *Maybe*? Did coyotes even live in the Okefenokee? My brain spun in useless circles, grasping for an answer—then Jax shot to his feet so fast it startled me.

"Winter!" he yelled.

A bark answered, bouncing back across the water like a warped echo, as if Jax's shout had boomeranged mid-flight into that familiar sound.

"Winter, quiet!" Jax said, followed by "Winter, stay!"

I scrambled to my feet. My heart pounded, clammy sweat slicking my skin. Winter was alive. *Alive.* Relief hit like an IV push—icy in my veins, sudden, undeniable—then vanished the moment Jax called, "I'll be back!"

What the hell is he doing? Reenacting The Terminator?

I splayed my hands. "I'll be back?"

Jax turned to me, his eyes distant, like I'd just yanked him out of a trance. For a second, it was like he wasn't there at all—his mind locked onto an invisible task only he could see.

"It's his signal," Jax said. "It means wait. Stay put, and I'll come get you soon."

"Why not tell him to come?"

Jax narrowed his eyes, sweeping an arm across the slough like he was presenting Tartarus. "Look at this shit show. His bark came from over there." He jabbed a finger into the distance. "If I told him to come, I'd be telling him it's safe, and he'd believe me. He'd try to get back however he could—walk, run, swim. Do you think this sludge is *safe*?"

My stomach dropped like an elevator with its cables cut. I could see it, vivid and awful: Winter plunging into the water, his tail wagging, legs pumping in that carefree doggy paddle. I could almost hear ripples brushing against his sides, almost see the disturbance behind him—the dark glide of an alligator closing in.

"Oh," I said. *That was smart Ellena, real smart.*

Jax's expression flattened, his anger buried beneath a blank stare. "Yeah. He's a good dog. Sharp as a whip—more so than a lot of people I've met."

I was just forming the start of a thought, about to lash out at him for the dig. *Okay, I had foot-in-mouth disease, but that didn't give him the right—*

"He knows a few hundred words," Jax said. "Border collies, you know? Knows the names of all his toys—every single one of the fifty we bought him."

"We?" Just like that, my brain flipped from rage to jealousy. And now I hated myself for my snap emotions. Why, oh why, couldn't I control my damn brain?

Then, as if he read my mind and he wanted to reassure me, Jax said, "My dad. He looked after Winter when I was on deployment. Must have bought him a hundred toys."

"Jax, I'm so sorry." *I'm an idiot.*

The bark echoed again, distant but clear, snapping me back to the moment and away from Jax's questioning look. *He must think I've lost it.*

Jax cupped his hands over his mouth. "Stay, Winter!" His voice carried across the water, firm but pleading.

He looked at me with a half-cocked smile, and I figured the next words out of his mouth were going to be something like *Well, I'm going to go find him, and you stay here, conducting whatever mad science experiment passes for your thought process.* But instead, he said, "He's a good dog, you know, he even knows how to open the latch on the doggy door if I forgot to open it. He'll be okay. He'll sit there until I come. He knows to..."

Jax's words kept spilling out—a steady stream of facts and anecdotes, like he was trying to fill the silence before it swallowed us.

That's when my thoughts cleared, and I realized it wasn't about me at all. He wasn't judging me. He wasn't blaming me. He didn't think I was crazy. He focused on only one thing: rescuing his dog. Perhaps it was the only thing keeping him from falling apart.

Sure, he obviously wasn't a SEAL. But even if he had been, would that have stopped the canoe from capsizing? No. Would it have saved Greg? No. Even if Jax had been a rescue swimmer and towed Greg to shore—what then? Greg had been a dead man walking, cooked from the inside out by radiation. We all knew it, even if no one had said it out loud. The water claimed him fast, but the alternative was worse—a slow, festering death, organs liquefying, skin sloughing away, marrow cooking in his bones.

And Winter? My chest tightened. If Jax had been able to swim, would Winter still be gone? Probably. And Jax knew it, too. No doubt he was consumed with guilt. That wasn't fair. Jax was just one man, stretched thin in a world that demanded too much. No amount of training or courage could've changed the outcome.

I didn't know why Winter mattered so much to Jax, but I had that *wee feeling in my water.* Without Winter, Jax would spiral. And if Jax fell apart, we were dead. Jax might not be a SEAL, but he knew where his cabin was. More importantly, he knew how to survive. Without Jax, we wouldn't last a hot minute. And I'd be damned if I let our only hope of living through this nightmare—especially when he couldn't even swim—float into the swamp alone.

Stop going in circles, lass, and focus on what's important right now.

"We need to go get him," I said.

Jax wiped his eyes, the gesture almost too fast to see, and hoisted an eyebrow. "How?"

"I'll swim and get the canoe."

* * *

The canoe bobbed like a coffin, fifty feet out where the lake turned to ink. I could swim the distance—hell, I'd done ten times that in the YMCA pool—but this wasn't chlorine and fluorescent lights. The water exhaled its own foul breath, thick with rot and time-bloated fish. Something moved beneath the surface—not the lazy ripples of wind, but the muscular push of things that had been down there so long they'd forgotten the sun.

Jax crouched beside me, his boots making a wet sucking sound as they sank into the mud. "You think you can do this?"

I nodded. "Yes. I can do it."

But Do I want to? About as much as I want an enema. Fear spread through my gut like blood in water, staining every corner of my body. The unknowns beneath that surface made my teeth ache. "What do you think? Is it safe?"

Jax studied the water, his face as still as a dead cypress. "Safe? No. Safer? I don't know. Alligators aren't as active in the heat of the day, but sundown's when they move again. If you're fast... perhaps. But water snakes? Different story. They'll be out for sure."

He paused for a moment, then said, "They're more likely to avoid you, but if you piss one off..." He let the thought hang in the thick, humid air.

"Great," I said, my eyes fixed on the canoe. "So, I'm swimming through death soup."

Jax's mouth twitched, but his voice stayed grave. "You'll be fine as long as you're fast. No splashing around. Stay smooth, stay quick, and keep your eyes ahead."

"Backstroke."

Jax frowned. "What?"

"With backstroke, I won't have to kick much. I can just float, dip my arms in. Less of me in the water means less of a buffet for anything peckish, right?"

He twisted his lips, tilted his head, and raised an eyebrow—a gesture that said everything and nothing.

Was he impressed by my feigned confidence? Exasperated at my recklessness? I didn't know. And I didn't care. There was only one way out of there, and it was in that damn canoe.

I crouched, dipping my hand in the water. The liquid was cool and thick against my skin, offering a steady resistance as it rippled outward.

I stepped into the water. A thin, shifting layer of something clung to the surface. Oil? Fallout? Gasoline? Dead things? I didn't want to know. Whatever it was, I had no choice but to get in.

It's just swamp detritus, I told myself, forcing the thought to stick. I closed my eyes, breathed in the bitter air, and focused on steady breaths. *I can do this. I have to.*

"Wait," Jax said. He jogged over to the riverbank, bent down and snapped off a branch. He returned with a long stick, broken to a point at one end. "Take this."

I took it, the rough bark catching against my palm. "You think I'm going to *stab* my way through the water?"

"No. But it might give you a chance if something gets too close. Better than nothing."

My first thought was, *I can't swim backstroke holding a spear.* Then I realized floating—slow and steady, stick in one arm, guiding my body with the other—might work.

"I have an idea. Are you okay with waist-deep?"

He nodded. "What are you thinking?"

"The water's flowing to the left, so if I set off from there," I pointed to the right, "and you push me off, it should give me some momentum. I could maybe reach the boat without making too much movement."

"That's a great idea. I should have thought of that."

I swallowed a comment about his swimming abilities—or rather, lack thereof. Then I waded out until the water creeped up my thighs and belly. The murk pressed against my skin, stinking like rusted playground swings and stagnant swimming pools.

Jax followed, keeping close enough that I could hear his breathing.

"Were you even in the Navy, Jax?"

"Yes."

"Not the SEALs, though."

"No. It was a cover story." The sound he made as he waded deeper wasn't quite a grunt, more like someone who'd just bitten into a sandwich and found something moving inside it.

"For...?"

"Long story. Rain check?"

"Just tell me how you ended up in the Navy if you can't swim."

"That's easy. OCS deferment—Officer Candidate School. They waived it because of my expertise."

"Expertise in what, exactly?" I needed a small nugget of truth to hold onto, some reason to not think he was a sociopathic serial killer hanging out in the woods with his hunting knife, because if I allowed myself to unravel that train of thought and let it loose—"

"Nuclear physics."

I stopped and turned around. "You aren't being serious..."

"I am. Master's degree. MIT. Look, Ellena, I couldn't say anything before because what I was working on was classified. It had been programmed into me to 'stick with the story' even if I was being waterboarded."

I coughed out a laugh. "Bet you wouldn't stick to your story then."

"I would."

"How can you be so sure?"

"SERE Training. Survival, Evasion, Escape school. Three weeks of simulated capture."

Jax was like one of those sliding puzzle boxes: every solution revealed another lock. But I'd figure it all out. Later. Not now, not when we were waist-deep in God knew what kind of poison soup. But I would eventually. I needed to know. *Had* to know.

"Okay. Later, right? You'll tell me everything when we—" I was going to say, *when we all get to safety*, but thought of Greg and stopped short.

Jax placed a hand on my arm. "I promise. When we've got Winter back, and we're somewhere safe, I'll tell you everything."

I nodded, lay flat on my back, and pointed my head toward the canoe. I balanced the stick against my chest. "OK, I'm ready."

He pushed me off, and I glided toward the canoe, making small circles with my right arm. When that pulled me off course, I switched arms. In under a minute, I reached the canoe. It lolled beside me, a corpse refusing to sink, its hull slick with pond scum. My fingers scraped against the splintered wood, seeking purchase, but each grab sent it skittering just out of reach.

My legs churned beneath the surface. The weight of my waterlogged clothes dragged at my shoulders, and somewhere in the gloom beyond the canoe, something broke the surface with a wet pop.

I didn't want to know what made that sound. I really didn't. But in about thirty seconds, I figured I was going to find out.

How the hell was I supposed to get a waterlogged canoe back to shore? I glanced at the bank and saw Maggie, Button, and Jax lined up, watching me like they expected me to sprout gills. Swim to shore with the canoe hoisted over my head? *Sure, no problem.*

I turned my gaze to the canoe. *Shit. Focus.* I grabbed the edge, testing its weight. Water sloshed inside, weighing it down. If I flipped it, I figured I might trap air underneath and lighten the load. I took a breath, braced myself, and shoved. The canoe rolled, and a pocket of air caught beneath it. Not perfect, but better.

I hooked an arm underneath, kicking to guide the canoe against the current. It wasn't pretty, but it worked.

From the shore, Maggie yelled, "You got this, Ellena! Just keep it steady, eh?"

"Sure, no pressure," I muttered, kicking harder.

The shore crept closer, mocking me with its glacial approach. Sweat carved lines down my face while my muscles throbbed in my shoulders and back. The canoe dragged behind me, its waterlogged bulk resisting every stroke of my trembling arms.

Something brushed my hand—soft, slick, alive. My throat clenched around a scream. It felt like a jellyfish, but this wasn't the ocean. Eel? Snake? *Just one touch. Just one fish passing by, that's all.*

Another touch. Then another.

I screamed.

Breathe, Ellena, breathe. Gran's voice cut through the panic, steady as a lighthouse beam: *Keep your head, lass. Panic'll drown you quicker than the sea ever could.*

"I'm okay!" I called to shore.

I kept kicking, kept moving. A minute later, I hit solid ground and dragged the canoe onto the bank. The first thing I did was check my legs. No tears in my pants, no bites. Just that phantom tickle—like spiders dancing under my skin. I rolled up my pant leg, but found only goosebumps.

"You did it!" Button said, clapping her hands, her voice bright against the gloom.

Maggie joined the applause, despite the shadows in her eyes. "Now that's what I call grit! You're a darn inspiration, Ellena."

I barely heard her. I was soaked to the bone, exhausted, and shivering. But I was alive. I'd done it.

Jax stepped in close, eyes searching my face. Before I could speak, he pulled me into his arms, his warmth driving back the evening chill.

"I think I may have just fallen for a water witch," he whispered into my ear.

For a moment, the fear melted away. I leaned into him, just for a breath.

I smiled, my voice quiet but sure. "Then it's a good thing she didn't drown."

* * *

I tipped the last of the water from the canoe, muscles burning as I heaved it upright.

Jax prowled the sandbank. He picked up a thick branch from a tangle of flood debris. He yanked it free, testing its weight in his hands. "This will do."

He pulled his knife from his belt and crouched down, setting to work. The first strip of bark curled away, landing near my boot.

He worked fast, stripping the wood in thin layers, exposing the pale grain beneath. No wasted effort, no hesitation. His hands were steady, his grip sure. The tapered end took shape, rough but functional.

"It won't be perfect," he said, "but it'll move us forward."

A few more strokes of the knife, and he flipped the branch, working down the handle.

Jax set the crude paddle in the canoe, pulled out the revolver, and held it out to me. Water dripped from the barrel. "The gun's yours. Keep it ready, okay?"

I nodded, tucking it into my waistband.

We scooped water from the canoe with our hands and an old plastic container we'd pulled from the mud. The canoe wasn't perfect, but it would float.

"Winter, bark!" Jax called over the water.

A single bark cracked the silence like a gunshot.

"Winter, quiet!"

The swamp swallowed Jax's words whole. Something rustled the leaves, a quiet reminder we weren't alone.

Jax squinted into the gloom as the sun dipped behind the trees. Then he pointed to the left.

"We'll take the canoe that way. There's a narrow pass—we'll have to push through some low branches, but it should keep us out of the worst currents. Tried it once, had to turn back."

He gestured toward a pine tree that rose like a broken finger against the sky. "That's Fenokee's Siren. Landmark tree. To the right is Alligator Alley. Left takes us toward Salmon's Knob. He's in there somewhere."

We pushed off, the canoe sucking free from the muck with a sound like pulling teeth. Behind us, Button's sobs pierced the air, thin as a cat's wail. Maggie sat beside her, whispering words that dissolved into the dusk.

I couldn't cry—not yet. Without the mission to focus on, I'd be right there with Button, hollowing myself out with tears. But I had a purpose. A rescue to complete. I clung to that thought like it was the only solid thing left in a melting world.

But that voice in my head, the one that lived in the basement of my mind where truth festered, wouldn't shut up. *Don't get your hopes up*, it said.

Jax dug the paddle deep with each stroke, calling to Winter every few minutes, his voice bouncing off the water. After the fourth or fifth call, the barking stopped. Instead, a rustle came from the reeds by the bank. Winter burst through, his orange life jacket bright against the twilight.

"There you are, boy," Jax said.

Winter paced the bank, ears twitching.

"Why did you stop?" I asked.

"Look left. See those gators?"

Three humps of ridged armor broke the blackwater, each crowned with unblinking yellow eyes, dull as sunken coins.

"It's feeding time. We scrape bottom, then we get stuck. Stir up that water, and it's like calling chow in the mess hall."

The alligators lay still as fallen logs, their snouts cracked open just enough to show vampiric teeth. The setting sun cast dull copper across the swamp, and they waited. Maybe for a groundhog's last mistake. Perhaps for something on two legs that thought it was smarter than sixty million years of patience.

"Winter, stay," Jax said, then paddled twice, coming within ten feet of shore.

The alligators sprawled thirty feet away, motionless in the shallows. Winter stood on the shore, just ten feet from the canoe where Jax and I waited. I eyeballed the distance. Thirty feet could vanish in seconds if the alligators decided a four-legged snack was worth the effort.

"Come on, boy! Come!" Jax's voice held the desperate edge of a man bargaining with fate.

Winter hesitated, his paws leaving dark prints in the mud.

Jax clapped his hands. "Come! You can do it!"

Winter whined, paced a little more, then launched himself into the blackwater.

I held my breath as he paddled toward us, orange vest bobbing like a buoy in a current. The canoe rocked as Jax leaned forward, arms stretched out.

Halfway across, Winter's yelp split the air.

I shot upright. "Winter!"

Winter thrashed in a frenzy, water exploding around him in white froth.

"Something's got him!" The revolver was in my hand before I even realized it, but Jax's fingers clamped onto my arm.

"Wait!" he said, eyes locked on the churning water. "I don't see anything. It's not a gator."

Another yelp—this one hesitant and thin.

Jax said, "Winter, come on, boy!"

Winter surged forward, dragging himself through the last stretch of water.

Jax grabbed Winter's vest straps and hauled him aboard. The dog collapsed between us, his wet fur releasing the swamp's decay-sweet stink.

I ran my hands over his fur. "Good boy, good boy," I whispered, fingers searching for wounds in the wet tangle. I half expected to see blood oozing from an alligator bite, but there was none.

Then my fingers found two perfect puncture marks on his hind leg, each weeping dark blood.

Winter licked my hand, as if thanking me for saving him. *Not yet, buddy. Don't thank me yet.*

"Snake," Jax said. "And we don't know what kind."

My throat tightened. I stared at the wound while a Carolina wren chittered from the trees, its call sharp and scolding, as though mocking our attempts to survive.

I pressed my hands against the bite, feeling Winter's warm blood seep between my fingers, but my mind was already racing ahead to what came next: venom spreading, swelling, his body betraying him one system at a time.

"Jax, I know we have to keep him calm, keep the limb still—but beyond that, I don't know."

Jax didn't answer right away. His eyes swept the water behind us, where a blob had just slipped beneath the surface, ripples spreading like a slow breath exhaled.

When he spoke, his voice carried all the warmth of a morgue drawer. "Here's what I *do* know. First, we gotta survive the night."

15 Expectant

I crouched next to Winter, cleaning the bite wound in the dim light of our makeshift camp. His flank quivered, and his breathing was shallow but steady.

Jax had jury-rigged a shelter from branches and leaves.

Maggie had coaxed a fire to life with scavenged wood. I hugged her, and considered mentioning Greg, but the words formed and dissolved before they could leave my tongue. My training warned against platitudes—grief-stricken relatives spat them back more often than not. But silence was just as wrong, like another loss Maggie didn't deserve.

I pulled back from the embrace and met Maggie's eyes. "If you ever want to talk about Greg, I'm here. No pressure. Just... whenever you're ready."

Maggie nodded. Her lips trembled before she pressed them into a tight line. "I appreciate it, Ellena. I'll keep that in mind."

I squeezed her shoulder, giving her space to decide what she needed. Sometimes the best comfort was just letting someone know you'd be there.

We sorted through what remained of our meager supplies. Some bags had sunk into the black depths, but Jax's backpack had stayed put, clipped to the canoe's grab line with a carabiner.

"That was smart," I said.

Jax shook his head. "Not smart. Muscle memory. I do it without thinking when I'm in the canoe. Wish I'd secured more. What are we missing?"

The pause stretched wide, ugly and raw. A change swept over Jax's face, chasing away whatever had been there before. "Maggie, I'm sorry—"

"Psht." She waved his apology off with a flick of her hand. "Greg's gone, I know that. And I can't deny that I'm sad. Sadder than I ever thought I could be. But it ain't your fault. Now, let's see what we've got here that's useful. Someone please tell me there's a water bottle because I'm just about parched."

Jax rummaged in his backpack and pulled out a canteen. He shook it in the air. "Full. Drink as much as you want. We should be at the cabin in two hours."

He didn't say it. He didn't need to. *We'll get there in two hours—unless some other crazy shit happens.*

But that kind of screwed-up luck was—hopefully—unlikely, I dared to hope. The boat had capsized because of Greg's dead weight, and we all knew it. Button had thrown up and rocked the boat, sure, but if it hadn't been for Greg's body... *corpse?*... shifting at the worst moment, the canoe would have stayed balanced.

My backpack was still wedged under the seat, which meant I had clothes—dripping wet, but still usable. And I still had Maggie's waterproof notebook, a granola bar, and two water bottles. I pulled one out, took a sip, then asked Jax, "You have water at the cabin?"

"Sure do. My dad drilled a well down to the aquifer. Radiation won't touch the water down there."

I blinked, trying to process his words. "The aquifer's 300 feet underground. How did he manage that?"

Jax shrugged. "Hired a well-drilling company. Cost him damn near 20 grand. I'd say it was worth it."

* * *

The flames licked upward, shadows twisting and writhing across the swamp like phantoms. Jax paced at the camp's edge in slow quarter-circles, his head turning at fixed points like a sentry marking time.

Maggie was asleep beside the fire on a bed of ferns, her whistling snores rising and falling in sync with the crackling fire.

I turned my gaze to Button, who sat nearby, knees drawn up. Her face, slick with sweat and shadowed by the firelight, looked better than it had earlier. Her pallor was gone, and something glinted hard in her eyes, like flint against steel about to spark.

"Feeling better?"

Button nodded. "I guess. Throwing up helped."

The fire snapped, sending embers spraying into the damp air. Button's response unsettled me—why didn't she seem worried? Shouldn't she be concerned about the possibility of radiation poisoning? Or asking me what I thought was wrong? Sure, I wasn't a physician, but I knew a thing or two about illness.

I said, "Look, about what you said in the boat..." I wasn't ready for this conversation, not fully, but the words came anyway. "It made me angry. I'm not going to lie. I needed time to think about it." I hesitated, my thoughts skittering like startled birds. "Button, it wasn't your fault."

"But it was," Button said, her voice small. "I could've said no. But I didn't know where it would lead. I thought I was helpin'."

I raised a hand to stop her. "Hang on. Let me finish."

"I pushed Eric into it," I said finally. The words felt forced, reluctant to leave my mouth. No, pushed wasn't right. Cajoled, maybe. Manipulated. "After I lost the baby..."

My voice caught, my hand freezing mid-motion against Winter's fur. Thunderclouds rumbled on the horizon and the fire crackled, but I was barely registering any of it. I was back on that maternity ward. The long hours of labor, the nurse muttering about decelerations, the midwife's furrowed brow. The sudden shift in tone when calm turned to urgency.

"Turn her. Now," a voice said.

Hands were on my body, and the beeping accelerated into chaos.

The midwife stepped out, her voice tight and angry in the hall: "I paged you an hour ago. This woman needs help now."

The doctor had arrived an hour later, sauntering in with musky cologne still clinging to him, snapping on his gloves like it was just another routine delivery. By then, it was too late.

A final push. Then, unbearable silence. The midwife's hands untangled the cord wrapped tight around my baby's neck. They carried away his limp, blue body twenty minutes later without a word.

"Ellena, you in there?"

Button's voice.

I blinked hard, dragging myself back to the present. Winter stirred beneath my touch, his eyes meeting mine before he huffed and looked at Jax again.

I exhaled a deep breath. "I blamed him. I told Eric it was his fault. That if we'd had decent insurance, I could've gone somewhere better. Maybe the Maddison Clinic instead of Jacksonville General. Then our son might have lived."

Guilt swept over me. Blaming Eric had been so wrong. We never could have afforded the Maddison Clinic's insurance plan—not with the $5,000 deductible and the 25% copay.

Button reached out, her fingers brushing my arm. "Ellena, I know. Eric told me. He said he wanted to get that bastard obstetrician. Sue him for negligence. Hire the best lawyer money could buy."

A thick and rotten breeze curled around the campfire. My mind skittered back to our front steps, where Eric had fumbled with his keys, hands shaking. I'd stood behind him, hospital bracelet still tight on my wrist.

"It's all your fault," I'd screamed.

Eric's face crumpled, eyes red and swimming.

Now, beside this dead-land fire, the memory tasted like ash in my mouth.

My gut churned. Eric's face floated in the campfire smoke—first whole, then peeling away like a radiation victim's skin.

"I'm so sorry," I whispered to Button, to the smoke, to wherever Eric might be. Alive in the prison hospital with his teeth falling out? Or scattered across the exercise yard in pieces too small to gather?

Button said, "Stop blaming yourself. So, you screamed at Eric. BFD. Since when does screaming at someone make them do anything? It wasn't your fault, not one li'l bit."

My smile felt brittle, like a pane of glass moments before shattering. "I wish you were right."

"I *am* right. Let me be right for once Ellena, please."

Maybe she was. But the guilt, the grief, the shock—it all wrapped itself up so tightly that there had come a point when I didn't even know which way was up or down, let alone what caused what or who was to blame for this or that.

I nodded. "I was worried about you earlier. The throwing up and everything."

"My stomach's, uh, been a bit queasy for a few weeks."

My mind clicked through the possibilities like tumblers in a lock. Not food poisoning—I'd been watching Button all day in that narrow canoe, and she hadn't begged for a toilet break. But had I been so focused on radiation sickness I'd missed what was right in front of me?

"You're not," I said.

Button met my eyes across the fire, shoulders rising in a half-shrug. "I missed my period last month."

16 Safe Haven My Ass

The following morning, the sunrise bled through the haze. Muted oranges and deep reds streaked the horizon, their colors diffused by clouds of ash in the sky. The sun was little more than a pale smudge, casting weak light over the rippling surface of the water.

There was no birdsong, no buzzing insects. Just the slap of the paddle cutting through the water and the occasional distant splash.

Nestled at Jax's feet, Winter gnawed at his hind leg, oblivious to my worried glances.

I adjusted my seat, trying to ignore the maddening itch on my arm. I bit my lip, trying to focus on anything else but the itch. But the more I tried to ignore it, the more the itch seemed to scream. Still, we were only a couple of hours from Jax's cabin and the possibility of—amongst other things—calamine lotion. *Just two more hours in this river hearse.*

Behind me, Button sat still as a headstone. Was she counting the minutes until we reached safety? Or imagining her belly swelling with something that might have too many fingers, too many teeth? Perhaps she was bargaining with God, promising anything if her period would just start tomorrow and pull her back from the abyss.

Maggie sat in the rear, staring at the water. Tears glistened in her eyes as she cradled a small bouquet of wildflowers. She scattered the petals over the water, her lips moving in a silent prayer. A goodbye to Greg, no doubt.

I hated myself for not getting to know him better. The truth was, I hadn't known Greg at all. I should have made time—but was that fair? When was I supposed to have squeezed in a card game, a chat, a beer? Between saving his life—twice? Between fighting alligators, rationing supplies, shielding the trailer from radiation? Between the fear, the restless sleep, the agony of knowing the world was lost? No. I wasn't being fair to myself. Greg was gone. I hadn't known him—that much was true. But that wasn't my fault.

I said, "What was Greg like, Maggie? I mean, before his accident?"

Maggie looked at me, eyes red and swimming. A flower petal drifted down from her palm and settled in a shallow pool of water at her feet.

I blinked. Water? I turned to warn Jax, but something stopped me— no, it wasn't just a puddle. The water was rising. It crept up Maggie's boots, higher with every stroke of Jax's paddle.

"There's a leak!" I yelled.

Everyone froze for half a second before erupting into action. We scrambled, searching for anything to bail the water out. An empty water bottle? *No good. Too small.* I yanked off my boots, the leather stiff and cracked from days of wear.

"Use your boots! Take them off! Now!"

Maggie moved sluggishly at first, but then she pulled off her boots. Button hesitated before yanking hers off as well. I scooped water with my boot, my arm muscles screaming as I hurled water overboard. Maggie and Button joined in, the splashing water mingling with our labored breathing.

I said, "Row, Jax! Get us to shore!"

I wanted to take it back as soon as I said it. Of *course* he was rowing to shore. It wasn't like he was up on the bow doing a pirate jig while we bailed water.

Jax said, "I'm going as fast as I can."

The canoe rocked with every movement and the rising water sloshed against our ankles. My heart pounded as I tried to ignore the sucking sound of water finding its way into every crevice.

The stern dipped, lifting the bow.

"We need to balance!" Jax said, looking back over his shoulder. "Maggie—shift to the center! Button, hold steady!"

Maggie shuffled forward and squeezed next to Button. The canoe steadied, but water still seeped in around our ankles.

I scooped another boot full of water over the side. My arms ached, and the water level wasn't dropping.

Jax nodded toward a clump of reeds and roots breaking the surface ahead. "Over there!"

The patch of reeds wasn't much, but it was something. The canoe lurched forward with each stroke as Jax steered us toward it.

When we reached the small rise of ground, peeking just above the swamp water, Winter hopped out and peed, like it was an ordinary rest stop, although his back leg hobbled in a limp where the water snake—or whatever it was—had bitten him.

Button toppled out of the canoe onto her side. She reached for the reeds. "We can use this—stuff it in the hole?"

Maggie shook her head, her lips pressed thin. "That won't work. Too dry." She turned to me. "You've got my notebook, right?"

"Yes, one sec."

I shrugged off my backpack and rummaged through the damp mess inside until my fingers brushed the notebook. It was wet, but I marveled at how the pages, though swollen, still held together. I passed it to Maggie, who shook it out and started flipping through the pages.

Her fingers paused on a page and started tracing the words.

Jax waited until everyone had disembarked, then overturned the canoe, and crouched low to inspect the damage. He ran a hand over the fractured edge—a thin, jagged line that had cracked under pressure.

"Stress fracture. Too many people, too much weight."

I crouched beside him. "The reeds won't work?"

"Not for this."

But he pulled a handful anyway, twisted them into a rough bundle, and wiped down the fractured hull.

"We'll need this dry. Help me out."

I nodded, grabbed more reeds, and rubbed furiously at the damp wood.

Jax snapped his fingers. "On guard."

Winter stopped sniffing the ground and perked his ears. He shifted his stance, his body taut and ready.

"Ellena, look here," Maggie called, holding up the notebook. She pointed to a diagram scrawled in her precise hand. "We can use this."

Her finger tapped the sketch of a water bottle cut into strips. "You've got an empty plastic bottle, right? Please say ya do."

I nodded, dug into my pack and pulled out a crumpled plastic bottle. "Here."

Maggie said, "Perfect. Jax, you got a knife?"

Jax unclipped a multi-tool from his belt and handed it over.

Maggie sliced the bottle into strips. "Get me some dry stuff. Anything small and brown and dry... leaves, moss..."

While I gathered more dry reeds, Maggie knelt by the mound, hands steady as she struck a single match pulled from a weatherproof case. The flame fluttered in the damp air, but Maggie shielded it with a cupped hand, coaxing it to catch on the tinder. She pierced one end of each plastic strip with the multi-tool's screwdriver, then threaded it onto a stick. Then she held the plastic over the flame just long enough to make it pliable. She handed the pieces to me. I pressed them into the crack while Jax smoothed the repair with the back of his knife, sealing the hole.

"Next," Maggie said, nodding toward the mud at our feet. "Put a layer on top t'seal it."

I scooped a thick handful of sludge, smearing it over the plastic patch like plaster. "Now what?"

"Wait," Jax said, straightening. He glanced at the sky, then at the water. "We give it a few minutes, then get moving. That storm's about to hit."

Lightning flared, an intense electric blue splitting through the thick, orange-tinged storm clouds. It lingered—far too long for normal lightning—searing against the heavy sky while thunder rumbled to the south.

We waited, the air around us thick with tension. Winter growled low in his throat, his gaze locked on a distant point I couldn't see.

I swallowed hard, brushing mud off my palms. "What is it, boy?"

Jax coaxed him into the canoe, where he sat at the helm, ears pricked, body rigid, staring into the distance.

We pushed off, the repaired canoe gliding through the blackwater. Every shift felt precarious, as though the slightest jolt might undo our patchwork fix. The landscape darkened, shadows stretching long and wide, while heavy clouds bruised the sky.

A distant, high-pitched howl sent a shiver racing down my spine.

I gripped the canoe's edge. "What was that?"

Jax said, "Could be anything. Dogs going feral? Coyotes?"

He shrugged, but his fingers tightened on the paddle.

We didn't look back.

* * *

More than an hour after patching the hole, the canoe bumped against the bank. Light rain was falling, but we had reached shore before the storm hit.

Jax got out first and steadied the canoe.

Winter rose and hobbled onto shore.

Maggie climbed out next.

I followed, wincing as pain flared in my arm with every movement. I hadn't noticed it during the trip, but now that we had reached our destination, the pain came roaring back, triggering a memory.

I had once spoken to a pilot who survived a small plane crash. As he recounted the story, blood dripped from the remnants of his arm, tendons hanging in loose strings. He described the bird strike down to the smallest detail—ten brown pelicans swooped up in front of the plane in a V-shape, each with a golden-yellow wash on its head. They slammed into the engines two at a time. He'd gestured toward the wreckage, oblivious to his missing forearm.

That was how it worked—under stress, the body forgot what ailed it.

Button remained in the boat, gripping the edge, her knuckles white.

"Come on," Jax said, extending his hand.

She took it and grimaced as she exited the canoe and put weight on her injured leg.

Jax tipped the oar upright so that the paddle fit under Button's armpit like a crutch. "That'll get you to the door."

I followed close behind but froze when the decrepit cabin came into view.

The structure crouched in the swamp like a forgotten corpse. Its wooden siding had bowed and grayed with rot and the porch sagged toward collapse. I stepped up, testing each board before shifting my weight. The windows were thick with grime—dead eyes staring out from a dead face, watching my every move.

This is it?

I wiped a window and peered inside. Holes gaped in the floorboards—black pits hinting at danger below.

My heart plummeted. I'd been clinging to Jax's promise of a haven, a place to regroup and recover. But what I was seeing was a tomb waiting for its occupants.

I glanced at the others.

Maggie's face was tight and unreadable.

Button's eyes were swimming with tears.

Only Jax and Winter—ears twitching as he sniffed the air—showed no hesitation about approaching the front door.

"Shall we?" Jax asked, not waiting for a reply before pushing the creaking door open.

He'd called this a "safe place." A "shelter better than the Airstream." Had I misplaced my trust? Maybe I should have listened to that wee feeling back at the campground. It looked like the Unabomber's hideout, not a nuclear bomb shelter. I glanced at the desolate landscape surrounding the cabin.

Nowhere to run. Nowhere to hide.

It was three against one—no, one old lady and two cripples against one. My legs gave way under me, like I was standing on a magician's trapdoor. For one endless second, my stomach kept rising while the rest of me fell.

Jax ran over and caught me just before I hit the floor. "Ellena, what's wrong?"

I waved him off. *Seriously? What's wrong? What do you think, Jax? Do you really think there's anything* right *about this dump?* "Give me a second."

We had trusted him, and now we were here, staring at the reality of it. *We're all dead.*

We needed antibiotics. We needed food, water, and shelter from the fallout. And this shithole was supposed to save us?

Maggie's boots hit the porch like hammers striking a coffin lid. The planks groaned beneath her. "Well, this ain't quite what we were expecting, Jax."

"It's not what it seems," he said, pushing the door open and tipping his head inside. "Step in. I'll show you. The outside's just for show."

Show. I knew the word but struggled with the context. *Game show? Show house? Show me the money?*

Winter stayed by Jax's side, limping on his back leg as he stepped through the door.

Button's crutch clicked over the uneven planks as I helped her over the threshold.

The interior was exactly what the outside suggested. Dust clung to every surface. Cobwebs draped across the corners, their threads glistening in the dim light. A rusted wood stove squatted in one corner. Vines had broken through the outside wall and were creeping toward the ceiling, though they looked winter dormant. The furniture—an old table, a few mismatched chairs, and a battered recliner—smelled of mothballs, as if someone had tried to preserve it, but looked like it might collapse if touched.

"This is your big plan?" I asked. "You better tell me I can pop a sugar cube and *The Magic Roundabout* will turn this into a lakeside retreat."

Everyone stared at me like I'd just cracked a too-soon joke about nuclear bombs. "It's a British TV show. Gran had me watch it... oh, never mind. What the hell is this, Jax?"

"It's to deter people," Jax said, his boot landing on what looked like a hole in the floor.

154

I tensed, expecting him to drop into the crawlspace, but he didn't fall in—he stepped *on* the hole. I moved closer, frowning as realization clicked into place. The holes weren't holes at all. They were trompe l'œils—black and gray paint, deliberately placed to trick the eye from a distance. From the window, they looked like gaping pits in the floor. *Great, instead of a decrepit dump, the cabin's a carnival fun house. What's next? Two-way mirrors?*

Jax moved to a bookshelf on the interior wall. Its shelves were stacked with old hunting magazines and weathered paperbacks.

"My dad grew up in a bad neighborhood in Atlanta's inner city. He always told me that if you want to keep burglars away, make sure your outside looks poor."

This triggered a memory for me—my Gran's voice, talking about keeping your door shining. Was this what Jax was saying? That a shiny door meant prosperity, cleanliness, while a crappy door...

"You've got something hidden."

A dungeon? I shoved the thought away. *Give him a minute, stop churning the crap in your head. Just breathe and panic after he shows you, not before.*

"Could say that," Jax said.

The bookshelf creaked and groaned as Jax heaved it aside, revealing a steel door embedded in the wall. The door gleamed, its surface smooth as polished glass. A mechanical combination lock was set into the steel.

"It's EMP-safe," Jax said.

He punched in a series of numbers. The lock's mechanism clicked in a pattern as delicate as a death's-head moth tapping against glass—hesitant, fragile—before the final tumbler dropped with a sound like a boot heel crushing that same moth.

Button and I exchanged wary glances before Maggie said, "And what exactly is behind door number one, Jax?"

Jax gripped the handle, twisted, and pulled the door open. He swept his arm wide, palm up, fingers pointing the way forward.

"Come and see."

17 Winter's Howl

The darkness beyond the doorway gaped like a hungry mouth—until I flicked the switch. Fluorescent lights sputtered awake, casting stark shadows across rows of canned goods and boxed supplies lining the metal shelves. They stretched floor to ceiling like a survivalist's shrine. Mason jars caught the weak light, vegetables floating inside like specimens in formaldehyde. The canned goods stood in perfect rows—fish, beans, vegetables, fruit—each section labeled in thick black marker.

Tools claimed one corner: axes, saws, hammers, and neat coils of rope. Medical supplies occupied another, dominated by a first-aid kit the size of a suitcase, its red cross faded to the color of old blood. Below it, bottles of antibiotics and antiseptics caught what little light reached the bottom shelf.

Everything gleamed with surgical cleanliness. Two bunks hugged one wall of the studio apartment-sized space. Not huge, but every inch was claimed with precision, turning what should have felt claustrophobic into something bordering on homey.

I sat down on the edge of a bunk, relief flooding through me. Not a dungeon then. Winter limped to my side and sat down. I noted the awkward angle of his steps, the way his back paw barely touched the ground. A pang of guilt jabbed at me—I should've looked at him earlier. He would have to be my priority now.

A sharp throb flared in my mouth, a brutal reminder of how little control I had over my own body. I pressed my tongue against the molar and winced. I bit down hard on my lip, trading one pain for another.

"Well, I'll be!" Button said, her wide eyes darting around the room.

"Jax..." Maggie broke the silence, her voice caught between awe and disbelief. "You didn't just dabble in prepping, did ya? This—is something else. I mean, come on! You expect me to believe you didn't see this war coming?"

Jax scratched the back of his neck, eyes sweeping the room as if seeing it for the first time.

"Later," he said, like that was enough of an answer. "Let's get tidied up, settled in. Get some food in us. And then I'll tell you why this is all here."

I caught something in his expression that made my gut clench—like spotting a shadow dart across the bedroom wall when I was home alone. Guilt or hesitation, I couldn't nail it down—but wrong was wrong. The Geiger counter, the in-depth knowledge of radiation, then the doomsday-ready cabin. He hadn't just prepared for a thermonuclear war—it was as if he'd had a direct line to the missile silos. What did he say was his area of expertise? Nuclear physics?

Anger flared in my cheeks. Anger at Jax. Anger at our situation. Anger at the whole fucking world. How the hell were we going to survive this? Sure, we had a few months of supplies—and then what? What would we do when the medicines ran out? The food? Was this just a futile attempt to put off the inevitable?

My tooth screamed for attention, now a white-hot poker jabbing straight into my jaw. I couldn't afford anger, not now. Flooding my system with adrenaline and tension would only sharpen the pain. Anger was luxury meant for people whose bodies weren't betraying them. I needed to stay frosty and fix what needed fixing—unless I wanted to end up hunting for pliers while my mouth became its own private torture chamber.

"Don't suppose you have Orajel in there," I said, pointing at the first-aid kit.

The question hung dead in the air. Of course he didn't.

"Actually, I do," he said, opening the box. "I've also got Dentemp, clove oil, and crown repair kits. Oh, and these." He held up a pair of forceps, grinning like a mad scientist.

I stared at the forceps gleaming under the fluorescent lights, their metal edges flashing with every flicker. My tongue found the throbbing molar again—a hot coal buried in my jaw. Part of my brain screamed at him to lock those metal jaws away in their case and never open it again. But the deeper, more primitive part knew the truth. One hard pull, one moment of white-hot agony, and the hellish beast in my mouth would be dead.

The relief would be worth any price. Almost any price.

* * *

After wolfing down our chili MREs, Maggie settled in for a nap while I got down to business, starting with Winter's wound. I cleaned the bite with alcohol and gave him a scratch on the head. He looked okay, but what did I really know about dogs? A limp and some pain were to be expected, but what about swelling? The area around the bite was swollen and red, no doubt, but how much was too much?

At least he was drinking water—that had to be a good sign. I decided to circle back to him after tending to other matters.

Next, I took Button's temperature. My stepsister's wound had gone from bad to worse, the flesh around the edges swollen and angry, like a bee sting turned into a full-blown allergic reaction. The thermometer read 101.4. Not death's door, but fever had a way of climbing when you weren't looking.

I dug through the first-aid kit, my fingers skimming over bottles that belonged in a hospital pharmacy, not a field kit—Augmentin, Azithromycin, Bactrim—enough serious medication to stock a small-town clinic.

"This is impressive. Where did you get this?"

"Online. They call him the Prepper Doc. Arizona, I think. Two-fifty and he fills up a case."

I opened my mouth to say more, but a jolt of white-hot pain shot from my back molar to my temple. I pressed my fingers against my cheek, trying to knead the pain away, but that only made it worse. The constant ache drowned out every other thought until my world shrank to a single point of agony. Even the soft rush of air over my teeth when I breathed made me wince. I bit my bottom lip again. It didn't help.

The Augmentin rattled in its orange bottle as I shook out a 125-milligram pill.

I dropped it into Button's hand. "One of these every eight hours, okay? You'll be fine."

Me? Not so sure about this damn tooth.

I rummaged through the rest of the med kit, found a bottle of codeine, and swallowed two pills.

Jax watched me, his concern clear.

I checked my own arm next. The skin had reddened around the gash and throbbed like a bruised bone, though that pain paled in comparison to my screaming tooth. At least the redness hadn't spread. My mind drifted back to the swamp water I'd waded through—I still couldn't believe I'd escaped without infection. I decided to save the antibiotics for when I really needed them, and cleaned the wound with alcohol. Wrapping a fresh bandage around my arm, I tried not to dwell on what might be brewing beneath my skin.

Next, I examined Winter's leg more closely. The skin beneath his fur had swollen to an angry red. It radiated heat.

"Jax. Can dogs take aspirin? And is Neosporin okay?"

"Yeah," he said, fishing a tube out of the med kit. "Here you go. Used it plenty of times."

His smile tilted, lopsided, as he dropped the crinkled, half-empty tube into my palm. I wasn't sure if he was apologizing for his obvious devotion to Winter or for the well- worn state of the medicine.

I cleaned the wound, spread the antibiotic ointment over it, and Winter's whimper cut straight through me. As I considered pain relief, Jax appeared beside me, holding out a bite-size treat between his fingers.

"It's a doggy pill treat," he said. "Aspirin inside. Whatever you do, don't give him ibuprofen or acetaminophen. It's toxic to dogs."

I raised my eyebrows. "Don't tell me you've got veterinary expertise too?"

"Nope." He pointed to a shelf where medical books stood like soldiers at attention. "Canine Medicine and Surgery for the Wilderness and Home."

I studied his collection—no novels, no fluff. About twenty books, all with one purpose: survival. Field surgery manuals, edible plant guides, handbooks on nuclear fallout and water purification. Respect bloomed in my chest. A person who read *Where There Is No Doctor* was a person who planned. A person who might keep us alive.

Then came the guilt—slow, creeping, insidious. Guilt for judging him. Even if he'd had inside knowledge about the bombs, that knowledge might be the only thing keeping us alive. What the hell was wrong with me? I was being irrational, on edge, too emotional, and it was like I couldn't stop it. Like I was unraveling, thread by thread.

Then the cavity woke like fire ant bites, flaring hot and needling deep. I pressed my fingers against my cheek, but the pain only burrowed deeper.

Jax asked, "Toothache still there?"

"I've been trying to ignore it. That pill hasn't kicked in yet. Should have had it filled a year ago, but I couldn't afford it. I just hope to God it isn't infected."

I reached for the thermometer but hesitated. A fever wouldn't tell me much yet. Instead, I ran my tongue over the swollen gum, wincing at the sharp jab of pain. No gumboil. Yet. But the ache was spreading, radiating to my temple and ear. *Not good.*

Jax watched me intensely. "Might be best to take it out before it becomes a problem."

I exhaled. "You offering? Because unless you've got actual dental training, that's a quick way to make this worse."

Jax just shrugged. "Seen it done more than once."

I eyed him, skeptically. "With what? A bayonet and a bottle of whiskey?"

"Something like that. We had this rule on the sub. Tooth starts screaming and no dentist aboard? Corpsman pulls it. When you're holding at 750 feet under an ice pack, an infected tooth isn't just a problem—it's a death sentence. No shore leave for a rotting molar."

The truth of it sank into my bones. Out here in the swamp, we might as well be at the bottom of the ocean. Any dentist still breathing was holed up in their own shelter—if they weren't already dead. There was no help coming, not that day or any other day.

My mind raced through the possibilities, each one darker than the last. Infection spreading, fever cooking my brain. Maggie and Button fumbling through bottles in a desperate game of medication roulette, thinking maybe *this* one will work, maybe *that* one. The tooth had me cornered, and it knew it.

"Jax, if you break it and leave a root behind, I'll be worse off than before."

He met my gaze. "I won't break it. I've got the right tool for it."

I swallowed hard, heart hammering. "You sure?"

"Yeah. I wouldn't be offering if I wasn't."

The truth of it sank deep. I had no choice.

"Do it quick, before I lose my nerve." My stomach fluttered like a crow caught on barbed wire. "Novocain?" *Please, God, let him say yes. Please, please, please.*

He walked to a box on a corner shelf, opened the lid, pulled out a bottle of Glenfiddich, and held it in the air.

"Nope, but I've got this."

* * *

I sat on the edge of the dusty dining room table, gripping it so hard my knuckles blanched. Jax stood in front of me, forceps in one hand, a bottle of whiskey in the other. He poured a generous shot into a tin cup and handed it to me.

"Drink up," he said, his voice steady, his eyes boring into me.

Fear? Hesitation? Determination? I didn't know and didn't care. I just wanted the fiery ball of agony removed from my mouth.

I downed the whiskey. The burn in my throat—usually pleasant—only added fuel to the fire.

The bottle tipped again—another shot, then another. By the fourth, my hands had steadied, my nerves dulled, though a hazy buzz crawled through my skull.

"Have you done... this... like..." The words faltered, the thought unfinished.

"Yeah. Took two seconds on the sub."

Jax set the bottle down and tilted my chin up with a calloused hand, studying my mouth. "This is gonna hurt."

I let out a laugh—sharp, dry, humorless. He needed an EMT course on talking to patients. "Tell me how it is, why don'you... don't... you."

The pliers gleamed in the dim light as he adjusted his grip. The moment they clamped onto my molar, pain shot through my skull. I gripped the table tighter, my toes curling in my boots.

"Okay, on three," he said.

He yanked on two.

White spots danced across my vision as something deep in my jaw ripped loose. My knuckles gripped the table's edge, and I imagined that my fingernails were carving half-moons into the soft pine. Metal scraped bone—a sickening vibration through my skull—then a wet crack, loud as a gunshot inside my head. Copper flooded my mouth.

Jax shoved a rag at me, and I spat into it, saliva and blood stretching in thin, glistening strands. The cloth darkened crimson. My chest heaved in ragged bursts, each exhale dragging a whimper from my throat. The room tilted, the edges of my vision swaying as tremors wracked me. Cold sweat beaded along my hairline and trickled down my neck.

"Well? Did you... get it?" I asked.

Jax held up the tooth. Yellow roots dangled like dead worms, bits of pink flesh still clinging to jagged edges.

I glared at him, grabbed the whiskey bottle, and took a long swig.

"I'm never... trusting you with pliers... again." My tongue felt thick, clumsy in my mouth. "That was... brutal. Are you sure you've done that before? Felt like you were trying to rip my... my damn jawoff. I mean jaw. Off."

Jax sucked his lips in, shrugged, and suddenly found the ceiling very interesting. Then he smiled—tight, almost hesitant.

"Pretty sure you just asked if I've done that before. Answer's... sort of. If I'd told you the truth, you wouldn't have let me do it. And that tooth had to come out."

Anger flashed through me like summer lightning, gone before it could strike the ground. Something else that had vanished—that spark between me and Jax—the one that had lit up the trailer. His eyes weren't hungry anymore. They inspected that bloody tooth, distant, indifferent. *No. Disgusted?*

As if he could read my mind—and to prove my point—he stepped on the pedal of an aluminum can, popping the lid up. He grimaced and flicked the tooth inside.

The whiskey made my thoughts swim in circles. Of course the spark was gone. Survival came first, right? Air, food, shelter—then whatever came next in Maslow's pyramid. I couldn't remember. Didn't matter. A rotting tooth had its own hierarchy: pain, fever, death. A tooth in the can was worth two in the mouth—wasn't that how the saying went? Before I could try and decipher the thought, it left my mind as quickly as it had come.

I watched him studying me, his brown eyes catching the lamplight, shimmering in the center. That spark wasn't dead. Not quite. It was still there. Maybe. Maybe not. Should I ask him? Or was I about to make a fool of myself? *Probably best not to say anything. Let him say it.*

But the whiskey spoke first.

"You and me. Back at the trailer. Was there something? I mean..."
Shit. That didn't sound right. Not at all.

"I mean... did you feel something... you know..."

Jax's grin spread. His eyes warmed.

My stomach rolled—once, twice—feeding the giddiness in my head.

He leaned in close, and I breathed him in. Smoke and sweat and something else, something from the trailer. Something Eric used. Not pine, but—Christ, that smile. It reached his eyes now, and my heart stuttered in my chest.

"Ellena." Those too-long lashes shadowed his cheeks. A dimple dug into one side of his mouth.

"Yes?"

Jax tilted his head and chuckled. "Can't understand a word you're saying. You're slurring worse than my Grandpa Pete on New Year's."

He handed me a wad of gauze. "Bite down on this to stop the blood flow."

I took the gauze and bit down, chewing on my humiliation. *You just made a fool of yourself, Ellena. Nice job.*

I reached for the bottle. *Just one more tot.*

He lifted the bottle out of my way. "I think bed's better than more booze right now."

I nodded, mumbled a muffled goodnight, then stumbled into the bunker and climbed toward my bunk. The ladder wobbled under my hands. Each rung felt like another step up Everest, and I thought I might succumb to exhaustion before I reached the summit. Eventually, I collapsed into the bunk, the sheet scratching my cheek like sandpaper, the metal frame pressing cold through my clothes like a mortuary slab.

Somewhere between sleep and waking, where thoughts unraveled like old sweaters, Winter howled.

18 No Response

I woke to a throbbing pain in my jaw and complete silence. No rustling from the others, no groggy voices, no soft steps on the vinyl floor. It was the kind of silence that settles in the moments before a tornado strikes—when the sky turns green, the light fades, and the wind falls still. Only the distant hum of the generator broke the silence. Something was wrong. I needed to get up.

I sat up too fast, and the room tilted around me. Two days of paddling on sips of water and scant food had left me drained. First priority: rehydrate. As my foot touched the bottom rung, I noticed Maggie, motionless on the bottom bunk.

I switched on the overhead lights and bent down. I hesitated, then gave Maggie's shoulders a gentle shake. "Maggie, can you hear me?" No response.

I pressed two fingers to Maggie's neck, finding a pulse—present, but weak. Her breathing was shallow, and her skin was cold and damp to the touch.

My grogginess lifted in a rush, like waking to a house fire. I peeled back one of Maggie's eyelids and her pupils reacted sluggishly to the light.

I frowned, my mind racing through the possibilities. Dehydration was likely. Since Greg's death, I couldn't recall Maggie drinking or eating much of anything. Low blood sugar was another possibility. Heat exhaustion crossed my mind, but Maggie's skin was too cool and clammy for that to fit.

Whatever it was, I knew I couldn't wait to figure it out. Maggie needed fluids, but swallowing anything in her state wasn't safe. Jax's medical box—if he had a hydration solution or IV supplies—could save her.

"Damn it," I said, scanning the cabin for the medical kit.

I'd seen it yesterday, but where? My eyes locked on the far corner, where the box sat next to two crates of batteries. I started toward the shelf, but a low whimper made me pause.

Winter.

He lay sprawled in the corner, his injured leg double its normal size, the skin stretched taut and shining with fevered heat. I knelt beside him, running my hands down the inflamed limb. I paused—there was no pulse at his paw. Beneath the surface, the rigidity confirmed what I already feared.

Compartment syndrome.

I'd seen it enough times to know the danger. Cooling or immobilization couldn't stop the advanced swelling. Without immediate release, the toxins trapped in his muscles would spread. A fasciotomy was the only option—and it had to happen right then and there.

But I'd only seen one once, during an ER observation. That had been in a controlled setting, with a trauma surgeon, bright lights, sterile instruments. It wasn't an EMT's job. Hell, it wasn't even a paramedic's. Fasciotomies belonged to surgeons, people with scalpels and training and steady hands. I'd failed the practical exam for hesitating—what if that same hesitation cost Winter his life?

And I'd never seen one performed on a dog. Their physiology was similar, sure. But similar wasn't the same. *And if I did this wrong...?*

My pulse thundered in my ears. *What about the bleeding? The risk of infection? What if I cut too deep? What if I didn't cut deep enough?*

But the limb was swelling fast. Time was running out.

"Ellena?"

Button stirred on her bunk, sitting up with effort, her face drawn with exhaustion—and something else. Sweat slicked her skin. "I had this dream... there were monkeys in here..." She plopped down flat against her pillow, as if sitting up had required all her energy.

I knelt, pressed a hand to Button's forehead, and felt the heat.

Button's eyes darted, unfocused, like she didn't know where she was. *Either that, or she's chasing imaginary monkeys.*

"How are you feeling?"

Button scrunched her face. "Are we at Gran's house?"

"No, we're at Jax's cabin." I pulled back the bandage on Button's leg. "Let me take a look at this."

A deep flush of red spread toward Button's knee. Heat radiated from the skin.

Shit. Shit, shit, shit.

Infection. Maybe cellulitis, maybe worse.

What antibiotic had I given Button yesterday? *Cephalexin.* But was that the right choice now? I wasn't sure. "Damn it."

Jax had a survival book—the answer could be in there. Hadn't I seen a field medical book as well? Whatever the solution, I needed help. I couldn't handle three patients on my own.

I tapped Jax's shoulder. "Jax, wake up."

He rubbed his eyes, his face shadowed by exhaustion. "What's going on?"

"Everything. I need your help." I wanted to scream, *Button's in trouble. Maggie and Winter too,* but held back. Overloading him now wouldn't help; he needed a moment to shake off sleep.

"We've got a medical emergency. I need you to grab your medical books, supplies—and the vet book."

What the hell am I thinking? Vet book? Think that covers emergency fasciotomies?

Jax bolted upright and flew out of his bunk. "What's wrong with him?" he asked as he dropped to Winter's side, eyes wide.

"It's called compartment syndrome. I can fix it." *I can maybe fix it—if I can keep my hands steady, if his physiology is close enough to a human's, if it's as easy as that surgeon made it look, if—* "But I need you to look in that vet book for me. I need a safe way to keep him immobile. A sedative, if you have one. Can you do that, Jax?"

He nodded and quick-stepped to the shelves. I followed, my mind racing as Winter's body shuddered in a way that made my stomach tighten. I had to act fast.

"Blanket? Sheets?"

He pulled a tote from a top shelf, opened it, and handed me a sheet.

I took it, stooped, and opened the medication box, scanning the rows of labeled bottles. My fingers trembled over the smorgasbord of choices— too many options, too little time—but I forced myself to focus. Winter's condition was deteriorating. I couldn't afford to waste time.

Okay, here's Praziquantel, Percocet, propofol—

"Find propofol in the vet book index."

Jax flipped to the back of the book. His hand shook as he turned the pages. I prayed it was nerves and not dehydration or some other ailment. One more patient to triage on my own was one patient too many.

"What was it?" he asked.

"Propofol," I said, forcing back my frustration. *Go easy, Ellena—he's not a professional.* "P...R...O..."

"Got it." He flipped through more pages, stopping near the middle. "It says... 'Not recommended for untrained use in animals. Requires precise dosing and monitoring. High risk of respiratory failure.'"

I glanced at Winter again. His whole body trembled in irregular waves, his muscles twitching beneath his damp fur. Oxygen-starved tissue, swelling pressure, pain so intense it hijacked his nervous system—his body was in full distress. He wasn't just shuddering; he was trapped in it, locked in the agony his own limb was inflicting on him. "Okay. How about... diazepam?"

He turned another few pages, eyes scanning. "It says... 'Safe for dogs in carefully measured doses. Used as a sedative and muscle relaxant. Can also help with seizures.'"

"Okay. Dose?"

"Uh... Dosage range: 0.1 to 0.2 milligrams per pound for sedation or anxiety. He's 45 pounds, so..."

I did a quick mental calculation. "Nine milligrams. That sound right?"

He shrugged. "I... uh... forty-five pounds times point 1 is, uh..."

"It's okay, Jax, never mind—I've got this."

I turned back to the box, fingers tracing the bottle tops as I looked for a numbing agent.

"Lidocaine. L...I...D..."

"Got it." Jax flipped the pages again, faster now. "Approved for veterinary use in dogs."

"Dose?"

"Uh, 81.6 to 102 milligrams for a single dose. But max dose... uh... this is confusing—lidocaine is usually sold in concentrations like 1%, meaning 10 milligrams per milliliter. So, for a 1% solution..."

"It's okay. 8.5 milliliters. That's the dose," I said, my voice steady despite the pressure mounting in my chest.

I located syringes, a scalpel, gauze, forceps, and iodine.

"What do I do?" Jax asked.

His posture was alert now, and ready for action.

"First, help me with Winter. Then we get antibiotics into Button. She's feverish. Could be cellulitis."

Jax frowned. "Cellulitis?"

"It's an infection. Not bad yet."

My hands hovered over the supplies. I didn't want to tell Jax that Maggie needed attention too. I figured it was best to throw the emergencies at him one at a time.

"Let's get Winter patched up first."

Patched up wasn't the right choice of words. *Butchered* was too much. *Experimented on?* Closer—but I wasn't about to say that out loud. Not to Jax. And not to myself.

Not that it would matter—he was about to see everything firsthand. *You can do this.*

I grabbed the book from Jax's hand. "Let me take a look at that. Take the supplies over to Winter."

I scanned the index, found "hind limb anatomy," then flipped to the page. Fascia tends to be thicker—check. No clean separation between compartments—check. Bleeding risk? High. Careful of the sciatic nerve—check. Avoid the saphenous vein—check. Cut too shallow, and it's useless. Cut too deep, and he bleeds out.

No pressure then. Just a living, breathing gamble.

I walked over to Winter and we both knelt next to him.

"He's going to be fine, Jax. But this is going to look worse than it actually is. I need to cut into him to relieve the pressure. There'll be a lot of blood."

Jax nodded, his jaw tightening as he moved to Winter's side. "I can handle it. Just tell me what to do."

His confidence was unnerving. He hadn't hesitated at the mention of blood. My mind flicked back to the swamp, to what he'd said about his training—about the things he'd seen. *Questions for another time.*

I said, "Hold him steady. Don't let him move when I'm cutting. No matter what."

* * *

Forty minutes later, Jax sat hunched on the floor, spine curled like a question mark. Winter's damp fur soaked dark patches into Jax's jeans. His fingers moved through the dog's coat in that absent way people touch things when their brain is somewhere else.

I stripped off my gloves and let my heartbeat settle, taking in the moment's wreckage.

Winter was still there. Still breathing.

My gaze traced the temporary sutures, the careful debridement, the dressing left open to reduce swelling. The compartment had been worse to take care of than I'd hoped—tissue dark, damaged, tough under the blade, the right spot almost impossible to find—but by some miracle, it had worked. The wound was open and draining.

The biggest risk now? Infection. With an open wound in a non-sterile environment, Winter faced a high risk of sepsis. Antibiotics and regular flushing should help—I hoped. Had I done it correctly? Would the swelling return? Worse, what if it turned necrotic? Amputation wasn't out of the question. A fasciotomy was one thing, but—*Och, Ellena, you're spinnin' round in circles, lass! Keep that up much longer and ye'll turn into a Hula Hoop.*

I flexed my fingers, realizing how stiff they were, how long I had been holding myself together. Across from me, Jax hadn't moved, his hands still curled around Winter as though some kind of Reiki magic could shield him from the pain.

I swallowed hard, allowing myself the smallest, quietest relief.

"Will he make it?" Jax asked, his voice hoarse.

"If he doesn't get an infection, yes. But I need to monitor him. He's not out of the woods yet."

Winter's chest rose and fell in slow, steady breaths, and for now, that was good enough.

I wiped my forehead with the back of my wrist. "Feels warm in here, Jax. Any chance you can turn on the AC?"

He walked over to the thermostat. "It's 78 in here. Can't turn it down lower. Conserve gas, you know?"

"Yes, sorry," I said, walking over to the sink. Maybe I need to hydrate. "No worries."

After washing my hands and drinking a full glass of water, I turned toward Maggie and Button, both lying motionless on the other side of the room.

"One down. Two to go," I muttered.

I wiped my hands on the rag, leaving rusty smears across the white cotton. The sharp bite of antiseptic burned my nostrils, mixing with the sour-sweet reek of infection that filled the small room.

I turned to Jax. "Winter's stable. I need help with Button." I gestured at the medical supplies scattered across the floor like a child's playroom. "Get me the antibiotics and water, please."

Jax grabbed the medicine while I knelt beside Button. My stepsister's skin was fever-hot under my touch, her face flushed as red as emergency lights. Sweat had soaked through her clothes, leaving them clammy and cold against my fingers. The infection below her knee had turned the flesh swollen and tight, puffed up like a carcass left in the sun.

Classic cellulitis. The fever had already sunk its teeth in, and without treatment, the infection would burrow deeper, turning her blood to poison.

I cleaned the wound with antiseptic, ignoring Button's feeble murmur of protest.

"Hold still," I said, pressing two pills into Button's trembling palm. "Take these. All of them."

Button swallowed with a grimace, barely managing the sip of water I held to her lips.

First dose down.

Jax sloshed water around in a plastic cup. "She gonna pull through?"

"She'll be fine if the antibiotics do their job," I said, wrapping Button's leg in clean gauze. "Help her drink. Small sips—not too much or she could choke."

Button's eyes found me through the fever-haze, glassy as marbles. Her breath smelled wrong—stale and overheated, like air trapped in a sickroom. "Am I... gonna die?" The words scratched out of her throat.

I leaned close and wrapped my fingers around Button's hand. "You're going to be fine." I hope. "I've got you, sis."

I moved to Maggie next, exhaustion dragging at my bones like lead weights. Maggie's pulse flickered weak under my fingers, but she stirred at my touch, a ghost of movement.

"Maggie, it's me, Ellena. You're dry as dust, but we'll fix that." The catheter slipped into the vein, the needle withdrawn in one swift motion. Saline dripped into the line, each drop a tiny hope. I injected glucose to the IV line, praying it would pull Maggie back from the edge where she teetered.

Jax slumped against the wall, his head in his hands. His breath came in ragged gasps, scraping against the silence. "How do you keep it together?"

I looked at him, sweat rolling cold down my back like melting ice. "I don't. I just keep moving."

19 Scratch

The following day, the sharp chemical smell in the bunker had faded to something duller, mixed with the copper-penny stink of dried blood and fever sweat. The generator's steady drone filled every corner of the room, humming in the background.

Jax sat against the far wall, his arms draped over his knees. Winter stirred beside him, each breath whistling through his nose. His body had curled into the shape of pain—muscles shuddering and ears pinned back—but the infection no longer owned him the way it had the day before. The gauze wrapped around his midsection rose and fell in a rhythm that had steadied, like a machine finding its groove after almost shaking itself apart.

I took his temperature. "101.5 degrees. Normal."

"That's what I want to hear," Jax said.

Button shifted in her bunk, mumbling through cracked lips. She was still feverish, though the antibiotics were doing their work beneath her skin like silent soldiers at war. No sepsis had taken root, which meant she'd gotten treatment in time. When she'd asked for water two hours ago, I had felt hope stir in my chest. The fever would break in a day or two. It had to.

Maggie was stable—as stable as could be expected. She was mid-sixties by my guess, and advancing age made it harder to shake off trouble. I recalled a case from a medical journal where nurses found a ninety-year-old man in a care facility unconscious with low blood glucose. It took five days of resuscitation and IV glucose before he stabilized. But Maggie had pulled through with barely a hitch. Something raw and primitive had kept her tethered to this side of death's door, a mix of stubbornness and pure will.

For the first time in days, I let myself sit and relax. Just for a second. The exhaustion hit me like a freight train—the kind that roars through small towns at midnight, leaving nothing but silence and fluttering debris in its wake. If I had the choice, I would lie down and sleep straight through tomorrow. But sleep and rest were not an option, not with three patients to tend to. And damn, I was weak. I needed to eat a proper meal and drink more water.

Jax's high-frequency radio sat on the table, tuned to a channel that should have been alive with emergency transmissions—some proof that someone was still out there. But the radio was silent. Not dead, just the faint hiss of an open frequency, a void where voices should have been.

Jax leaned forward, twisting the dial in slow, precise clicks. Each click landed on the same faint hiss. His fingers tightened around the knob, knuckles whitening, but he kept at it—like the next click might be the one that made the world talk again.

"Try... lower bands," Maggie said, her voice like sandpaper on old wood. "Nighttime skips better there."

Jax nodded, already twisting the dial. Static hissed through the speakers as he hunted for a signal. His forehead creased deeper with each empty channel.

"But it isn't night," I said.

"D-layer's weakened. She's right." He caught my blank look. "That's how the signal travels. Fallout affects it."

I knew as much about radio signals as I knew about quantum mechanics, but I knew enough to recognize the wrongness of the silence. The question rose in my gut, cold and heavy. "We should be picking up something, right? Even if it's weak?"

Jax said, "Yeah. Unless—"

I wasn't in the mood for unfinished thoughts. "Unless what?" I wiped my forehead with my sleeve, removed my hoodie, and placed it in a pile on the floor.

Jax flicked the radio off and dragged a hand down his face. When he spoke, his voice was quiet. "Unless there's no one left to send a signal."

The words settled between us, heavy as the swamp air outside.

Maggie shifted, her breath catching on something deep in her chest. "Not no one. Somebody's always out there."

Jax ran a hand through his hair, looking more exhausted than angry. "Then where the hell are they? Military's got bunkers with comms. Government agencies, too. Hell, even some preppers should broadcast something. But we're getting nothing."

I leaned forward, resting my elbows on my knees. "Could it be EMP damage? Or maybe they don't want to broadcast?"

Jax shook his head. "That's not how this works. EMPs would've knocked out a lot of comms, sure, but the military's got hardened systems. They'd be back up by now. And even if official channels stayed dark, someone with a ham radio should be screaming into the void."

He stared at the radio like it might crackle back to life. "Which means, either no one survived, or the ones that did don't want to be found."

* * *

The following afternoon, the cabin felt... almost normal.

Jax had tidied the main room, sweeping away dust that had gathered thick as desert sand. The main floor wasn't much—just a rough-hewn space with a small couch, a table, and chairs that looked like they'd been collected from six different yard sales. I kept sidestepping those trompe l'œils, my feet refusing to trust what my mind knew was a solid floor. But it was something, a place to *be* rather than just exist.

We were comfortable venturing out of the bunker and into the exterior cabin, because the silence outside had grown absolute—no distant engines, no planes in the sky, no trucks on forgotten highways, no boats on the blackwater. It was becoming clear that there wasn't anyone nearby.

The bunker still held our supplies, our real lives sealed away behind that door. But out in the living room, with cards scattered across the table and a half-finished Scrabble game waiting, it was like we'd simply booked a substandard Airbnb and were about to have a laugh about how the listing photographs must've been AI-generated.

I stared at the Scrabble board, deep in thought but unable to decipher the letters in front of me. PRATGER. I couldn't think of a single word. Not one. My brain didn't want to think beyond sleep.

"Unless 'pratger' is suddenly a word, I'm swapping these," I said.

I shoved my tiles into the cloth bag, the wooden pieces clacking against each other. My hands trembled as I drew seven new ones, nearly dropping them onto the floor.

Across from me, Jax leaned forward, squinting at my face. "You're white as a sheet. Everything alright?"

"Yes. Maybe I need to lie down. Exhaustion, I think. This trip..."

He nodded. The last week had taken it all out of us.

Maggie adjusted her tiles with the smug patience of someone who had already won. She was a ruthless Scrabble player, and she made sure we all knew it.

"If I put 'Quixotic' right here," she said, tapping the board, "that's a triple-word score and a double-letter bonus on the Q." She placed the tiles

173

down one by one with a series of clicks as the pieces hit the board. "And, since I used all seven letters from my rack..." She leaned back with a smug smile. "That's a bingo. Which means..."

Jax squinted at the board, muttering under his breath. "Q's ten... plus X... triple-word..." He sat back, scowling. "You've gotta be kidding me."

Maggie grinned. "One hundred and fifty-five points."

Jax let out a low whistle. "Glad we weren't playing for money."

Button groaned from her spot on the couch, draped in a blanket and flipping through *Call of the Wild*. "This is why I don't play Scrabble."

I smiled. Button was back. Her fever had dropped to 100.4 that morning—holding steady and almost normal.

Winter, curled up beside Jax on his egg crate bed, flicked an ear at the sound of our voices but didn't stir. He was still healing, still weak, but the antibiotics were doing their job. My amateur veterinarian stint had been a gamble—no, not a gamble but a necessity—and it had worked. And now, he was almost back to sticking to Jax like a shadow—albeit a slow, hobbling one.

Jax sighed, shaking his head at the board. "You hustled us, Maggie."

Maggie shrugged. "Never said I was bad at it."

I leaned back, stretching my arms over my head. A day or two ago, we'd been fighting for survival, wondering if one of us wouldn't wake up the next morning. Now? We were playing board games like the world hadn't ended.

Jax plonked down TAP over the E in QUIXOTE. "Six points," he said with a heavy sigh.

I looked at my tiles again. HERPROO. Nope. Coffee might help.

"I fold—" I shook my head, tongue thick in my mouth. "I mean... I quit. Scratch? Shoot. Coffee anyone?"

* * *

The kettle rattled in my unsteady hands as I scooped instant coffee into two mugs. Steam curled around my fingers as I filled them, then I grabbed two electrolyte drinks for Button and Maggie. Before I could load the tray, the floor pitched beneath my feet like a ship's deck. Black spots swirled at the edge of my vision.

I clutched the counter and waited for my vision to clear. I needed food. Reaching for a granola bar nearly sent me sprawling, the wrapper crinkling in my grip as I took a few deep breaths, then swigged an electrolyte drink.

Perhaps caffeine would cut through the fog. If not... my body begged for horizontal, for darkness, for sleep. Button, Maggie, and Winter had turned the corner—they'd be okay without me hovering for a few hours.

I opened the door and found Jax seated in a rocking chair, staring out of the window. Maggie had cleared away the game, and still sported a winner's air of victory.

I gave Button and Maggie their drinks then handed Jax his coffee. "Penny for your thoughts?"

He exhaled, rubbing the back of his neck. "Just thinking about my dad. I told you he built this, right?"

"I think you said something, yes. Your dad was a prepper, right?"

Jax nodded. "Not the crazy, YouTube-conspiracy kind. Just... always convinced something bad was coming. Civil war, government collapse, something. Had shelves full of canned food, enough guns to stock a small militia."

I frowned. A nuclear bunker didn't feel like typical prepper stuff—or did it? In my mind, preppers had compounds and truckloads of guns, not nuclear war bunkers and HF radios. But what the hell did I know? I waved a hand around the cabin. "So, why did he build this?"

"I called him about a year ago and said, 'Dad, I'm not allowed to tell you anything, because it's classified. But that civil war bunker you're gonna build? Make it so that it could last a very long winter.'"

I raised an eyebrow. "And he listened?"

"Yeah. I got him to figure it out—without my violating clearance. Most of this? His work. I just improved on it."

I wiped sweat from my brow, wondering why it was still so warm inside. Hadn't it barely broken sixty degrees that day? "Sounds like he was a great man. Wish I could have met him."

"He was. Thanks, Ellena."

Something about the way he spoke disorientated me. I slumped in my seat, my stomach flip-flapping like a fish out of water.

I glanced at the small enclosure Jax had set up outside—a patch of fake grass, just enough for Winter to do his business when he got up and going again. It was the sort of thing you didn't bother with unless you cared—really cared—about the ones you were trying to keep alive.

"Looks like Winter's going to be a spoiled puppy when he gets up on his feet," I said.

Jax broke into a grin. "Nah. It's keeping Button off my back with the indoor toilet business."

He nodded toward the sky. "You see that?"

I followed his gaze. The clouds were rolling in, thickening at the edges, heavy with the promise of rain. But between them, one star shone through, bright and sharp, visible even through the plastic. Sirius maybe? Hard to tell through the haze.

"That's the last one we'll see for a long time," he said.

I swallowed hard, my throat clicking like a broken music box.

No more stars. Just darkness stretching out longer than any night had a right to last. But it was all theory, wasn't it? Just like when they'd built the first atomic bomb, sweating bullets over whether they'd ignite the atmosphere and torch the whole planet. They'd done it anyway. And nuclear winter? I remembered reading about it somewhere, in one of those science magazines gathering dust under my coffee table. How the smoke and ash would kill off plants across continents, how the effects could last a hundred years or more. But they'd done it anyway.

Because that's what people did—they pushed buttons and pulled triggers and hoped like hell someone else would clean up their mess. Only this time, there might be no one left to work a mop.

Jax reached over and took my hand, and I almost jumped out of my skin. His fingers were warm, rough—solid. Real. I stared at those fingers wrapped around mine like a steel trap lined with velvet. Living flesh pressed against living flesh, and each ridge of his calluses sent messages to my brain I didn't want to decode.

Time stretched like a rubber band ready to snap. His grip neither tightened nor loosened. Just stayed there, as steady as a foundation stone, telling me without words that whatever came next, he would be right there with me.

I didn't look at his face. Not yet. The reality of his hand was enough to process. More than enough.

He squeezed my hand. "Thanks for saving Winter."

I almost told him, *you helped*. But the words caught in my throat. It had been me, hadn't it? The scalpel, the sutures, the choices.

Jax turned my hand over, his thumb following the lines of my palm like he was reading my future. Each gentle caress sent little electric jolts up my arm.

He lifted my hand, pressed his lips to my knuckles, and time stretched like warm toffee.

I didn't pull away.

My lungs emptied in a rush. The armor I'd been wearing since the world went sideways cracked and fell away as my fingers threaded through his.

He studied my face, questioning.

A flicker of warmth sparked low in my belly as it hit me—he was about to lean in for a kiss.

Jax lifted a hand to my cheek, thumb brushing before settling there.

Then his hand moved to my forehead and his expression shifted. "Jesus, Ellena, you're burning up."

20 Followers

When my eyes cracked open, there was Gran, sitting beside my bed in the shelter's dim light. Her gray curls caught what little illumination filtered through, her blue eyes warm and steady as childhood memories.

My tongue felt like it was coated in glue when I tried to speak. But before I could say a word, Gran pressed a cup against my lips. Peppermint tea, my addled brain insisted. But the taste betrayed me. Bitter. Rotten. I gagged, spitting the liquid across the silver blanket. A crinkling silver blanket—familiar yet foreign.

"None of that," Gran said, and the voice was pure authority, the kind that had commanded every childhood illness into submission.

I turned away, but Gran's grip found my chin with surprising strength. "You'll drink, or you'll die, lass."

Death was easier than drinking poison. Sleep was easier than both.

I slipped under again, into a dream where I was two-years-old, bare feet in beach sand, chubby legs pumping toward waves that stood like concrete walls. Laughing. Then hands yanking me back as the water crashed down. Gran. Always Gran.

Gran smiled, solid as bedrock. Then she was gone.

I shivered in the stale air, cold sinking into my bones.

Am I dead?

Reality flickered, fuzzy and intermittent. The weight of the blanket pressed down like a shroud, and I shoved it off. A wet rag brushed my forehead, and Gran's voice cut through the static. "There you are."

No, not Gran. Maggie.

"She's awake?" Jax asked.

"You betcha."

Jax knelt beside me, his skin the color of milk left out for five days. "Are you okay?" I asked.

He chuckled. "I should be asking you that question. Welcome back."

"How long was I out for?" I asked.

Maggie let out a breath that seemed to deflate her whole body. "You've been cooking for a full day. We tried the same cephalexin you used on Button's gator bite, but it was like chucking darts at a speck of rice. The survival guide might as well've been written in chicken scratch. We thought it was an infection in your arm from that damn gator claw, but then your breath started smelling like something crawled in and died, and we started second guessing everything. Hours, Ellena. Hours of not knowing."

Jax dragged a hand across his face. "Then Button and I started puking."

That explained why they looked one step from the grave.

Maggie's voice dropped. "Took us too long to figure it out. The swamp water, when the boat went over. Could've been that, could've been the well water. Either way, something mean is swimming in your guts. Lord knows why I was spared." She shook her head. "The book said Metronidazole's our best shot, but we were shooting in the dark. Bacterial, viral—might as well have flipped a coin."

I drew in a shallow breath. Every inch of me screamed in pain, like it had been through a meat grinder, but I was on the living side of dead. The words "viral" and "bacterial" drifted through my head like dead leaves in a gutter—meaningless debris my fever-fried brain couldn't process. All I could push past my cracked lips was, "Thank you."

Maggie looked at me, fear as raw as a fresh wound. "We almost killed you. Made us realize something. You're our lifeline, Ellena. If you die, we all follow."

21 Static

We'd been in the cabin for five weeks. The sun had long since vanished behind clouds as thick as steel plate, and the world had gone gray. That first week, heat soaked my clothes and dripped down my back, turning every breath into work. Now the temperature dropped after sunset, the thermometer creeping toward freezing, mocking our Floridian camper preparations. Our bags held the evidence: tank tops crumpled into wads, Button's bottles of Off! standing useless on the shelves. We'd packed for swamp weather, not a nuclear winter.

The wood stove's heat barely kept the night's chill at bay. Our firewood stack had dwindled to about two months' worth. After that, we'd have to venture into the dead woods to gather more. Without the Geiger counter, we'd never know if the wood was hot. One load of contaminated fuel, one lungful of radioactive ash, and we might as well dig our graves.

I flipped open my notebook, the pages crackling like old parchment. I had tracked our supplies since week one—medicine, food, fuel, toiletries. The lists grew shorter. The empty spaces stretched longer.

Jax had stocked the cabin with enough provisions for one or two people and a dog—for a year at most. An extra two people had whittled that down to six months, if we were lucky. Some supplies—coffee, toilet paper, bandages—were already running low.

Somewhere out there, store shelves might still hold what we needed. But venturing out meant gambling with death. Fallout didn't come with warning signs, and no one knew where the hotspots lurked.

Not that Winter cared. Still thin but getting stronger, he would've charged through the dust, tail high, chasing sticks and scents only he could smell. Inside, his claws clicked across the floor as he chased the knotted rag Button dangled overhead. She jerked it away at the last second, and he spun like a top, his tail whipping with joy.

"You're teasing him," Jax said from the table, watching him.

Button grinned. "He likes it."

Winter barked and lunged, snagging the rag between his teeth. Button whooped as he shook his prize, thrashing it like fresh kill.

I leaned in the doorway. A few weeks ago, Button burned with fever while Winter fought the snake venom that nearly took his leg. Now they rolled across the floor like old playmates.

Maggie said, "They're thick as thieves. Should rename him Shadow the way he follows her around."

I smirked. "Yes, but good luck getting her to admit she likes it."

It was funny how things had changed, considering how my stepsister used to talk about dogs. A dog-loving coworker at the credit union gave her a ride home once, and the husky hair coating those seats sent Button into a fury. She burned through a whole lint roller trying to save her Balenciaga pants, spitting out the word "mongrels" like poison. After that, every dog bore the name.

But now there she was, whooping it up like she'd found religion.

Winter flopped onto his back, the rag clenched in his jaws. Button scratched under his chin. "Alright, alright, you win. Just don't drool on me."

* * *

We gathered around the dinner table where the heat pooled like the last sunlight before a storm. The table was quiet, save for the clink of forks against tin plates. The meal was simple—canned tuna, rice, and the last of the green beans from Jax's stash. It was warm. It was food. For now, that was enough.

Winter had a mix of tuna and rice, which he wolfed down. He turned away from his empty bowl and darted after a tennis ball that Button had thrown.

Jax set his fork down. "We should talk next steps."

"Yup, we gotta move, eh," Maggie said.

"Exactly. This place wasn't set up for four people and the long freeze. We need to leave, but the problem is—"

I said, "We don't know where to go. We haven't heard a peep from the radio."

No whispers. No emergency broadcasts. Nothing.

"Even considering the atmosphere blocked signals after the detonations, it's been over a month," Jax said. "By now, some radio signals should have broken through. That means either the atmosphere is still screwed, or there's no one left to send signals."

Silence hung over the table until Button spoke.

"We could go south, where it's warmer?"

My first thought was sharp—*Sure, Button, let's all grab our hobo sticks and walk to Miami*—but I kept quiet. Button was trying to help, I reminded myself.

Stop being so hard on her.

Jax shook his head. "Not safe. We aren't getting any signals, so we don't know if anyone's even alive in South Florida. If they hit the state, targets would've included Miami, Tampa—with MacDill Air Force Base—and Jacksonville with its naval base. Pensacola might've been hit too. Orlando's a possibility, but I wouldn't bet on it."

"I bet taking out Disney World would be a 'real boon for morale,'" I said, making air quotes with my fingers.

Jax said, "Right. And I'm not even taking into account..." His voice trailed off as he looked at everyone in turn.

I opened my mouth to ask him... taking *what* into account?

But Maggie cut in first.

"I don't get it. Why would they bomb Winter Garden of all places, eh? Makes no sense. I've been there. Lovely place. Far enough from Disney to be away from the crowds."

Jax turned his fork over in his hand, his mind somewhere else.

I watched him, dread curling low in my gut. "You're thinking about something."

Jax didn't answer right away. Instead, he set the fork down and leaned back in his chair. "I was thinking about the Blitz."

Button frowned. "Like, the London Blitz?"

My skin prickled. Gran's wartime stories echoed in my mind—London under siege, first the Blitz bombs screaming down, then the V-2 rockets. Silent killers. No warning. One moment peace, the next—rubble where St. Paul's Cathedral might've been. Calculated terror, designed to break not just buildings but spirits. Maximum civilian casualties. The words spun in my brain like a demented clock set to lightning speed. And now Jax spoke of a new "Blitz." The word tasted like copper in my mouth. Was that the goal again? Maximum casualties?

Jax rubbed a hand over his jaw. "The first strike is bad enough. That's what you expect—nukes hit major targets, military installations, infrastructure. But the second strike? That's the real killer."

He glanced around the table. "The second biscuit. That's what they called it. If we lost enough cities—D.C., New York, L.A.—the President had a second option. The Blitz."

My forehead creased. "Wait a sec. You're telling me they had a backup plan? To just... what, go and finish the job?"

Jax nodded. "Thousands of warheads, all fired at once. No strategic targets. No infrastructure. Just people. Civilian centers. Major cities, every high-density population area they can get. Random targets as well—think, national treasures like Mount Rushmore or the Alamo, wiped off the map."

A chill crept up my spine. "But why? How does that make any sense?" But I already knew the answer. Nothing about war made sense. A series of images flashed in my mind. Napalm. The My Lai massacre. Dresden burning. Sarajevo under siege. Bodies stacked like cordwood in Kigali.

Jax let out a breath, shaking his head. "To make sure there's no winner, that's why. If we go down, we take them with us. No enemy left to invade. No country left to pick through our bones." He tapped his fingers against the table. "Russia's got the same plan. China, Iran, Korea too, the hell knows who else. Doesn't matter. What matters is that when it happens—when those second strikes launch—there's no coming back."

The silence that followed ached. Empty and cold and endless, like staring into a black hole.

Winter plopped a ball into Button's lap. She tossed it, and he sprinted after it, but when he reached the ball, he didn't bring it back.

Button said, "Winter. Bring me the ball."

When he didn't budge, she snapped her fingers, then twirled a finger in the air. "Oh, oh, oh... What was it you said his name was back at the campsite, Jax? 'Winter is coming,' right?"

"Well, I'll be," Maggie muttered, slumping back in my seat.

Jax held up a hand. "My dad named him. Got Winter after that phone call I told you about. He had a dark sense of humor, my dad."

"But how did you know about all of this?" I asked. His secretive military background—that's how. The SEAL cover story. The "expertise" in the military. His knowledge about radiation.

Realization hit me like an icy wave. "You were part of it."

Jax met my eyes. Sadness was there. He shook his head—not in denial, but in shame—lips pressed inward, gaze dropping to the table. "I was."

I drew in a sharp breath and covered my mouth.

"Look, guys, I was in the Navy. I was following orders." He paused. "Shit."

His next words came slower, dragging something dark behind them. "I was in the military, as you all know. I was a submariner—nuclear sub—but I got a special deployment to Jamaica—to work in the deep subterranean missile silos there. It was supposed to be preventative, you know? Stop a war."

His exhale was sharp enough to cut glass. "But it wasn't meant to stop anything. It was one giant war game. A giant psych-ops experiment. And then, when I found out about the grand plan—the Blitz—I went AWOL."

"The go-bag," I said. "You were on the run."

It was more of a statement than a question. He didn't need to answer. But he gave a slight nod. "Vasquez tipped me off that the Master-at-Arms team were on their way. That's when I hightailed it to the campsite in the canoe."

I watched the confession splinter across the table. AWOL Submariner. Jamaica. Silos. Each piece refused to fit with the last. He followed orders until he didn't. Until he couldn't.

The silence stretched.

Button was the first to break it. "So you're saying... that the Blitz might've already happened?"

Jax shrugged, but there was something bleak in his eyes. "We haven't picked up a single signal on the radio. Not military, not civilian. Not even emergency broadcasts. That tells me two things: either communications are down or there's nobody left to use them."

I closed my notebook. "Damn."

I felt the weight pressing down on me. I had clung to some small, stupid hope that someone was still out there. That there were still governments, still cities, still people.

Jax clenched his jaw. "You know what they don't tell you about nuclear winter? It's not just the cold. It's the dust. The ash. The way the world gets dark. Crops die, animals starve. People do too. Even with stored food, rationing—it's the inevitable starvation that gets you."

I stared down at my plate. Suddenly, the food tasted bland. It wasn't just starvation that was a problem. Vitamin D deficiencies, infectious disease, hypothermia, radiation sickness, dehydration, sepsis—the slow unraveling of the human body, one system at a time.

I let out a breath, leaning back against the chair. "So what do we do?"

Jax took a bite of tuna, chewed it, and set his fork down. "I wish I had answers. All I know is, we need to make some kind of plan, because it's going to get a lot colder. We can last here until next winter just about, but the truth is, we'll have to severely ration food. I planned for myself, Dad, and Winter—not two extra people."

The silence stretched, broken only by Winter lapping at his water.

"I have an idea," Button said.

Can't wait for this. I stopped the thought dead. Button had proven her strength. Time to quit the cutting remarks. "Go on then."

"My Uncle Hank. He's in Colorado—"

"That's a bit far from here." Jax's chair dropped forward with a thunk. "Might as well say he's in Timbuktu."

"Give her a chance," I said, holding up a hand.

Jax gave a tight smile, lifting his hands in mock surrender. "Sure. Why not? Enlighten me."

"He's high up in the military. He told me to get to Colorado, to this survival community, up near Grand Mesa. Said I should get out there if I could, but that was the day it happened. And he said if I needed help, if anything happened, I should call him at 8pm. He said he'll be listening. But my cell phone obviously ain't working."

"No shit," Jax said, his chair wobbling on its back legs. "Survivalist community, huh. Bet he's got an HF radio then."

"HF?" Button asked.

"High-frequency, military radio. Long distance communication. Same thing we've been listening to static on. Damn, this is good, Button. If he's high up, he might be able to tell us what's out there... assuming he's still alive."

"But you said no one was broadcasting on it," Button said.

"I didn't say no one was broadcasting. I said there's nobody on the regular channels. If your uncle has a dedicated frequency, we wouldn't be able to find it. Assuming a one hertz tuning step, there are about twenty-seven million possibilities. What frequency did he give you?"

"I, uh..." Her index finger traced slow circles in the air as she searched for words. "July 24 at 2 and March 9 at 7:50."

"Those are dates, not frequencies." Jax raked a hand through his hair, cheeks flushing. "I think—"

Button leaned forward and cut him off with a raised hand. "July is month 7, so 7-24-2—"

"7.242 Megahertz!" Maggie said, clapping her hands. "Well, I'll be. Genius!"

My heart skipped a beat. "Gran's birthday. Wow, that's a coincidence."

Button said, "Not a coincidence. Uncle Hank gave me a few to choose from and I picked that one so I'd remember it. I miss her, you know?"

I did.

22 White Lies

I sat at the dining table. Across from me, Button stared at Jax's HF radio, hands clenched in her lap. Winter dropped a ball there, and she tossed it. He skittered after it across the floor.

The radio dominated the table, its black metal casing scarred with years of use. Knobs and dials were scattered across the front panel—some labeled in faded white, others worn smooth. The microphone cord coiled across the surface, its handset resting by Button's knee. Outside, the wire antenna vanished into the trees. Inside, only static answered: a dead-channel hiss filling the space between them.

Jax turned the frequency dial at 8 PM—the time Button's uncle had specified.

Nothing.

The same nothing as the last three nights.

Jax exhaled through his nose, shoulders tightening. "We'll keep trying."

Button nodded, but I saw the truth in the tension of her jaw. Hope had an expiration date.

Jax moved to switch the dial, but then—

Crackle.

A burst of static. Then—

"—nybody out there? Over."

Button sucked in a sharp breath. "Oh my God. It's Uncle Hank!"

Jax grabbed the mic, steady but quick, and keyed it. "Uncle Hank, this is Jax Mercer, transmitting on the agreed frequency. Do you copy? Over?"

He released the mic, and the radio spat out another burst of static. He glanced at Button, but she just gripped the edge of the table, knuckles white. Then—a crackle, a voice.

Jax repeated himself, slower this time. "Uncle Hank, this is Jax Mercer. I'm calling on behalf of Button. Do you copy?"

The seconds stretched. Button's hands twisted together.

Then—

"Where the hell is Button? Is she okay? Over."

"She's fine, Sir. She's right here."

I didn't realize I was holding my breath until Button choked out a sound somewhere between a sob and a laugh. "Uncle Hank!"

"Over," Jax said.

"Button! Jesus, kid. I thought—" Hank's voice cut in and out, but the relief in it was thick enough to break bones. "Where the hell are you? Over."

Jax held the mic in front of Button, who wiped at her eyes, laughing. "We're in Georgia. We're okay. We're alive."

Jax said, "Over."

"Georgia?" Hank's voice darkened. "Who's with you? Over."

"My name's Jax, Sir. Jax Mercer."

Button leaned in. "He helped us through, Uncle Hank. We wouldn't be alive if it weren't for him. And Ellena's here too."

A pause, then Jax said, "Over."

"Ellena's there?" Uncle Hank said. "That's great news. Okay, we need to plan for you to get out here. Do you have a vehicle? Over."

"Sir, this is Jax. Affirmative on the vehicle. But, uh, Colorado's a ways from here and we're hoping you can help us navigate to a safe zone. We're in the Okefenokee swamp in South Georgia. Over."

"Roger. No safe zones in your area. Stand by for route details. Over."

Jax keyed the mic but hesitated, like he was collecting his thoughts.

I took a deep breath. Then two. Then three. *What did he mean by "no safe zones"?*

Jax said, "Confirm status of Southeast. Florida? Any known safe zones? Over."

More static, then Hank's voice came through, clear as if he were standing right beside us. "No safe zones means just that, son. They got the major targets. Tampa, Miami, Jacksonville. No surprises there. But they also got civilian targets. Sanibel. Palmetto Springs. Many more."

I gasped, the sound shattering the quiet like a rock through plate glass. Palmetto Springs.

I locked eyes with Button, and in that frozen moment their shared look carried one thought, hard as a bullet. *Eric.*

"Put Button on the line, over." Hank said.

Jax gave Button the handset.

She stared at him, wide-eyed. Winter plopped the ball in her lap, and it just sat there. Six feet away, he crouched, staring at it like it might launch at any moment, while Button sat frozen.

Jax nudged the handset toward her. "Hold to talk. Let go to listen."

She took the handset and pressed down the transmit key. "Hi, Uncle Hank. It's me, Button."

A beat of silence.

Jax nudged her. "Say 'Over.'"

Button cleared her throat. "Over."

"Glad you're okay, Button. And glad Ellena's with you. We need a medic. Family is welcome here. Who else is with you? Over."

"Well, Jax. He's... he'll get us there, Uncle Hank. And Maggie—she's..." Button looked at Maggie, then at me, then to Jax, as if she were triaging us all.

Jax leaned in. "What Button's trying to say is that there are four of us, over."

Button let go of the transmit key and fumbled the mic. She stared at Maggie. Jax, and me in turn.

A sharp pause. "Copy that. I'm sorry, son, but we don't have room for outsiders. Family only. If I bring in strangers, these guys will riot. Over."

Button pressed the transmit key. "They are family, Uncle Hank. Ellena got married." She met my gaze head-on when she told the lie. "And Maggie's Jax's mom. She's a gardener—knows how to grow food. Over."

A burst of static. Then—"Ellena got married again? Well, I'll be damned. Congratulations. Over."

Button pressed the key again. "We'll be seeing you soon, Uncle Hank. Jax will take it from here to sort the route. Over."

My mouth dropped open, and I snapped it shut. Who was this ballsy person who had invaded my stepsister's body? I avoided looking at Jax. My face was already burning with heat, and I wasn't about to risk going scarlet if I met his eyes. We were going to play married? Could we do it to survive? Heat crawled up my cheeks as I turned to Button and mouthed, "What the fuck?"

Button shrugged and mouthed, "Sorry."

Hank said, "I've got people still moving out there—truckers, old vets, preppers. Not many, but enough. I can set up a route: safe houses, fuel stops. It'll take time. You'll have to reach the first checkpoint on your own. Can you do that? Over."

Jax nodded—pointless, since Hank couldn't see it—then grabbed the mic from Button. "Copy. Standing by for first checkpoint coordinates. Over."

"Alabama. Marker is I-65, Fort Deposit exit—about four-fifty klicks west of you. There's an old Army buddy of mine there, callsign Rattlesnake. Holed up at an old truck stop, used to be a Love's. You'll be able to get fuel, food, a place to rest—but you can't stay longer than a night. Over."

Jax pressed the mic again. "Copy. We'll make it. What's the next contact point after that? Over."

"After that, you're looking at..."

Static crackled through the speaker.

Jax tightened his grip on the mic.

A beat of silence. Then, "Conway, Arkansas. Ex-National Guard runs it. They've got defenses, fuel, and trade, but it's not a charity stop. You'll have to barter for what you need."

Jax glanced at me. We had little to trade—maybe ammo.

"Best bet is to keep moving after Rattlesnake's," Uncle Hank continued. "Conway is... stable for now, but they don't like outsiders hanging around. Over."

My stomach knotted. Three hundred miles to Alabama, another five hundred to Arkansas—eight hundred miles through a world gone to hell.

Jax exhaled. "Copy. Anything past Conway? Over."

Static. Then, "That's where it gets tricky. There's a refueling stop in Pawhuska, Oklahoma, but it's unreliable. If you can't reach them, you're on your own until you hit the Rockies. Over."

"And what about you, Sir?" Jax asked. "How much longer will you be monitoring this frequency? Over."

"Every night at 2000 hours. Same frequency. If I stop answering, assume I'm compromised. Over."

Jax nodded. "Copy that. Over."

"But Button, kid, you listening?"

Button leaned in, gripping the mic with both hands.

Hank said, "You gotta be smart. You gotta be careful. You hear me? Over."

Button let out a shaky breath. "Yeah, Uncle Hank. I hear you. Over."

"Alright, then. Move fast. Move quiet. And don't stop until you hit that checkpoint. Copy?"

Jax's voice was steady. "Copy. We'll see you in Colorado. Over."

A pause. Then, "Uncle Hank, you're breaking up. Say again. Over." The radio static crackled on.

"No copy on last. We're moving to the first checkpoint. Over."

Jax placed the mic on the table. "That's it then. We set out in the morning."

"How are we going to get to Colorado?" I asked. It was a fair question. The tin-roofed shed next to the dirt road wasn't big enough for a car. A riding mower, maybe.

"We head to my dad's place, just north of us. He's got an old F-150 that won't have been fried by the EMP. It's bulletproof."

"Bulletproof? Seriously?" Button asked.

Jax laughed. "Not presidential bulletproof. I mean it's built to last. Parts are easy to find. No computer junk to mess with. It'll get us cross-country with a bit of spit and polish."

23 Bulletproof

The morning air bit at forty degrees, clouds massing overhead like a ceiling of crushed concrete.

From the passenger seat, I watched Jax make his final circuit around his UTV—an off-road vehicle and a rolling patchwork of scrap and stubbornness. A week's worth of supplies—tent, food, water jugs, fuel cans, and the medical kit—strained against the bungee cords holding them down. A plastic hula girl bobbed on the dashboard; her endless dance broke into spasms with every vibration. The whole rig looked like someone had ripped it from a National Lampoon movie set. I just hoped it wouldn't fall apart before we made it out of the swamp.

Jax had spray-painted ZOMBIE RESPONSE TEAM across a highway sign bolted to the side. He stepped back, arms crossed, assessing his handiwork like a man proud of his masterpiece. But his smirk wavered when he saw my gaze, and the joke wilted in the frosty morning air.

Too soon, Jax. Too soon.

"This thing's barely roadworthy," I muttered, nudging Winter's ribs with my boot. He lay curled at my feet, chin resting on his paws, wedged under the dash in his den.

He let out a low growl—not the ferocious, teeth-baring kind, but one that meant, *Hey, watch your feet, lady.*

"Sorry, bud," I said.

Behind me, Maggie and Button took their places on what passed for seats—a wooden pallet cushioned by blankets, with bike handlebars zip-tied to the roll cage for "safety." As they settled in, the pallet beneath them groaned in protest, shifting the weight of the whole rig. The UTV rocked, tools clanking in their milk crates but holding steady under the tension of their straps.

"Better than walking." Jax gave the strap one last tug before climbing into the driver's seat. His grin was all false bravado—like if he faked optimism hard enough, the rest of us might believe it too.

Button gripped the handlebar. "Yeah, well, let's just hope this here death trap holds together."

Her snarky comment didn't irk me like it would have in the past; I almost found it amusing. Button had recovered from her battle with cellulitis, although gray and purple mottled her leg. It would take a few more weeks to return to normal. *Snark away, Button.*

I smirked. "And this is coming from someone whose bedroom floor looks like Shein's return pile after a buy-one-get-ten-free sale?"

"Och, listen tae yerself—that's the pot giving the kettle a right telling-off for bein' black." Button said, laughing so hard she snorted.

Tears streaked down my cheeks. Button had known some of Gran's sayings all long.

I thought back to before the bombs, when Button and I clashed constantly. Back then, I'd written Button off as shallow, but had Button just been reacting to my defenses? My prickliness? Probably.

Gran had another saying, something about getting back what you give out. *Ye cannae spit in the well and not expect foul water*—that was it.

I'll do better. For Button. For us. I'll do better.

Maggie snorted, shifting on her blanket cushion. "That 'bulletproof' F-150. You sure about that, Jax?" She exhaled, watching her breath curl in the cold air.

Jax said, "Not much is bulletproof anymore."

My stomach dropped. Not even ten miles into a thousand-mile trip, and the cracks were already forming. We had to believe we'd make it—I had to believe it. Because if I didn't, what else was left?

Jax must have seen something in my face because he backpedaled. "If there's a problem, we can fix it. Dad's garage is full of spare parts."

But the words were out, and some truths, once spoken, can't be stuffed back in their box. They run wild like hungry dogs, impossible to leash again. The rest of the group knew it too—that's why we sat rigid, shoulders hunched against reality, watching ash drift down from rustling tree limbs like dead moths. A thousand miles stretched ahead of us through nuclear winter's nursery, and our hope had shrunk to match the hibernating sun—a dim disk barely bigger than a quarter.

His attempt at reassurance—talk of spare parts in his father's garage—only made it worse. It was like offering a Band-Aid to someone bleeding out. We all knew what waited for us out there in the wastelands. We'd seen the clouds thickening on the horizon, black as fresh-poured tar.

The real question wasn't whether we'd make it—just how long we could keep pretending we would.

Behind us, the rusted yard cart groaned, metal shrieking at every bump. Its wheels wobbled like loose teeth. We pulled onto the northern trail, our last safe harbor shrinking behind us.

I stared out at the landscape, trying to ignore the way the UTV rattled beneath me. Five weeks after the bombs, and the Okefenokee was a cemetery. No alligators lounged on the banks. No kingfishers flashed blue across the water. The wading birds—ibises, spoonbills, wood storks—had vanished, an avian rapture sweeping them away before the humans even sensed death coming. The cypress trees loomed like blackened skeletons, Spanish moss hung limp and gray, rotting in the poisoned air.

Jax cursed under his breath and jerked the UTV to a stop. He reached under the seat, yanked out a wrench, and slammed it against the dash. The engine, which had rattled like a blender full of rocks, sputtered into a passable rhythm.

Button pointed at the cargo rack. "Ellena, that strap by your head's lookin' loose."

I reached up and gave it a tug. The fuel can wobbled, but the knot held. "It's fine. But we should check the others before we lose supplies all over the road."

We stopped. Again. The trip had turned into a crawl, every bump and shake rattling something loose. We'd be lucky to make it halfway before nightfall.

A rabbit darted across the path, its fur patchy, ribs jutting like prison bars. The silence pressed in—no car engines, no animal shrieks, no insect hum, just a whisper of ghoulish wind through the trees.

"Should be an hour to Dad's," Jax said, his voice loud in the dead air. He climbed back into the driver's seat, twisted the key, and the rocks rattled to life in the engine.

I flinched as the UTV hit a pothole, jolting me hard enough to make the hula girl's head snap sideways. "Tell me about this truck again," I said to Jax, adjusting my grip on the roll cage. "Tell me it's going to start."

"It'll start," Jax said, but his knuckles had gone white on the steering wheel.

Something in the yard cart popped loose, bouncing behind us like a freed hubcap. Jax checked his rearview mirror. "Loose bracket."

We pushed north toward Waycross, toward whatever waited for us in that bulletproof truck. The UTV groaned and sputtered—a symphony of desperation—but it moved.

Right now, the only thing that mattered was keeping the wheels turning—one more mile, one more breath, one more inch away from the grave we hadn't dug yet.

* * *

An hour later, the UTV skidded to a stop, tires grinding through the gray-white powder blanketing the ground. Jax's dad's place sat ahead—a squat, single-story building with a metal roof, an oversized garage hunched beside it like a sentinel. A rusted chain-link fence circled the property, more memory than barrier now.

A gunshot cracked through the winter air. My shoulders tensed. Not a hunting shot—wrong time of day. Someone defending their property, most likely. The houses were scattered wide, quarter-mile apart at least, which meant no neighbors to call for help if trouble came. No one to hear a scream, or a shot. Except us.

Jax pulled the UTV up to the garage door. "Stay in the truck," he ordered, yanking the key from the ignition. "Dust is too thick. Let me open the garage first."

I stretched my stiff legs over the driver's seat once Jax climbed out. The house looked untouched—windows intact, front door secure. Like time had frozen here five weeks ago, but the dust had settled thicker than in the swamp, coating everything in a deep layer that spoke of our proximity to King's Bay and one of the blast zones.

Jax punched a code into the keypad next to the garage. The metal door shuddered, then rolled up with a reluctant groan, revealing a hulking shape inside. "Told you it was here."

We climbed out into the garage's protective gloom. Jax scooped Winter up from the UTV's footwell and set him down on the garage floor, pointing to a corner. "Go potty."

Button scrunched her face, then looked at me with resignation and shrugged. A dog's gotta go when a dog's gotta go—that's what the look said. Winter wouldn't be safe outside, not unless he wanted a new Cesium-137 coat.

"Let's see if this beauty will start."

The word "beauty" brought back a memory. Eric and his Rio—that ridiculous tin can he'd pampered like a show car, polishing the rims until they gleamed, buffing the windshield to mirror brightness. The ache of those memories surprised me—not just for Eric, surely dead now—but for how the good parts of our marriage shone brighter now that the bad had faded.

The F-150's door creaked as Jax pulled it open. He slid into the seat, turned the key, and—nothing. Not even a click. Silence. Complete silence.

Button groaned. "Well, that sure is a kick in the teeth."

Jax muttered and tried again. The dead quiet was damning.

"Battery's dead," Maggie said, arms crossed. "Ain't been run in what—years? You thought you were gonna luck out?"

Jax said, "No worries. There's a spare."

Maggie huffed. "Ain't the battery, son. If it's been sitting this long, the alternator's likely shot too. You can jump it, sure, but soon as you pull the cables, the battery'll drain, and we'll be dead in the water."

Button slumped against the truck bed. "So what now? We just leave it? Haul ourselves to Colorado in that fun wagon out there?" She jerked a thumb toward the garage door.

Maggie rolled up her sleeves, her bangles glinting in the fluorescent light. "Yeah, no. That's not what I said."

Jax blinked. "You know how to fix alternators?"

Maggie's eyes narrowed. "What, you thought I spent all my time reading tea leaves?" She cracked her knuckles. "My first car was a '75 Pontiac that had no business still running. Learned how to keep it alive by necessity. Now quit gaping and help me find some damn tools."

Jax dove into the garage's shadows, rummaging through his dad's stockpile.

Maggie popped the hood and traced wires with the confidence of someone who had done this a hundred times before.

"Well?" Jax emerged, arms full of clanking tools.

Maggie grunted, wiping grease from her hands with a rag. "Alternator's not as bad as I thought. Belt's loose, terminals corroded. Ain't no miracle fix, but I can get it running long enough to get us the hell outta here."

Jax handed her a wrench. "I could kiss you."

Maggie smirked. "Shame on you, being a married man and all." She shot a quick wink at me. "Alright, you clean the connections and I'll get this puppy running."

* * *

While Jax and Maggie worked, Button and I took charge of lunch. Tomato soup, some crackers—and, unexpectedly, some peppermint tea.

As I glanced around, the familiar colors and wall decorations stirred a strange sense of belonging, as if Gran had left her mark here somehow.

The engine coughed to life in the garage, stuttered, then roared, the sound echoing off the concrete walls.

Button whooped. "Now that's what I'm talkin' about!"

Jax and Maggie stepped inside, grinning, with their grease-smudged thumbs raised in triumph. Their smiles were contagious, and the room filled with quick, celebratory high fives—a brief, bright spark against the gloom.

Jax spread the maps across the kitchen counter, running a finger along the back roads northwest. "Alright, we're here—just south of Waycross. Our destination is that way." He tapped the spot Hank had given us. "Fort Deposit. If we leave first light, we might get there by nightfall."

Button said, "It's only, what?—three hundred miles? That's like, five hours."

Jax said, "We have to go slow. Unknown dangers—potholes, slick roads. Also, we should cover the taillights."

Maggie nodded, her expression tight with understanding. I opened my mouth to ask why covering the taillights mattered, but Button beat me to it.

"What's that for?"

"We're less likely to be shot at," Jax said.

"Oh, dear sweet Jesus," Button said, then heaved and ran for the bathroom.

"Wow. That was unexpected," Jax said. "Was it something I said?"

I shook my head. "She's fine." As if that would explain it. I wanted to just come out and tell them that Button was pregnant, but that wasn't my call to make. "Weak stomach."

Maggie raised an eyebrow, her stare boring into me. She knew. *She wasnae born yesterday*, Gran would have said. *Nor the day before that.*

Maggie leaned over, peering at the map. "You got a plan, or are we just flipping a coin every time we hit a fork in the road?"

Jax exhaled through his nose, grabbed a pencil and circled a few areas on the map. "Albany could be hot, but who knows where else got hit? We're going to drive slow and navigate around any radiation." He scratched a rough line westward. "We need to cut up through back roads, keep away from interstates. If we hit a jammed highway, we'll burn fuel maneuvering around it. Or worse, we'll have to backtrack."

I asked, "How will we be able to tell where the hotspots are without a Geiger counter?"

"Ah," Jax said, walking to the kitchen. He opened a cabinet of clutter and fished out an identical Geiger counter to the one he'd been carrying before. "I got Dad one for Christmas."

"Let's hope that one lasts longer than yours," I said. We were putting our lives in the hands of a mass-produced gadget that might crap out when we needed it most. Kind of like people, I thought—until I looked around.

Button. Maggie. Jax. They'd saved my life.

Button, who—if I had to guess—would've been the first to die in a post-apocalyptic world without her Hermès bag and Goop face cream. But now, in the after, Button had blossomed into someone who was sharp, sassy, and almost completely likeable.

Maggie, a stranger who'd offered us shelter without hesitation.

And Jax—the glue holding us all together.

We were going to make it. We were a cobbled-together family, but a family all the same.

I studied the map, chewing my lip. "What about fuel? If we take back roads, we can't count on gas stations having anything left."

Jax nodded. "Yeah. We'll need to siphon. Trade if we find friendlies. That means keeping an eye out for farms, remote stations, even old fuel depots. I say we fill every spare can before we hit the state line. Overpack supplies for trade."

Maggie pointed to the roads Jax had marked. "Bridges. These routes cut through river basins—if a bridge is out, we'll have a hell of a backtrack."

"Yeah, I know," Jax said, scratching his head. "That's why we need backup routes." He tapped an alternate path. "If we get boxed in, we head north and skirt around Columbus. Hell of a detour, but it should be clear of bomb damage—unless one of those Blitz missiles landed right in our way."

Button laughed. "Yeah, great. Let's swap radiation poisoning for frostbite."

To Floridians, anything north of the state line meant hypothermia—and Button had never been farther north than the Okefenokee. No wonder she believed it.

Maggie laughed. "Oh, suck it up, sweetheart. A little cold ain't gonna kill ya."

Button elbowed her and grinned. Maggie feigned a direct hit, and they both chuckled.

I asked, "What about other survivors? We're bound to run into people."

Jax's face darkened. "Yeah. That's the other problem." He pulled out a red marker and slashed circles around a few towns. "Some places might be fine—farm communities, small settlements. But others?" He shook his head. "Desperate people do desperate things. We keep our distance, watch for signs of life before rolling in. No stopping unless we have to."

Button raised an eyebrow. "Define 'have to.'"

Jax met her gaze. "I mean unless this truck's out of fuel or one of us is bleeding out from a stray bullet."

* * *

The following morning, I woke to the scent of coffee cutting through the stale air. The house sat in dead silence, broken only by the soft click of Winter's claws on the linoleum. Through grimy windows, I could see that fallout dust clung to everything, turning the familiar landscape into something alien. If I didn't know better, I might almost mistake it for snow.

I found Jax in the kitchen, his back to me as he worked the French press. Winter thumped his tail once in greeting but didn't budge from his post by Jax's feet. His golden eyes tracked my every move.

"I'll wake Button and Maggie in fifteen," Jax said without turning.

The living room beckoned, and I drifted to the bookshelves. Romance novels lined the shelves, their spines cracked and faded like old memories. Nora Roberts. Sandra Brown. Danielle Steel.

"Mom's books," Jax said, stepping up beside me. His presence filled the space with a static charge. "Dad kept everything after she died. Take one, if you want."

None were my style—romantic suspense, historical romance—but then one title caught my eye: *Love in the Time of Cholera.*

"That was her favorite. Must've read it twenty times."

Dog-eared pages fell open as I thumbed through the book. I skimmed the back cover, and something tightened in my chest. True love beyond reason. Not about the plague at all. But wasn't that what my feelings for Jax were? An infection of the heart, spreading through my system every time he came near. When his hand brushed mine, when those deep brown eyes locked onto mine—my pulse lurched like the UTV slamming into a pothole at full speed.

The room around me blurred. If someone told me I had to stay here forever with him... well, that should have terrified me. But it didn't. Not really. Because right now, it all felt—hell, right. Me, Jax, that house with its peeling paint and creaking floors. I belonged. And for a moment—a single, stolen moment—I let myself forget. Forget the nuclear winter, the fallout, the ghost-gray ash drifting on the wind, the dying sun, the dwindling supplies. Right now, it was just me, the coffee, and Jax.

But that thought didn't have time to settle before reality slammed back in. Because even if, by some lunatic miracle, Jax lost his damn mind and said, Hey, screw it, let's just stay here, ride this out, whaddya say?— even if I could somehow let myself believe in that fantasy—the truth still stood, cold and sharp-edged. Colorado needed medics. And I wasn't a person who turned her back on the dying. Technically, I wasn't an EMT anymore—but did a piece of paper matter now? Did anything official still exist—anyone left to stamp their approval? I'd saved lives. That should count for something.

"Got something for you," Jax said before disappearing into the bedroom. He returned with his fist wrapped around something small. "Mom would've liked you. And after what you did for Winter..." His voice roughened.

The necklace caught what little light remained—a silver shooting star, delicate as a wish.

"It's beautiful," I said.

His fingers were warm against my neck as he fastened the clasp. When he stepped back, barely a foot separated us. I could smell the coffee on his breath, feel the heat coming off his body in the cold room. His eyes dropped to the shooting star resting against my collarbone, then climbed back up to my face.

The air between us thrummed like a live wire. His hand came up, hesitated, then brushed a strand of hair from my face. The touch sent electricity down my spine. I leaned into it without meaning to, the way plants lean toward sunlight.

All those days—watching him stand sentry, feeling his shoulder brush against mine in the Airstream while radiation storms raged outside, the gentle way he'd patched up my clawed arm—it all flooded in.

The embrace came natural as breathing. I felt wetness on my cheek— not my tears, but his. His chest shuddered once against mine.

"Couldn't have made it this far without you," he said.

My hands found his face. His stubble rasped against my palms. I pulled him onto me—or maybe he was already falling forward. Our lips met, a taste of salt and coffee and the end of the world. Through the window, clouds shifted, revealing only darkness where stars used to be. Winter whined at Jax's feet, but neither I nor Jax moved to pull away.

In fifteen minutes, we'd wake the others, and face whatever hell waited between here and Colorado.

But for now, in this abandoned house with its rusted fence and tin roof, we held onto something that felt like hope.

24 Oregon Trail 2.0

We loaded the truck like soldiers prepping for a long campaign—every supply, every spare part placed and secured. The garage surrendered its treasures: fuel cans, tools, parts that Jax's dad had stored away like prayers against that very day.

Rain hammered the roof by the time Jax hit the garage door button. The door groaned up, revealing a world turned liquid silver.

Jax slid behind the wheel without a word. I claimed shotgun, slamming the door shut as Maggie and Button squeezed into the back—crammed into the narrow jump seats like sardines with an attitude.

Maggie grunted, wedging herself sideways. "Heavens, who's this seat made for? A toddler with no knees?"

Button shifted, her shoulder jammed against the window. "I think I just dislocated a rib."

Jax glanced over his shoulder with the faintest smirk. "Quit complaining. We'll switch it up every hundred miles."

"Darn right we will," Maggie muttered, trying—and failing—to stretch her legs. "I'm not surviving nuclear fallout just to be taken out by a cramp."

"Survival training," Jax said, adjusting the mirror. Then, without looking at me, he added, "Right, Mrs. Mercer?"

I froze, my hand tightening around the seatbelt. My glare could've melted steel.

Button snorted from the backseat, grinning. "You two are adorable."

"You're lucky I don't have a ring to throw at your head," I said.

Maggie huffed. "How about you two lovebirds get this show on the road before the blood congeals in my legs, eh?"

Laughter rippled through the cab, the kind that came easy despite exhaustion, despite everything. Even Winter's ears pricked up, as if trying to get in on the joke.

Jax started the engine, the cab filled with the low growl of the truck—and the sound of shifting bodies in the back, settling in for a long, uncomfortable ride.

Winter snuggled into the space on the bench seat between me and Jax, his warm body pressed against my leg, his steady breathing a reminder that we were still alive, still moving forward.

I pressed my forehead against the window's cold glass, watching the rearview mirror. The rain blurred the house into a faded photograph. Jax didn't look back. Neither did I—mirrors showed the past, and my eyes were on the road ahead.

We had a destination. Uncle Hank promised normalcy, though normalcy now meant bitter cold and rationed meals. We were pioneers heading west, just like the old wagon trains—only our Oregon Trail was paved with nuclear ash and lined with horrors worse than dysentery.

But I wasn't alone anymore. The thought filled me with warmth: I had people now. Real people. Family.

For a moment, terror clawed up my throat. This fragile thing we'd built—this cobbled-together tribe of survivors—felt as delicate as a spider's web in a storm. The road stretched ahead of us like a gangrenous tongue, ready to devour everything I'd found and leave me hollow again.

I forced myself to anchor in the now.

What do I see? Jax's hand on the steering wheel, steady as bedrock.

What do I hear? The crunch of tires on gravel, taking us further toward our future.

What do I feel? Winter's fur under my fingers, real and warm and alive.

What do I taste? Tuna. They'd better have goddamn toothpaste out in bumfuck Colorado.

As we pulled onto the main road, the truck's headlights pierced the rain like searchlights sweeping through fog.

I felt the shooting star around my neck and made a wish.

Jax's hand found mine in the dark. "Ready for a fun road trip?"

"Yes," I said. And meant it.

The sequel to Fallout in Georgia is now available on Amazon!

Dust in The Rockies

After nuclear strikes destroy most of the United States, EMT Ellena Reed—stripped of her license for freezing when it mattered most—leads a group of survivors west toward a rumored bunker in the Rockies. Her stepsister, Button, is ailing. Nuclear winter is setting in. And there are reports that Yellowstone is about to erupt. Every encounter forces impossible choices: trust armed strangers or risk the journey alone; travel west while other survivors head east; hold on to humanity or do what it takes to survive. Ellena must decide who lives and who dies—and find a way to live with those decisions.

ABOUT THE AUTHOR

S.E. Glen is a writer with a background in mathematics and the author of a published statistics textbook. She has also been an M.C. at The *Comedy Zone*—proof that numbers don't always tell the whole story. A lifelong fan of psychological thrillers and survival fiction, S.E. Glen blends tension, dark humor, atmospheric horror, and character-driven suspense in her storytelling. When not writing, she can be found researching obscure disaster preparedness techniques, testing the limits of caffeine intake, or trying to convince her border collie that the world isn't actually ending just because they lost their ball. *Fallout in Georgia* is her first novel.